MW01128591

THE CAIRO PUZZLE

LAURENCE O'BRYAN

Copyright © 2017 Laurence O'Bryan

All rights reserved. No part of this publication may be reproduced, distributed, or transmitted in any form or by any means, including photocopying, recording, or other electronic or mechanical methods, without the prior written permission of the publisher. For permission requests, write to the publisher at the address below.

Ardua Publishing

5 Dame Lane,

Dublin 2,

Ireland

http://arduapublishing.com

Ordering Information: Contact the publisher.

This novel is a work of fiction. Any resemblance to actual persons, living or dead, is entirely coincidental.

"Who determined its measure, surely you know?

And who laid its cornerstone?

While the morning stars sang together, and your

angels shouted for joy?"

JOB 38:5-7

1

The chanting was louder now. It seeped through the closed windows of the taxi, competing with the Arabic pop music the driver had been swaying along to since we'd left the airport. As we jolted forward another foot he turned to me, shrugged. Sweat prickled on my brow. He grinned. His teeth stood out, ivory white, against the dark stubble on his bony, sun beaten face.

I stared out the window at the line of policemen blocking the traffic heading into Tahrir Square. They were dressed all in black and had their helmet visors down. They held long metal sticks in front of them. Anxiety twisted in my gut. Henry's words came back to me, as if he was behind me, whispering in my ear. I'd called him just before the British Airways flight to Cairo took off.

"If you go to Cairo you might well get yourself killed, Isabel."

The taxi lurched forward. Horns blared around us. Men in black t-shirts moved past us. Some of them held black flags. One of them noticed me. He shook his fist in my direction. My jaw tightened. I looked away. I'd read the stories about the attacks on foreign women, during the violent demonstrations when the current military ruler had taken power. I felt for the stainless steel pen in my bag. It was still there. If some bastard with a hard on for a Western woman smashed the taxi window to try to pull me out, he'd find out that not every female was easy prey.

"We get to hotel soon, madam. Don't worry." The driver's grin lasted longer than it should have, as if he was enjoying our situation.

A boom shook the taxi. The chanting hesitated, but only for a second. Then it returned, with added roars of defiance. Someone banged the roof right above my head. I stared out the front window, holding the steel pen tight to my thigh. The driver was unlikely to help me if they tried to break in. Was I crazy, coming here? In the distance, the afterburner of a fighter jet blazed like a comet through a purpling evening sky.

The muzzle of a shiny black pistol appeared at the window to my left. It was pointed straight at my face. My lips opened, but no sound came out. Don't move if a gun is pointed at you was the memorable, though obvious advice I'd received on a kidnap prevention course in my way too distant past. My mouth dried as I waited, as if I'd stuffed it with blotting paper.

Would I ever find Sean? Would I ever see his face again? I stared into the muzzle of the gun. I knew I'd never see the flash that killed me, but I was calm, as my hand slid towards the door handle.

2

One Week Earlier

It was April 30th, a month since my husband Sean Ryan fell into that water filled pit in Nuremberg. His body had still not been found. I'd been told he could have been swept far down the river Pegnitz, and might eventually be found by a fisherman, months from now, tangled in the reeds that grew along the bank.

I'd flown back to London three days after I left the hospital in Nuremberg. Alek, my son, needed me. The chance of finding Sean alive had passed, the kindly German policewoman said. The black hole inside me hadn't.

How I'd survived the past four weeks I had no idea. I'd been prescribed Xanax by my doctor, but after taking half a tablet I threw the rest away. Mostly, Alek had kept me sane. He asked about his father every day, and I almost burst into tears every time he did, but it's not right to burden a seven year old with despair. I could see in his face that he knew there was something going on. Something bad.

Jenny, my sister, had also kept me sane. But I would have to admit the truth to Alek soon, and to myself. It was time to arrange a service for Sean. Time to make arrangements.

But I wouldn't. I couldn't. I was angry. Angry at the German police. Angry at their whole damn country. And angry at myself, most of all. And now I was clutching at any old straw that floated by. This was my time for clutching at straws.

I looked up at the red brick building. The east end of London had changed since I'd been there, the Olympics had forced it to, but Charnal Street, near Hoxton Square, hadn't been penetrated by even one shiny new street lamp.

I pulled my jacket collar tight against chilly rain and pressed the dirty plastic buzzer beside Dr. Candio's card. Some of the other buzzers had scrawled out names beside them. One had a card with a smiling woman's face on it. Two had their buzzers missing completely.

I was regretting coming here.

I could be home in Fulham. Jenny was cooking tonight. She'd been staying over almost every second day for the past week as I sunk lower. I bit my lip, listened, as the ember of hope died slowly. All I could hear was the animal thrum of traffic from Old Street, the traffic artery leading out of the City of London. I pressed the bell again, hard. Then I took out my smartphone to check Dr. Candio's website. Again.

Indian Astrological & Mantra Card Reading & Psychic Consultations, 2PM to 8PM, read the symbol cluttered page. I peered closer.

A loud bang sounded from above, as if a window had been shut. I looked up. Rain pelted down.

"Who?" said an angry voice from a tiny speaker near the buzzers.

"Isabel Ryan. I called earlier."

Nothing happened.

I stamped my feet. I wanted to bang the door. I bit my lip again instead.

The faded black, heavily scuffed door opened with a squeak. I caught a glimpse of a snarl on the face of the man standing behind it. He was six foot three, at least, thin, wiry-haired, pale complexioned. His face was elongated, rat like. He was wearing a dirty kaftan, which went down to just above his ankles.

"Doctor Candio?"

He nodded.

A young man appeared behind Doctor Candio. He brushed past him, heading out. He was disheveled, sunken eyed, slack jawed. He stumbled into me, smiled, like a junkie looking for a meal ticket. An aroma of urine filled my nostrils. I stepped back. He shook his head, staggered away.

The stairs Dr. Candio led me up were dark. The carpet covering them oozed with dirt. You could no longer tell what shade it had originally been or if the stains on it were patterns.

His room was on the top floor. It had a low ceiling, the walls covered in large symbols scrawled in black and red on the yellowing wallpaper. I took them in, uneasiness growing inside me. There were swastikas, swords, cups, squares, circles, diamonds, crosses, moons, spaceships, Celtic swirls and Egyptian looking hieroglyphs.

On shelves half filling the walls to the left and right, on four low tables in the corners of the room, and on a big old cabinet between the high windows that looked out onto the thin trees of the square, there were statues of multi-armed gods, brass pots, incense holders, dusty glass bottles, beads hanging in ropes, ivory elephants, statues of Jesus and Mary in various sizes. The array glistened in the light from a bare, single yellow bulb above our heads. It felt as if I'd entered a shrine. But to what?

5

"What do you want?" asked Doctor Candio. He gave me a wide smile, as if he was practicing something he'd been told to do, which he didn't believe in. The gaps in his teeth, on both sides, on the top row, made the remaining ones stand out like tombstones.

"Has your husband left you, for another?" A deck of black cards appeared in his hands. He shuffled them. His hands moved fast, almost in a blur, as he cut them again and again. After a few more seconds he placed them on the red Formica kitchen table in the middle of the room and motioned for me to sit.

I wanted to leave.

I sat.

He took the chair opposite, shuffled the cards again, arrayed them in a semi-circle in front of me. He smiled. I half expected him to leap over the table at me.

"I will pay you for a reading, but I also have a question for you." I paused, unnerved for a moment by Doctor Candio's wide eyed glare.

Now he was moving his facial muscles, as if exercising them. Flashes of anger and peacefulness, ugliness and fear appeared, then passed away in a second.

"One hundred pounds is the reading fee."

I paid him from the purse in my handbag.

"What is your question?"

"Why do you use this symbol?" I pointed at one of his business cards. It was lying scruff-eared on the dirt-ingrained table. The symbol was in the form of a single flame inside a square, but the shape was the same as the symbol they'd found in that room under Nuremberg. The symbol that no one I'd asked in Germany had any clue about.

"Why do you ask?" Candio leaned towards me, his face coming to within a foot of mine. I could smell urine. His expression was curious, his eyes wide, his mouth slightly open. Drool was gathering on his lower lip.

"It was in a room where my husband disappeared."

"Where was that?" His smile had a lustful grin to it now.

"Nuremberg, in Germany."

"Why do you think this has any relevance to your husband's disappearance?" He pointed at the symbol on his card.

I took a slow breath. Should I reveal more? What harm could it do?

"My husband was researching this symbol."

Candio leaned back, picked a card from the array on the table with a flourish. He turned it up to face me. The symbol on it was a black horse with a pale green rider. Above the rider was the word Plague in an old Germanic looking font. Below the horse was a sequence of Egyptian symbols, a pyramid, a beetle, Isis, with the sun above her head. The last symbol was a square with an arrow inside it.

I moved my hand to touch the card. My hand was trembling. The tremble passed up my arm and through my body. Had he picked this card because he knew what happened in Germany in the last month, how thousands of refugees had died from a rapidly spreading illness, which the medical authorities were still struggling to contain?

Or had the card been picked for some other reason? My hand touched the edge of the card.

He slapped his down on top of mine. It felt hot, clammy, as if something was burning on his skin. I jerked my hand away.

I felt infected.

"Leave at once. Do not return. You have seen your card," he shouted. He smashed his other hand down on the table as if he was determined to frighten me. The black tarot cards and his faded business card all jumped inches into the air. I stayed still. He stood, shook his fist at me.

"You and your husband are cursed. Get out! Out!"

I headed for the door, one eye on Candio. He was bobbing up and down, a finger pointing in my direction. I wanted out. I'd seen enough.

"Evil clings to you!" screamed Candio, jabbing his finger at me, as if I'd admitted to killing babies.

"You're one sick hustler," I said.

I slammed his door hard, headed down the stairs. "Weirdo," I shouted to the building as I went down. When I reached the first landing a navy baby pushchair smashed into the floor in front of me.

I stopped, looked up in time to see a black foot-tall wooden sculpture of a snake flying in my direction. I stepped back. It smashed into the spot where I'd been standing. A violent shiver passed through me. He could have killed me.

"Go! Your fate is sealed. You are dust."

His parting shouts echoed in my ears as I closed the front door. As I walked away fast I was shaking. Not just a little, but inside, as if my brain had been scrambled.

My hand felt hot, too, where he'd touched me.

There was a pub on the corner near the Tube station. I went inside, found the ladies, scrubbed my hands, again and again.

They were still trembling, but with anger now.

I felt enraged, but stupid too, for bothering to go to see him just because of that stupid symbol. Was I going crazy with grief? I'd seen Sean in my dreams. I am sure that's normal. But there were symbols around him. And there was a fire in front of him, which I touched. The flames felt like ice. And I'd heard his voice. All around me. Calling my name. Sometimes even when I was awake.

***

His voice came back to me when I went into the bathroom to wash my salty tears away. Light played at the edges of our bathroom mirror, noises echoed from the street.

And now I felt roasting, as if I was ill. I went back into the bedroom, turned on the light, opened up Sean's laptop again.

I'd looked through every file, every program on it over the past month. There'd been a saved blog post article in his browser about Egypt. I found it, opened it.

It was about a recent discovery in the new chamber they'd found in the Great Pyramid outside Cairo. A picture of one wall of the chamber filled the top of the article.

I spent the next two hours, until the dawn lit our room, researching Cairo and its ancient monuments. I started with Wikipedia and moved to YouTube. The Great Pyramid, the largest of the three main pyramids near Cairo, was, depending on who you believed; hiding the game reset button for our virtual reality world, an alien construction project by the beings who brought human DNA to Earth, which humans still hadn't found a way inside, or a storage center for seeds and knowledge from before the flood. Or possibly all three.

The Sphinx, in front of the Great Pyramid was either built in 2,500 B.C. or 10,500 B.C. if you wanted all the related stars to line up at the Spring equinox. I ended up on an English language Egyptian news site called The Daily News Egypt. I scrolled through articles looking for anything connected with the new passages they'd discovered in the Great Pyramid using thermal imaging.

That was when I saw it.

An article about a new Saudi built hospital in Giza, on the outskirts of Cairo, called *Dar al'amal*, showed a picture of a white private jet with the Arabic letters of the hospital's name on its side. The article spoke about how the best medicine in the world was now being practiced in Cairo. Proof of this was that patients were now being flown in from all around the world to be treated there. The first example of this were flights from Germany, which had started a month before, to help the German medical authorities with their ongoing emergency.

It wasn't just Egyptians who were being flown to Cairo either, the article stated. I read the whole article three times. Then I searched for other instances of medical flights taking people out of Germany. There were none. Other countries had offered staff and equipment, but no one else had taken patients out of Germany.

I was clutching at wickedly thin straws, but I hadn't even found a straw to clutch at in the last month.

I looked up flights to Egypt.

As I booked a hotel near Tahrir Square in the center of Cairo, the tremble in my hand returned. This had to be crazy. I pressed the **BOOK NOW** button.

3

Now

The driver had his hands up. His smile was gone. The gunman was motioning for the car window to be opened on my side. I pressed the electric window button, my hand shaking, expecting the glass to shatter at any moment.

The gunman was dressed in paramilitary garb, loose black trousers, a thin black armored vest and a black cap with a gold emblem, a stylized bird. He bent down, the muzzle of his gun lowering.

"Which hotel?" he said. His accent was cultured, his skin paler than the crowd still surging around us.

"The Excelsior," I said.

His eyes were cold, piercing blue. "You are coming to Cairo at the wrong time. What is your name."

"Isabel Sharp."

"Why are you here? Are you a journalist?"

"I'm looking for my husband."

He nodded. He swung his arm. Two other men, dressed as he was, moved to the front of our car and pointed our driver to a laneway to our right. A yellow plastic barrier blocked it. It was being removed as I watched. My driver grunted, shrugged and headed down the lane. The buildings on each side rose high above us. The first windows were two stories up, but the lane was empty. We picked up speed as we made our way down it.

I turned to look out the back window.

The man who'd stopped us was staring after us. As I watched he took what looked like a phone from his shirt pocket and began tapping at it.

It took us less than two minutes to reach The Excelsior. The driver took my bag from beside me and handed it to a doorman in a baggy brown suit. The driver smiled at me as I paid him in Egyptian pounds. I gave him an extra fifty pound note at the end and he bowed.

"May Allah keep you safe," he said, as he backed away from me. "Pretty lady."

I coughed. The air was dusty and heat was pricking at my skin even though the sun was lowering over the buildings around us. The doorman was holding the double height glass doors open for me. I followed him in. The pale green marble of the giant foyer glistened as if it had recently been washed. Wicker chairs lined the walls. Behind the reception desk two young men in brown uniforms waited, smiling.

The foyer felt empty, though there were groups of two or three people talking together to my left and right. It seemed as if the hotel had been built for an influx of tourists which had never arrived. On the wall above the reception desk hung a giant painting, gilt framed, of the pyramids. A golden light shone from behind the Great Pyramid.

"Welcome to Cairo," said the smiling young man, as he took my passport. "I hope your journey from the airport was easy. Our traffic can be a shock." He handed me a card to sign. My name had already been filled in.

I headed for my room. I needed a shower, badly.

4

"It works, I can assure you, Excellency." The old man leaned forward. He pushed his gold rimmed glasses back up his nose. His smile was wide. His eyes gleamed as he placed the glass beaker on the polished mahogany table.

The older man in the tight fitting pin striped suit stared at the beaker. He swept his improbably black hair back over his head with a thin hand mottled by age.

"If you have succeeded, doctor, this will be the breakthrough that will have every pharmaceutical company in the world asking you to work for them." His gaze locked on the doctor's face.

"Have no fear, excellency. I would never leave your service. You have been more than generous to me and my family." The doctor glanced down at the beaker.

"The name Ahmed Yacoub is inscribed in our hearts." He held his right hand to his left breast, clutched it through his white cotton shirt. His head bowed.

Ahmed Yacoub stood. He picked up the beaker and walked to the high windows overlooking the Nile. Dark latticework shutters blocked the sunlight, but if you stood close enough you could see across the jumble of rooftops and minarets all the way from old Cairo to the Great Pyramid. It stood out against a skyline lit by a red sun descending into a bank of yellow cloud.

"There is a sandstorm approaching." He sipped at the beaker.

"Three days it has waited out there," said the doctor. "We have shuttered our villa in Giza."

Yacoub sipped again. "It tastes like apple tea."

The doctor smiled. "It works a lot better than apple tea." He licked his lips.

"And you have given the formula to the production team?"

"Yes. All the safety tests are done. We will help millions. Manufacturing costs are low. Rich and poor will benefit from this."

Yacoub sniffed at the liquid. "Our distribution strategy will be decided by our Swiss partners, doctor."

The doctor closed his eyes for a moment, then bowed. "Is your wife in the city?"

Yacoub looked away. "She is in Paris, shopping. Our summer party is coming up in two weeks."

"You may want her to hurry back." The doctor grinned.

Yacoub drained the rest of the liquid, placed the beaker down in front of him. "All donors have been compensated?"

"Every one." The doctor stood. "I will return tomorrow. The effects will last much longer, but I want to be the first to congratulate you on how well you look."

"I can assure you, you will receive more than words if you have achieved what you promised."

The doctor held the high back of the ebony chair. His fingers moved over the bird's head carving, as if caressing it.

"The formula does not fail, excellency. The health of your guest proves that. You have seen his recovery, have you not?"

Yacoub shrugged. "I have not seen him, but I've been told he watches Netflix the way you pursue your secretaries, doctor." He swept his hair back.

"I will take my leave, excellency. Enjoy your evening."

As he walked down the wide stairs towards the front door of the mansion he saw two young women sitting on the Persian carpet under the glittering chandelier, which dominated the entrance hall. They were sitting cross legged, their faces covered to their eyes by red scarves thrown back. They were talking to each other in whispers. They turned, glanced at the doctor. Then their laughter filled the hall.

As he left the building behind he hurried towards the multistory car park at the end of the street. He'd parked his Toyota on the top level, as he'd been instructed to always do, to avoid being seen. As he rode up in the elevator he thought about his own wife. Perhaps she too could benefit, as he had done, from a daily dose of the elixir. He smiled as he crossed the concrete of the car park and weaved between the parked cars to find his own.

He clicked on the fob and the car's lights flashed. It would be good to turn on the air conditioning and listen to Mozart on his way to his home in the exclusive suburb of Zamalek, Cairo's wealthiest neighborhood, on the island of Gazirah.

He closed the door behind him and reached for the stereo system controls.

A soft clunk made him turn his head. Something flashed across his vision. The first he knew about the thin wire that had been dropped over his head was when it bit into the flesh of his neck.

He reached for it, but it was already too late. It had cut his windpipe and was progressing fast towards his spine. Blood poured like a waterfall across his white shirt and pooled on his trousers. The only sound was the noise of air escaping from his windpipe, like a burst bicycle tire.

Then a tinkle of laughter filled the car and the two sets of hands, which had held the wire, released the ivory handles that had allowed them to pull it tight, leaving the wire dangling down the doctor's back.

They adjusted their niqabs as they went down the concrete stairs. The slit for their eyes was less than an inch wide as they walked out into the street. They followed two other niqab wearing women and mingled at the end of the traffic lights with a dozen others.

5

I turned on the TV, switching the channel to CNN as I unpacked. The room had two double beds, and was at the end of a long corridor.

The news at the top of the hour started. A suicide bomber had detonated himself in a market in Damascus. One hundred and twenty people had been torn to shreds, mostly women buying food for their families. The item closed with a shaky video a passerby shot of shattered buildings with dust drifting in the air. The buildings looked like the broken teeth in some long defeated giant's skull.

The next item came up on the screen, a view of the White House, and a discussion about the American president's health.

I switched the TV off, went to my bag and took out the printouts of Sean's picture I had made before I left London. He was smiling. The picture had been taken during his last visit to his family home in upstate New York. His cousin had taken it.

I breathed deep. The pain in my heart had been continuous since he'd disappeared. Some days it lessened, if I was busy, but always it was there, like a hot stone pressing into my heart. Now I was in a strange city it had grown again. I still couldn't believe he was gone. It couldn't be true.

I'd been told I was in denial. But I didn't care. If I saw his body, I'd accept his death. I'd told myself that over and over, but another part of me knew I was fooling myself.

I looked away, a rush of sadness welling in my eyes. I went to the window, gripped the curtain. Just once more, please. Let me see him once more. I pulled the white net curtain with the barely visible pattern of pyramids to the side and looked out.

The buildings visible from my fourth floor window were offices and apartment buildings with advertising signs in Arabic at street level. On one, on each floor, there were hoardings for some cola drink, with a symbol on the giant red bottle I'd never seen before. There was also a man at a window opposite. He was wearing a white shirt and staring at me. He had a phone to his ear.

I dropped the net curtain. His gaze had been intense. The tightness in my chest grew. I gripped my arms around myself, sat on the bed, took out my phone and went to the guide app for Cairo I'd found.

The hospital I'd read about which had taken a medical emergency victim from Nuremberg was in Giza, on the outskirts of Cairo. The *Dar al'amal* hospital was near the Faisal station, the stop before Giza on the Cairo Metro. I had to decide whether to take the metro in the morning and use one of the women only carriages, marked with a red sticker, or take a taxi.

The travel advice I'd read said tourists should avoid rush hours on the metro. Apparently the volume of people using the system meant that some of the stairways became packed and you could barely move at times, especially where the metro lines intersected.

What I needed was a driver who could help me at the hospital too.

When I woke the rumble from outside the window and the honking of horns made me wonder where I was. A sliver of sunlight on the pale green carpet told me the sun was long up. Breakfast in the restaurant was bread, cheese, sliced meats, fruit and strong coffee. The waiters were all young men who smiled deferentially as they served. Maybe I was being paranoid, but I spotted two of them looking my way.

I asked at reception about taxis to the hospital and a driver who spoke English. He arranged one for ten-thirty.

Before we left the hotel I asked the driver, Mahmood, would he come in to the hospital and translate for me and point me in the right direction. And drive me back to the hotel.

"I will do all of that, but the charge will be forty dollars," he said, as he held the door of his yellow cab open for me.

"No problem," I said.

"What is it you need to find at the hospital, madam?" He started the car and pushed out into the traffic, staring at me for most of the time in the rear view mirror.

"I need to know if my husband, Sean Ryan, has been treated there in the past month."

"Hospital records are not always easy to see. You may have to pay." He rubbed his fingers together.

"Whatever it takes." I thought for a second about what I'd just said, then added. "Within reason."

"Of course, madam."

After a few minutes he turned to me. "Did your husband go missing from the hotel?" His tone was kind.

"No. I read there was an American being treated at the hospital."

His eyes widened. "Your husband, he is an American?"

I nodded. The rest of the drive was in silence, except for the constant bleat of car horns outside.

The drive took forty minutes. We spent half of it sitting in a traffic jam on a wide boulevard with dirty looking palm trees down the middle. Most of the women on the street had their hair covered, some with the full black sack that made them look like walking shadows, others wore western clothes. A few wore white face veils. Most women were in groups.

The men had a beaten down look and wore dusty t-shirts, ill-fitting suits or long Arabic shirts, galabeya, reaching to their ankles. Some had small white turbans on. The streets hummed with activity and there was a dusty smell in the air, as if we were passing a cement factory.

The hospital was behind a high iron steel fence. Two security guards with black machine guns hung over their shoulders guarded it. Another sat in a security box with dirty sandbags piled up to window level. We had to weave past concrete barriers to get to the gate, where the car was examined, and a guard with a mirror on a long stick checked the underside for explosives.

The driver turned to me. "This is not a good day to visit a hospital in Cairo, madam." He pointed beyond the security barriers.

Three ambulances were pulled up to the side of the building. Medics surrounded the back doors of one of the ambulances. Green suited hospital staff were carrying a stretcher out of it. As the security gate opened the stretcher was rushed towards a set of glass double doors to the right of the main entrance. It had EMERGENCY and a string of Arab letters above the entrance in white lettering on a red sign. To the left of the entrance were gold luggage carriers, like you might find at a top hotel.

"I have to find my husband."

He shrugged, drove towards the entrance to an underground car park. The hospital towered above us, at least six stories and as we entered the car park I heard the clatter of a helicopter approaching. As we disappeared underground I saw the flash of helicopter blades descending to the roof of the hospital.

The clatter of the blades could still be heard as I got out. The driver, shaking his head, motioned for me to follow him. His galabeya was cream and below it he wore new looking blue Nike runners. They looked wrong. I hurried after him.

The anxiety I'd been feeling at being in Cairo was overlaid now by a sense that I was coming to some crossroads, an expectation that I might find answers here. In my brown leather handbag I had pictures of Sean. I held it tight to my side, as if by keeping it close to me I was holding onto him in some way, and that if I lost it, I would be saying a final goodbye to him.

As we walked up the stairs I remembered the email from the Institute of Applied Research in Oxford, where Sean worked. It had asked me when I was planning to have his memorial. It was the third such email I'd received. I hadn't answered any of them. But I'd have to when I got back to London. If the trip was an absurd wild goose chase, which a part of me knew it could be, I couldn't deny the truth of Sean's death any longer.

I stopped as the glass doors opened to the reception area of the emergency department. Someone was screaming. Whether it was a woman, a man or a child I couldn't tell. The screeching, like an animal in pain, filled my head and sent tingles of fear creeping up from my stomach.

The driver, standing to my side, shook his head. "I told you this is a bad time, madam."

Two armed guards, like the ones at the entrance, stood in front of us. Their machine guns were slightly raised, as if they were expecting an attack at any moment.

An urge to leave, to turn, to walk away, came over me. I resisted. My hand became a fist. If this was what was needed to make sure I had followed up every possibility of finding Sean, so be it. I'd spent days in Nuremberg searching for him. I'd even visited the local government office, which looked after the rivers, the *Staatsamt für Flüsse*, in Nuremberg, and I'd spent two hours with them going over where bodies were found after people fell into the Pegnitz.

Then I'd spent a day walking the areas they showed me on a map, getting shouted at by Germans who didn't like trespassers, and jumping fences to get closer to the river at every opportunity.

A local police vehicle had eventually stopped me, as I came out of a pathway beside a warehouse. After checking out my story they'd dropped me back at my hotel, where I'd sat on my bed and cried, until the tears wouldn't come any more.

But I hadn't given up. I wouldn't now.

The guards waved metal detecting wands over us. The screaming had changed. It was more a keen now, a wail of suffering. Eyes darted to the doors the wail was coming from. A line of people were waiting near a glass window. Yellow chairs to the left, bolted to the floor, were filled with people, mothers, children, men with prayer beads and small books they were reading from, a young couple in western clothes whispering to each other.

The wail filled me with dread deep down inside, every time I breathed in.

"Not there," said the driver, as I went to join the line. He pointed at a door, marked ADMINISTRATION and with a series of Arabic squiggles above it. He pressed a buzzer by the door and we waited. I forced myself to breathe deep.

"Is this security normal?" I said to the driver.

"These days there is high security everywhere that deals with foreigners or members of the government." He glanced towards the people waiting.

I followed his gaze. Only then did I notice that some of the men waiting were standing stiffly, as if the families they were near weren't their own. That they were guarding them.

The door opened. A man in a loose cream suit looked at us, then beckoned us in. The room was tiny and had another door at the back. He pointed at two chairs, started speaking in Arabic. My driver answered, pointed at me, but didn't sit.

"Tell me your husband's name," said the administrator.

"Sean Ryan."

"Please spell this name."

I did. He typed it slowly into a computer in front of him. Then he peered at the screen.

"I am sorry. We have no record of such a patient. We cannot help you. Perhaps another hospital?" He smiled solicitously. There was a pause. He looked at the door, as if expecting me to leave.

"But he was brought here by airplane a month ago, from Nuremberg. Please check again. Perhaps he was registered under a different spelling."

He glanced at the computer screen. "We have no similar names on our registry. I checked the two private wards for foreigners and the general admissions."

I should have guessed. If anyone had brought him here, they wouldn't have registered him in his own name.

"May I know the name of the patient who came here from Germany by air ambulance a month ago?"

His smile disappeared. "We do not give out patient information. I am sorry for your loss. But you must look somewhere else." His hand waved fast between us in a dismissive gesture. He looked at my driver and started speaking fast in Arabic, glancing at me.

Eventually the driver touched my shoulder. "We must go, madam."

I felt like brushing his hand away, but instead, I stood and walked out the door. In the reception area a group had just entered. Three women were carrying a girl of eight or nine towards the line of people at the glass window. They were shouting in Arabic and waving at the people to get out of their way, while holding the girl up by her armpits.

The girl was dressed in a long black tunic, similar to what the women were wearing, but without the tight hair cover, just a thin black veil on top of her head. She also had nose piercings and a white band around her middle. She was slumped and behind her a trail of blood stood out against the cream marble floor.

The women behind the glass window shouted back at them, then turned and screamed at someone behind her, who I couldn't see.

The driver was beside me. "This is a family matter, madam. Nothing to concern yourself with."

Inside my stomach the anxiety was turning to anger. I looked the driver in the eye, clenched my jaw.

"I understand. Wait for me at the car. I will be there in a few minutes." I nodded towards a door, which had a picture of a small black woman in a long dress on it. He took the hint.

As he exited the reception area I followed the group of women, directly behind them, as they were ushered through double doors into the emergency area. One of the medical staff, a young man with a beard, stared at me with green eyes. I smiled, sailed past him.

The area beyond was filled with cubicles with green plastic curtains separating them. Relatives waited by beds. A few beds were empty. I kept walking. There was a pair of doors at the end of the corridor. Above them was a sign in Arabic and the word Wards. I pushed through them. My mouth was dry. Every nerve in my body tingled. Any second now someone would shout at me.

But no one did, and as I kept walking the doors behind me closed and the hubbub of noise quietened. Two male nurses in white passed. Then a doctor in a white coat came towards me. He looked European, Italian maybe, or Spanish.

I put up a hand as he came near.

"Where are the wards for the foreigners?"

He smiled and pointed behind him. "Up the stairs, just here. Take a left and you will see them."

I took the stairs fast. The corridor to the left was quiet. It had a set of yellow double doors blocking my way and a security guard with a machine gun standing in front of them.

I slowed, reached in my bag, found my passport, held it towards the guard as I came up to the door.

"I have come to see my husband," I said.

He looked at the passport, then took an iPhone from a jacket pocket.

"Please hold it open and here," he said. He held his hand to his chest.

I held it as he asked. He took a picture of me, then opened the doors with a swipe card and pushed at the one nearest door to him to allow me though. A rush of relief pulsed through me. I'd made it.

6

"The fountain of youth, that is what we are pursuing," said Ahmed Yacoub. He turned, pointing at the pyramids beyond the sloped glass windows. Behind the pyramids a wall of yellow dust stretched from horizon to horizon.

The bank of TV cameras and smartphones on tripods were a blaze of red recording lights in front of the wide ebony table in the top floor reception area of the Yacoub Holdings skyscraper near the Nile in the upmarket central Cairo suburb of Garden City.

The thirty-two floor building was the second highest in Cairo. Its square column design with a pyramid of glass on top replicated the column from the Hall of Records at Karnak from 1400 B.C. At night it was lit with blue light. In the middle of the day you could still see blue lights inside the apex of the glass and steel pyramid above you, when you were in the open plan reception area under the glass pyramid.

"What about grave robbers, Mr. Yacoub? Isn't it likely that anything our ancestors left inside the Pyramid of Khufu was robbed thousands of years ago?"

Yacoub leaned forward. "The thermal scanning in 2016 revealed the existence of a passage from the Queen's Chamber. We have now assessed the King's Chamber, too. Our results are better than I could have hoped. Some of the floor stones are warmer than the others. This means there is air behind them. And there is no damage to these stones, which means they have not been moved since the Great Pyramid was built four and a half thousand years ago."

He pointed behind him at the Great Pyramid. "The room we are searching for is the Hall of Records." He paused. "A hall, which holds ancient books of healing and magic. Books from which Moses learned how to part the Red Sea but, more importantly, the books which explain how each of us can become young again. And all the ancient treatments that were lost long ago. Cures that have been hidden from us. Until now." He smiled, waved at the man on his right. "The Director of the Supreme Council of Antiquities will be with me when we break through into the room in the next forty-eight hours. And a few of you lucky media people will accompany us."

His gaze swept across the assembled journalists. It met the blue eyes of the CNN reporter whose smile always caught his attention. He smiled back at her, breathed in deeply, puffing his chest out.

"Those selected will be informed later today." He stood, shook hands with the Director, who stood beside him grinning like a happy schoolboy. Camera flashes illuminated the glass pyramid above his head. They could be seen from the streets below, like fireflies in a glass bowl.

7

The corridor was short and had two doors, one on each side, and a nurse's desk at the end, where a female nurse in white was leaning over and writing something. She looked up as I approached. I smiled.

The nurse smiled back. She was pale skinned and had blonde hair. As I came near another nurse came out of the door on my left. I glimpsed three beds and a window with palm trees fronds brushing against it and blue sky beyond.

One of the beds was occupied, but all I could see were feet under a white sheet and electronic monitoring equipment blinking beyond the bed. Pressure built in my chest. My mouth was dry. Could that be Sean?

"I am looking for my husband, Sean Ryan," I said as I reached the nurse. I was tempted to just barge into the room and see if it was him, but I restrained myself. I didn't want to get thrown out before I'd even started.

The nurse looked me in the eye and without even checking she said, in perfect English, with only a faint accent which I couldn't place, possibly Irish, "We have no patient here by that name. I am sorry."

"Perhaps in the other wards for foreigners?" The pressure in my chest grew. Was my quest over?

"I know all the foreign patients by name, Mrs. Ryan. We have no one here by that name."

I reached for my handbag, found the pictures of Sean, pulled one out, passed it to her.

"You haven't seen this man in the past few weeks?" The nurse studied the picture, passed it back.

"No. I am sorry, I haven't." Her eyebrows went up and an is-there-anything-else look came onto her face.

"Are you sure?" I could sense a needy element creeping into my voice. I raised my volume, as I continued, "A man was brought here from Germany by plane a month ago. I think that was my husband. Please, look again." I put the picture in front of her on the white plastic covered counter.

She didn't even look at it.

"I am sorry, I have not seen your husband. I can't help you. Have you tried the other hospitals in Cairo?"

I let the wave of pressure building up inside me out.

"But who was the person you flew in here? It has to have been my husband?"

Her expression hardened. "No patient has been brought in here from Germany in the last year, since I started at this hospital. Mrs. Ryan, I don't want to call security. Your husband is not here. He hasn't been here. There is nothing more I can say." Her eyes narrowed. Her hand went towards a green phone sitting on the desk beside her.

"Ok, I'm going." I raised my hands in a defeated gesture, turned, walked back along the corridor. As I passed the door where I'd seen the patient in a bed, I went through the door.

"Mrs. Ryan! I am calling security!"

That meant I had some time. A minute. Maybe two. Enough. I walked towards the bed. The person in it had clean white bandages around his head. He could easily be Sean. He was the same height and build. My legs moved faster. The man appeared to be sleeping. I reached out for the hand lying on the bed beside him. Something caught in my throat. What the hell?

8

In Whitehall, in central London, in a War Office building transferred to MI5, the Assistant Head of Counterterrorism Investigations, Henry Mowlam, was sitting in a glass walled corner office with three flat screen monitors in front of him.

His recent elevation in status was not entirely to his liking. It was the first time an Assistant Head had moved his desk screens to his office and several of the staff in his unit, who had been on the same grade as him until recently, had started using nicknames for him. Henry the IT, was the kindest of them.

There were twelve Assistant Heads of Counterterrorism. The twelve apostles. But three of them were on sick leave and two others were near retirement, and still writing reports in long hand for their assistants to type up.

Henry was watching the larger screen on his desk intently. The window high on the wall, showed clouds racing across London's sky. On his screen was the square in front of the El Morsy Mosque, which opened onto the port road in Alexandria, Egypt. The crowd filling the square had already grown to block the road. Friday afternoon prayers were over and the faithful were not heading home. The imminent arrival of the U.S.S. Mount Whitney, the flagship of the Sixth Fleet, for a two day official visit, had stoked a suddenly volatile situation in Alexandria.

Henry's concern was not only for the lives of the 325 servicemen and women on board the Mount Whitney, he was also concerned that the attack on the Basilica of St. Theresa in Cairo earlier that day was the signal for a general popular uprising against the Egyptian military dictatorship.

Crowds were also gathering in Port Said and Aswan. No British lives were directly at threat, yet, but the possibility of a coup attempt had to be considered.

The current general in charge in Egypt was a friend of the west, but there were known groups in the Egyptian military who would prefer an alignment with Syria. Anything could happen if that occurred; outright support for Hamas, to prove the new leader's anti-Israel credentials, rejection or appropriation of western investments in Egypt, a further collapse in the Egyptian economy, leading to another great wave of Muslim immigrants floating across the Mediterranean, upsetting the balance of power in Europe.

His second screen showed the Basilica of St. Theresa in Cairo. The damage from the attack was still visible. An improvised explosive device had been used. It had the hallmarks of the work of returning combatants from Syria.

As he watched, two policemen moved extra barriers to the side of the smoke blackened church. Then a red warning box opened with another video playing on Henry's screen. He clicked on the box, held the edge of his desk.

The screen showed the entrance to the Egyptian Navy Officers beach club just outside Port Said. The metal barrier was up and two white uniformed bodies could be seen beyond it. The camera was facing up the laneway that led to the club.

A black Toyota Landcruiser was sitting with its lights on in the laneway. Beyond it there was another car. It was reversing. In the windscreen of the Landcruiser he could see a reflection of the entrance to the beach club. Sparks flew across the screen.

There was a firefight going on.

He clicked at the screen, looking for controls over the camera. There were none. Why the hell hadn't the Egyptians upgraded their security cameras!

He picked up the headset on the table in front of him and clicked on the audio and video connection to the British Embassy in Cairo. His fingers tapped at the screen. He could send a secure email to his CIA counterpart, the U.S. naval intelligence counterpart, and various British military and civilian Foreign Office employees in a few seconds, but first he had to make sure that the Ambassador and staff in Cairo would go into lockdown.

9

I stood beside the patient, leaning over his bandage swathed face, my heart hammering. Footsteps were pounding behind me.

"Mrs. Ryan," came a shout.

I looked at the man's neck and in a second I knew two things. This was not Sean, I knew every inch of him. The lumps on this man's neck were wrong, and this man had been tortured. The bandage around his chest had lifted where his neck fell away and at the edge I could see a weeping weal, which stretched up under the bandage.

My stomach turned. A hand gripped my arm.

"Mrs. Ryan, come." I looked at the man holding me. He wore a black uniform with a peaked cap with a bird emblem on it.

I didn't resist. My eyes swept the room as I turned. Sean wasn't here. It felt as if a hole was opening inside me. This was it. All chance of finding him was gone. I looked around as I walked away. At the foot of the patient's bed was a white dressing gown. A Macy's label at the neck caught my eye.

I didn't say a word, just walked fast out of the ward, almost pulling the security guard holding my arm. When we reached the main exit the guard released me.

"You must leave," he said. He pointed at the exit door.

I raised both hands, palms towards him. "I'm going." I looked back as I went through the door. The guard was watching me.

The taxi driver was smoking, leaning against a wall in the car park near a no smoking sign. I walked up to him, smiled.

"Did you find your husband?" He dropped his cigarette, stood on it.

"Not yet." I rummaged in my bag. "Can you find any ambulance drivers here and ask them if they saw my husband?"

He looked at me, shook his head. "I am not a detective, madam."

I smiled. "Will an extra hundred Egyptian pounds help?"

"Two hundred."

I nodded. He reached for the photo of Sean.

"Can I have a cigarette," I said. I hadn't smoked in ten years, but an urge to smoke had come over me. I needed something to take the edge off the numbness creeping over me.

He passed me one, lit it for me. His smile lingered as he stared at me. I looked away, took only a little smoke into my lungs, then blew smoke down to the ground.

"I'll pay you when we get back to the hotel. Ask every driver you can find."

He was gone for at least thirty minutes. I paced up and down the car park, near where his taxi was parked.

He held the photo up as he came back.

Laurence O'Bryan

"Sorry, madam. I found two drivers and none of them saw your husband. There are two other drivers. They will be on duty later, if you want me to come back." He shrugged. "Another hundred for that." He paused, smiled. "I can come to your hotel later."

"Yes, do that." I thought about giving him my number, but I wanted to see his face when he told me what he had found. I didn't want to hear stories over the telephone.

We were back at the hotel twenty minutes later. A black mini bus was parked outside. An older man with thick gray hair and a bushy beard with streaks of white through it stepped out of it as we pulled up. He was carrying a white plastic box under his arm.

"Make sure you go back to the hospital," I said, as I paid the driver.

He smiled at me. "For you, madam. I will do whatever you want." His smile was a little too friendly. I felt uneasy. I had to be very careful about what I did next.

I looked around, quickly. "I will be with my friend, so just call my room or leave a message for me at reception," I said, as I pointed at the bearded American.

"You know him?" said the driver.

"Yes," I lied. The thought that I had picked the wrong person to lie about loomed suddenly inside me. "Why?"

"He will bring shame on us all."

10

Ahmed Yacoub stared through the latticework window of his villa. In the distance, the Great Pyramid was lit with blue lights. Behind it the wall of the sandstorm, which had been brewing to the west, over the Sahara, waited. It had been moving south, so the weather forecasters claimed, but with a change in the wind expected over the weekend, it could engulf Cairo.

At the other end of the room an ebony table had a large screen laptop computer on it. It was showing live video from a Facebook page, set up only in the last few days.

Victory for The People, was the name of the page. The live video showed flickering images from the Navy Officers Club at Port Said. A second video, stopped, but waiting to be restarted, showed a confrontation at Tahrir Square in central Cairo. Army tanks and a mass of protesters faced each other. Men had been streaming into Tahrir Square from mosques all around Cairo for hours, and they were still coming.

A shout went up from the crowd. Yacoub walked quickly to the laptop to see if the moment of victory had come. The view on the screen was changing, as the man holding the smartphone panned across the quickly darkening sky. A rattling noise grew. Then he saw it. The blades of a helicopter rising fast into the sky.

He knew what that meant. The general in charge at the Navy Officers Club at Port Said had given up the fight and was heading away as fast as he could.

Yacoub picked up his smartphone, pressed at the call encryption app and then at a contact name icon. A male voice came on the line. His Arabic was guttural, from peasant stock Yacoub's family had long elevated itself from.

"Do you know where he is going?" said Yacoub.

"Inna afeal, I do," came the reply.

"What time will he leave Egyptian airspace?"

"In twenty minutes, no more."

Yacoub cut the line. He clicked a different contact icon. Another male voice answered.

"One general has departed by helicopter. Tell your people the revolution can be won this time."

He scrolled down the Facebook page, started the audio on the live video feed from Tahrir Square. The mob was chanting. A minute later a hush descended. A lone voice rang out from a loudspeaker.

He could barely hear what was being said. But he heard the words *waqad tashghil alkalb - the dogs are running.*

A cheer rang out from the crowd. It grew in waves as it passed out along El Tahrir Avenue towards Kasr Al Nile Bridge. The head of the crowd surged towards the tanks guarding the government offices. A burst of gunfire rang out, like a string of fire crackers being let off.

Whether the soldiers were firing over the heads of the crowd or at them was hard to tell. The crowd hesitated, split. Many were now running, pushing at anyone in their way, their heads down.

Yacoub smiled. It had started. It would be a long night.

He stood, went to a solid ivory side table, hit the brass gong on it with the small bronze hammer in the shape of a bird. A few seconds later the door at the side of the room opened. The two young women who came through it were dressed all in black, though their faces were uncovered. Each had a smile on their thin, pockmarked faces.

They stood respectfully on the far side of the table, and bowed.

He smiled at them. "I have another important job for you."

11

"Do you need a hand," I called out. The man with the beard was taking another box out of the car.

He turned to me. "No. I got it."

I stood beside him. "Let me help you, please. I'm trying to escape the attentions of a taxi driver. I don't want him to think I'm staying here alone." I inclined my head back towards the driver, who was standing by his car observing us.

"If you want to help you can stand here and make sure no one runs away with any of this while I get a trolley." He smiled at me. "Where are you from, England? My name's Mike Bayford. What's yours?"

I told him. He came back a minute later. I helped him put the boxes on the trolley, walked with him through the doors of the hotel. The taxi driver was pulling away into the traffic.

Mike stopped near the elevators. "What are you doing in Cairo on your own, aside from attracting the attention of taxi drivers?"

"I came to look for my husband. He's missing." I looked away. I didn't enjoy pouring my troubles out to strangers, but if it helped in any way, I would, every minute of every day.

Mike shook his head. "This is not a good time to be doing anything in Cairo."

"No?"

He turned, pointed at a TV screen visible through the doors into the restaurant area. A cluster of visitors were sitting on chairs around it.

"Wait there. I'll be back down in a few minutes. We can talk, okay?"

I looked at him. His beard had flecks of dust in it and his clothes, loose jeans and a blue shirt with baggy chest pockets were also splattered with dust.

"Yeah, maybe it'll be twenty minutes. I need a shower."

I went into the restaurant. The small group by the TV were guests, a German couple on holiday, two French businessmen, a Canadian woman working for a medical charity. I'd been introduced to them all by the time Mike came back down.

What struck me was that each of them could easily have watched what was going on in their rooms, but they clearly didn't want to. It was six-thirty. Outside it was getting dark fast.

"Don't leave the hotel until all this is over," said the Canadian woman, leaning close to me as Mike sat down on the other side of the table. He was staring at the TV screen. His hair was damp and he'd put on a clean white shirt and khaki trousers.

The image on the TV screen showed Tahrir Square. A huge crowd had overwhelmed a row of tanks. Dozens of people were dancing on top of them. Black flags were being waved.

Mike leaned towards me. "I'll be leaving here at seven in the morning."

"On an early flight?" said the Canadian woman.

"No, our project to open the hidden rooms in the Great Pyramid is coming to a climax this weekend." He rubbed a hand through his hair, then turned to the TV.

"We were supposed to have a press preview of what we discovered at nine in the morning, but I have no idea what's going to happen with all this going on." He waved dismissively at the screen.

"I reckon the Egyptian people are allowed to fight for democracy," said the Canadian woman.

Mike turned to her. "Democracy ain't what they're fighting for. Sure, many of them are moderates, but the Muslim Brotherhood will get in if they're allowed to stand again, and they want Sharia law, jihad, and the destruction of Israel."

"The international community won't allow that to happen," said the Canadian woman.

"Maybe, but a lot of people will die in the process."

"What makes you think you're going to find hidden rooms in the pyramid?" I sat up straight. "Isn't that the fantasy of hundreds of thousands of Egyptologists?"

"Millions, if you include the amateurs."

"So, what is it you've got the others don't?"

"There's been some recent discoveries that make us confident we're on the right track."

"What discoveries?"

"Anomalies in the temperature readings of the stone blocks, which make us think that some of them have air behind them, passages and a few other things that point in the same direction."

"And you want to see where they lead," said the Canadian woman.

"Yes."

"And what are the other things?" I said.

"A manuscript from the era has been discovered and translated."

"What is it about?"

"It claims that Osiris, the Egyptian god of regeneration, is entombed in the Great Pyramid."

"Isn't Osiris the god of the dead?" said the Canadian woman.

"No." Mike shook his head. "He's the god of the afterlife, and resurrection."

"I never heard that," said the Canadian.

"Well, it's true," said Mike. "Ancient Egyptians buried corn mummies, small mummies a foot or two long during the festival of Khoiak, with images of Osiris on them, and seeds and mud inside as proof of the resurrection from death, which Osiris can bring about."

"When was this festival?" I'd read recently about ancient Celts burying objects around Europe, at Spring festivals.

"At the end of August, when the Nile flooding reached its height."

"You'll be going to the pyramid in the morning?" I said.

"You bet. The earth would have to swallow me up, for me to miss this." His eyes narrowed. "You might want to come with me, Isabel. There'll be someone there who should be able to help you. You do know everything you want done in this country relies on who you know?"

"Who?" I leaned towards him. If there was any chance of getting help I'd take it. I did not want to leave Egypt with every hope dashed.

"It's only one of the richest men in Egypt. Ahmed Faisal Yacoub."

An ember of hope bloomed inside me as I watched him talking.

"The man who wants to live forever," said the Canadian woman.

"Why do they say that?" I leaned forward.

Just then a shout rang up from the crowd watching the TV. We all turned to see what was happening. On the screen the camera was turned skywards. A gray dusk on the horizon indicated where the sun had recently gone down. Visible against the dusk were three helicopters swooping fast towards the crowd, which was still jamming Tahrir Square.

Hisses and boos rang out from the crowd. Then an Arabic roar of defiance.

It was met by slivers of fire streaming from one helicopter straight into the crowd. Panic ensued. Then another roar. But in the middle of the crowd there was a rubble of bodies and flags.

My mouth was wide open. My stomach had turned. I gripped the edge of my seat. A groan went up in the room.

"What kind of an army opens fire on its own people?" Mike shouted.

I stood, went to the reception, then out to the front of the hotel. It was dark, but a distant clatter told me we weren't that far from Tahrir Square. As the wind changed I heard a distant roar.

An intense longing for Sean filled me, as if a stone had grown inside me. An urge to go back to London gripped me. What if he'd been knocked unconscious and had recovered in some German hospital, finally remembered who he was and gone back to London?

I shook my head. That had to be wishful thinking. Deep inside I knew I should have done more to stop him going to Nuremberg. I could have saved him. If only I'd insisted on him not going there. I had an easy excuse to stop him, the riots in Germany. Why hadn't I used it?

A series of flashes lit the skyline. Something tightened inside me. I knew the taste of fear, how it makes you more alert, jumpy, but this was different. This was fear and anger all rolled into one. I brushed a hand across my eyes. I was not going to go back to London. I was going to finish the job here, follow every lead, and only then go home, and if he still hadn't shown up, we would have a service for him. And I would accept the truth.

I felt a hand on my shoulder, turned.

"Are you okay?" It was Mike.

"Yeah, I'm good. I just miss Sean. A lot." I tried to smile. It came out crooked.

"Come with me in the morning. I ain't going to let any of this stop us. The crowds are dispersing. Meet me out here at seven. I don't expect a lot of press will turn up tomorrow, but we'll be recording everything for a documentary we're making. If he comes, Ahmed Yacoub will help you. I'll make sure he does."

"Thanks. See you in the morning." I headed for the reception area. The sky was quiet.

I spent twenty minutes looking up Ahmed Yacoub on the internet. Mike was right, he was one of the richest people in Egypt. His father had prospered in the 1950's, thanks to an import and export business he ran dealing in German cars and Egyptian cotton. He was a contributor to the Palestinian cause and, one website claimed, he'd helped Yasser Arafat, the number one enemy of Israel for decades, when he was living in Cairo. That financial support was critical to the rise of Arafat, it was claimed.

Ahmed Yacoub's father had employed many German refugees after the Second World War and it had led to the founding of what was now the son's largest enterprise, a pharmaceutical business that spanned the Middle East and was on the verge of breaking into the U.S. market with some revolutionary new products.

12

Henry Mowlam was still at his desk in central London. It was a little after nine. Two of the staff from his team had invited him for a drink an hour before. They'd be in the basement with pints of Greene King in front of them right now. He was tempted.

But the new shift had started and the situation in the Middle East was livening up.

The attack on the crowds in Tahrir Square in Cairo by an Apache AH-64 helicopter gunship was receiving worldwide coverage on a variety of news channels. A Twitter storm had followed the images Tweeted of the wounded and dying.

Copycat demonstrations had sprung up even before the attack, in Liberation Square in Baghdad, in Martyr Square in Damascus and, of most concern, in Deera Square in the center of Riyadh, in Saudi Arabia.

He had received no advance intelligence about any plan to coordinate these outbreaks, and none of the leaders in the other Arab countries had deployed their armies to protect themselves, but that didn't mean there wasn't a plan behind what was happening.

The overthrow of non-Islamic governments and the recreation of a pan Arabic Caliphate was the aspiration of hundreds of millions of Muslims. Just because the nation states created at the end of the First World War had existed for a hundred years, did not mean they would exist for another hundred.

The question was, could the West do anything to keep a lid on the situation? Were the forces at play beyond manipulation?

What was needed was a distraction. He scrolled through his newsfeed of stories from Arabic newspapers, which had been published that day on their websites, and which had been translated in the past few hours.

One caught his eye.

EGYPTIAN BILLIONAIRE REVEALS SECRETS OF THE GREAT PYRAMID

AHMED YACOUB, MAJORITY SHAREHOLDER IN YACOUB HOLDINGS, ONE OF THE LARGEST PHARMACEUTICAL COMPANIES IN THE WORLD, HELD A PRESS CONFERENCE IN CAIRO TODAY. HE ANNOUNCED THAT A SECRET ROOM IN THE GREAT PYRAMID OF KHUFU HAD BEEN DISCOVERED. MR YACOUB STATED THAT DISCOVERING THE "FOUNTAIN OF YOUTH" WAS HIS NEXT OBJECTIVE. THE FABLED FOUNTAIN OF YOUTH IS A WATER SOURCE WHICH RESTORES THE YOUTH OF ALL THOSE WHO BATHE IN IT. STORIES ABOUT THIS FOUNTAIN WERE RECOUNTED BY THE GREEK HISTORIAN WHO WROTE ABOUT EGYPT IN THE 5TH CENTURY B.C. IT WAS ALSO FEATURED IN TALES

ABOUT ALEXANDER THE GREAT, WHO CONQUERED EGYPT, AND IN STORIES BROUGHT TO EUROPE AND MADE POPULAR THERE BY RETURNING CRUSADERS.

THE DISCOVERY OF ANCIENT HEALING RECIPES HAS LONG BEEN THE GOAL OF THE FOUNDER OF YACOUB HOLDINGS. IN THE PAST HE HAS FUNDED PROJECTS IN LOWER EGYPT, IN JORDAN AND IN BAGHDAD LOOKING FOR ANCIENT TEXTS. IF HE SUCCEEDS EGYPT WILL, ONCE AGAIN, BE AT THE CENTER OF THE WORLD FOR MEDICAL TREATMENTS.

13

I reached for my smartphone as soon as I woke up, and checked my messages. It was a stupid ritual, but every morning I hoped a message from Sean would be there waiting for me. My ordeal would be over. I could almost taste what it would feel like, but every morning that feeling eluded me, like a wisp of vapor vanishing in a second.

It was torture by hope. And every morning when there was no message from him, the hole in my heart opened a little wider. I'd cried every morning for a week after he'd disappeared, but now there was only this growing emptiness, as if a part of me was being sucked out every day.

At seven I was down at reception. A cup of coffee in my room was all I'd had, and it was all I needed. My sister had told me I was getting thinner, that I needed to keep my strength up, but many days I just didn't want to eat at all, if Sean wasn't with me. And when I did eat, food tasted weird, dry, and it stuck in my throat. I think the worst part was not knowing what had happened, expecting every day to hear news. Every hour. Always waiting. I needed to know what happened to him. I had to know.

At the front of the hotel Mike was loading plastic boxes into the black mini bus I'd seen him exiting the day before. I offered to help.

"You look beat," he replied. "Did the noise keep you up?"

I shrugged. "I heard a few jets sweeping over, was there more?"

"Not much. The crowds dispersed, but there's another demonstration called for this afternoon. I want to get this job done." He dropped the last box in through the back door of the mini bus.

"You should leave Cairo too. Once the bloodshed starts, you never know how far it will go." He looked concerned. "Or who they'll target next. Foreigners often get blamed in the Middle East. This is not a good time to be a lone woman here."

"My flight back to London is on Monday. I'm not going to run away before that unless they storm this hotel." I gave him the best pretense of a smile I could muster.

He opened the side door of the mini bus.

"Let's go, then."

The traffic, heading towards the pyramids, in the western suburbs of the city was as bad as any I'd seen anywhere in the world. That included London during the Olympics, and Istanbul at the end of Ramadan. The demonstrations the evening before had definitely not encouraged people to stay at home. If anything, the city was like an ant's nest that had been smoked. Cars were heading in every direction, despite the early hour. Horns blared all around us, and for a while, at one intersection, I thought we were going to get stuck. Then we reached a wide avenue with palm trees down the middle and the traffic eased.

Mike turned to me after a long conversation in Arabic with the driver.

"We'll be there in fifteen minutes. Do you see the pyramids?" He pointed past the driver, through the front window.

The pyramids, almost directly ahead, grew larger by the second. It was unreal seeing them dominate the horizon, like in a Hollywood movie.

"Will Ahmed Yacoub be coming today?" I stared at the pyramids as they grew larger every second.

"Yes, he'll be here from nine."

"Do you know he's claiming he'll discover the fountain of youth?"

"Yes, he's using our dig to get some media coverage for his pharmaceutical business." He shrugged. "I knew he'd pull something like this. But we'd never have got the money to do this dig properly, or the permissions we needed without his help. I don't expect to find any more than an empty chamber. He's said an inscription on a wall is all he's looking for." His tone softened. "But there's a possibility we'll find more. That's what I love about all this."

"You believe in the fountain of youth then?"

Mike snorted. "I have no idea. It's could be a war story brought back by Alexander the Great's soldiers after they conquered Egypt and the same thing again after the Crusaders took Cairo and lost it again. There isn't any other pool, anywhere in the world, where old people can get in at one end and come out younger at the other and head for a party. It's a myth that's medically impossible. But there could be something to it. Some medical treatment to make us young again."

"And Yacoub is going to sell this to millions."

He put a hand on my arm. "Forty percent of the population here is illiterate, Isabel. They'd believe anything someone in authority tells them. As long as he's not damaging anyone's health, what the hell do I care. People have been selling pyramid myths to tourists here since before the time of Christ."

"It's all a bit strange."

"It's the total strangest, Isabel. The Great Pyramid was the tallest man-made structure in the world until the Eiffel Tower. They had to place eight hundred tons of stone into it every day to get it finished in twenty years. Some of the granite blocks are two hundred tons, for God's sake. We only have a few cranes in the world now, which can move that sort of weight."

I shook my head. "Truly amazing."

"It's more than amazing. The pyramids are at the exact center of the largest land mass on earth. Exactly half way between the top of Siberia and the tip of Africa."

"How did they work that out?"

Mike shrugged. "No one knows. And there's more. How did they get the site level to within a fraction of an inch over thirteen acres? We'd need top of the range laser tools to do that now, and we'd still struggle with leveling a site that size. And how did they align the edges of the Great Pyramid to face true north, south, east, and west to within a fraction of a degree of arc, which modern engineers weren't able to do until satellite positioning arrived." He took a breath.

"But you know what is the biggest question for me?" He raised his hands in the air. "Why level it so accurately? Why position it to face true north? And why make it so big that the whole thing took decades to build, and you'd need to manage teams tens of thousands strong to get it built?"

"Maybe it was useful in some way we don't understand."

"Like keeping people young again?"

"Maybe."

A memory of a conversation with one of Sean's colleagues, Neil Briars, the previous Christmas came back to me.

"You think he'll be selling people a placebo?"

"Placebos work, don't they?"

"All you need is for people to believe," I said, echoing Neil Briar's words to me.

We turned onto a side road. In the distance I could see the Sphinx.

"We'll be at the research center in a few minutes. The Egyptian government officials will start coming in from eight. You can come up with me to the Great Pyramid. I need to check everything is ready for sliding out the capstone to the tunnel that leads up from the King's Chamber."

"Is it safe?"

"We've had video camera probes up beyond the stone. That's how we know there's a passage. We've tested the air quality too. We foresee no danger."

"But there could be anything at the end of the passage?"

"Yeah, sure. That's why there'll only be a few people in the King's Chamber when we move the stones. Most of the experts will be outside watching on monitors. It's a big event. We'll stream live on a hundred media websites all over the world."

"You couldn't have sent a robot probe all the way up this passage?"

"No, the angle is too steep. When a previous team put a robot walker through another tunnel its motor conked out because of the angle. And the limestone used in the construction of the passages and much of the Great Pyramid, has a very high water content. This has an unusual effect on electrical signals inside the pyramid."

We slowed as we approached an entrance on the left. Six military personnel with black machine pistols were standing in front of a locked gate. As we stopped in front of the gate they raised their weapons and pointed them at us. Flood lights came on.

"What the hell is going on?" said Mike, in a low voice.

14

Ahmed Yacoub stood in front of the full length mirror. He was naked. His belly stuck out, as if he was pregnant. The bedroom had a canopy covered bed large enough to hold a party on, a floor to ceiling window overlooking Cairo, and a gilt covered desk that could have been in Louis XIV's bedroom.

The carpet was chocolate brown and as thick as the skin of a lamb. On his left a young woman, also naked, with large breasts, was holding a syringe up, expelling tiny drops into the air.

"Don't waste any," he said.

"I won't, master." She held it out. "Are you ready?"

He closed his eyes. "Do it."

She pushed the needle into his buttocks. He trembled. She wrapped her arms around him, extending one hand down to under his belly.

"Where is your sister?" He sounded angry.

"She will be here soon. Would you not like just me this morning?" She rubbed her breasts against his back.

He shook his head. "Get my phone," he said, pointing at one of the gilt-edged side tables beside the bed. He walked to the window. Cairo was engulfed in a dark mist below him. The horizon was lit with the first false dawn of a new day.

She passed him the phone. He pressed at it until his encrypted call app opened. He clicked at one of the stored contacts, put the phone to his ear.

"You still wake early, Ahmed," came a thin voice a few seconds later.

"This is the most important day for Egypt in a generation, why would I not wake early to enjoy it." He smiled, put a hand on the thick plate glass. In the apartment block below him lights turned on. A woman came to the window. She looked up. He stared back at her. She disappeared.

"You have made the second transfer?" came the voice in his ear.

"Our Swiss partners will make the transfer in one hour. They are waiting on news that we have all survived the night."

"Have no worries on that account. Special forces have taken up positions at all your facilities. They have orders to shoot to kill."

"Good. The Egyptian Republic will thank you when all this is done."

"I'll thank you when every transfer has been made, Ahmed." The line went dead.

On his back he could feel four hands stroking him. He turned. The two young women pressed their naked bodies into him.

He smiled. The effects of the injection were beginning to be obvious. One of the girls giggled. The other one grabbed him.

"Tell me how our doctor friend struggled again," he said in a low, rasping tone.

One of them leaned close to his ear. She began whispering.

The other laughed as she watched the effect on his manhood. The whispering went on. His hands became fists and his face grew red.

"Stop!" he roared.

They moved away, bowed low, knelt, their foreheads touched the carpet.

"Get the prisoner!" he roared.

15

I took my passport out of my bag, handed it to the khaki clad soldier at my window. Mike was holding his out through the other side. Our driver had his hands in the air. He was talking fast to another soldier. Others, with their guns trained on us, were standing nearby. The red metal gate to the compound, topped with barbed wire, was closed.

Mike joined in the conversation in Arabic. Within seconds he was shouting. An officer with red epaulets on his shoulders, who had been standing at the cement block security cabin, strode forward. He pushed the soldier at the driver's window aside and peered in at us.

"I am sorry to detain you, professor," he said, in perfect English. "But we must check everyone who comes in here while we are on security alert." His gaze slipped towards me.

"You have an assistant with you today?" His words were not aimed at me.

"She is my guest. Is there a problem?"

"I will be back shortly." He went to the security cabin to the left of the entrance. Sandbags had been piled up on the side of the cabin facing the road. They had Arabic writing on them.

"I've never seen them so jumpy," said Mike. "I hope they let the media through when they get to the pyramid."

"It's an important day for Mr. Yacoub. I expect he doesn't want anything to go wrong." I was wondering if they'd start asking why I was in Cairo, and if I should tell them about Sean being missing.

The officer walked towards us, our passports in his hand. He passed both of them to Mike. "You are free to go in, professor." He glanced at me. "And to bring your guest, but she is your responsibility when she is here."

I leaned forward. "Has the security situation improved since last night?"

He stared back at me, as if wondering how to answer me.

"The crowds in the city dispersed last night, Mrs. Ryan." He paused, pointed a finger at me. "Our response to the attacks on our military personnel were appropriate. Please make sure you report that when you get back to your job in London."

I stared back at him. How did he know where I worked?

He leaned in towards me. "You are most welcome here." His face was impassive. As we drove through the metal gate, which had opened, I looked back. The officer had his phone to his ear and was talking into it.

"What was that about?" said Mike.

"I work for a group that helps people who want to leak wrong doing."

He didn't reply. I stared straight ahead. A square concrete building, four stories high, loomed in front of us. Palm trees stood around it and a car park, mostly empty, stood in front of it. Beyond the building I could see the Great Pyramid. We were separated from it only by a wire fence with floodlights and black hooded cameras at regular intervals. After the fence rough stony ground sloped upwards towards the pyramid.

The driver pulled up in front of the building. As we got out Mike turned to me and said, "I wish you'd told me where you worked when I met you."

"Why?" I followed him to the front door. It was made of dark glass. All the windows of the building had closed blinds behind them. A camera above the front doors pointed at us.

"Mr. Yacoub is very picky about who he invites to his events, that's all." He swiped a card over a card reader, then held the glass door open for me.

"He's afraid of stuff getting out about him?"

"He likes to spin things his way."

"Tell him not to worry. I'm not planning to meet any whistle blowers here. All I want is help to find my husband."

Mike stopped at the bottom of a set of wide white steps leading up. The stairwell went all the way up the inside of the building. Glass barriers at each level controlled access from the stairwell.

"I understand, but you'll have to wait here." He pointed at a square of white leather chairs nearby. "I'll be back soon." He smiled. "I just need to check everything is ready."

The atmosphere between us had chilled to below freezing.

I stepped towards him. "You have my word, Mike. Nothing I see here will be repeated anywhere, posted anywhere or spoken about to anyone." I put my hand on my heart. "I have zero interest in what your boss is up to."

I put a hand out towards him. "Please, I need to find out if my husband was admitted to any hospital here in Egypt. That's all. Then I'm leaving Cairo forever."

Mike blinked, leaned towards me. "Don't worry, Isabel. I'm going to help you, I just have to be seen to do the right thing. Yacoub is one of the most paranoid people I've ever met. And I've met a few paranoids in academic land."

He leaned close to me. "If your husband ever came to Cairo we will find out. Yacoub has access to every database in Egypt." He put a hand on my arm. It lingered there a second longer than it should have. His eyes opened as he pulled away, as if he was stopping himself showing any glimpse of how he felt.

I sat down on one of the chairs, stared at the glass table in front of me. I knew the effect I had on some men. It was a pain in the ass. I bent my head. Where the hell was Sean? Why did I have to go through all this crap?

A faint buzzing sound sent me twisting my head to see where it was coming from. Then I remembered. My phone might be on silent. It does that to itself sometimes when I push it into my bag. I fished it out. I didn't know the number. Was that an Egyptian number ringing me?

I tapped at the phone, put it to my ear.

"Mrs. Ryan, come quick. I have news of your husband. You must come now!" It was the taxi driver who'd taken me to the hospital.

I stood, as if a bolt of iron had shot up through me.

"What news have you found. Tell me." My stomach somersaulted. Tears pricked behind my eyes. My words caught in my throat. Could he really be alive?

"Come. You must come. A nurse saw him. He saw your husband. He is going off his shift in one hour. Come to the hospital now. I will be there to translate."

I looked around, went to the window, pulled a blind up. Could I get a taxi from the street outside?

"I'm coming. I'll be there. Where do we meet?"

"In the car park, where I was parking last time." He sniffed. "And Mrs. Ryan, bring cash. We will have to pay him."

My heart twisted. Was this a scam? Oh my God. Was I being taken for a desperate fool?

"Okay." I put the phone back in my pocket, walked to the reception desk.

A security guard dressed in black looked up as I approached. He had a small black bird insignia on his breast pocket. It looked as if he was covering reception until the day time staff appeared.

"Please call Mike Bayford for me," I said, leaning over the desk in my eagerness to get out of the place. Mike might be able to call me a taxi.

The guard looked at me as if I was an alien.

"Professor Bayford, please." I raised my voice. I looked up. A black suited guard at the next level, by the stairs, was looking down at me. I glanced at the main door. Was I going to be able to get out of here?

"Professor Bayford!" I repeated, with a desperate edge to my voice now.

At last, the baffled look on the guard's face was replaced by a smile. He nodded, reached towards a black phone on the desk in front of him. He pressed at the keypad, put the phone to his ear, then spoke a stream of Arabic into the mouthpiece, all the time staring at me.

I paced the reception area, from the door, back to the desk, where the guard was absorbed in watching me. Minutes passed. I took out my phone, thought about calling the taxi driver and asking him to come out and pick me up. I looked at my watch. It was seven-thirty. The nurse was probably getting off work at eight. I looked up the stairs. Mike wasn't coming. I had to make a decision.

I headed for the door, yanked it open, sprinted across the car park, heading for the main gate. There had to be taxis in this area. It was near the pyramids. They'd be dropping tourists out here. But what if I was wrong? What if taxis didn't pick lone women up on the street here?

I stopped, looked back at the building. Torn is not a feeling I am used to. I know what to do mostly. I base decisions on gut feel and my knowledge of the options. But my gut was telling me to be careful and my knowledge of this part of Cairo was minimal.

I stared at the building, weighing up the options. How long would it be before Mike reappeared? Was he in a meeting, which the guards were afraid to break into?

I looked at the gate. A memory of Sean, smiling at me, filled my mind. I had to take this chance. I ran on. The soldiers on this side of the gate were already staring at me, three of them with their guns pointed in my direction. Another one had a phone to his ear.

As I got near, the rough, almost white gravel crunched under my feet. My heart was pounding. I waved, trying to appear as friendly as possible. The three soldiers stood together now. Two of them were whispering to each other. A sickening feeling filled my chest. They were talking about me. I knew young Egyptian women usually didn't go out alone.

I also knew that a woman's honor in this country was a prize her family would kill for.

I strode the final few yards to the gate.

"Please let me through," I said, pointing at the gate.

The soldiers looked at each other, shrugged. They had stupid blank looks on their faces. I was tempted to shout at them.

The officer who had spoken to us appeared from the gate house.

"What is wrong Mrs. Ryan?" He stood about three feet from me. He was taller than I'd thought. His expression was a mix of pity and feigned friendliness.

"I need to get back into the city. Please open the gate."

"Professor Bayford is on his way. Please wait here." He pointed at the building behind me. I looked around. Mike had appeared. He was with the driver. They were heading for the mini bus. I crossed my arms.

The mini bus arrived. Mike got out.

"What happened, Isabel?" His tone was angry. His lips pressed together, as if he was controlling himself.

"I got a call from the taxi driver I was with yesterday. He's found someone who might have seen Sean. I have to get back into the city."

He shook his head. "Isabel, be careful. People are going to take advantage here, if they think you'll pay for information."

"I know, but I have to do this." I was surprised at how strongly my words came out. There was a touch of desperation to them. I made a fist and held it tight to my side. My heart was beating faster than it should have. Was I clutching at stupid straws?

"Isabel, why don't you let my driver take you there? Where exactly are you going?"

It crossed my mind not to tell him, but he'd find out anyway if I used his driver, and even if I wanted to hide it from him he could have me followed. Why shouldn't I trust him?

I'd told him about the hospital already. I also needed his help. I was more likely to get it if I trusted him.

"I'm going to the hospital I visited yesterday. He's waiting for me there." I looked at my watch. It was twenty-five to eight.

"I have to go." I reached out, touched his arm.

His expression softened. "Be careful. Don't promise anyone money for information."

He walked to the mini bus. I followed him. He spoke a long stream of Arabic to the driver, then waved me to get in.

"Good luck. I hope you find out what happened. The driver will wait for you. He'll bring you to the pyramid when you're finished. He'll be coming back for me. You could arrive in time for the opening ceremony, if you get this business done fast." He paused. "That's if you want to come to it."

"I do. This could all be a wild goose chase."

"I'll leave your name with security. Good luck." He opened his arms.

I hesitated, then hugged him.

"Thanks."

A minute later we were heading back into the city. The driver turned to me as we stopped at a traffic light. He smiled, as if he knew my mission. I looked away. Was I about to get taken? Our trainer, almost ten years ago, when I went to work for the British Consulate in Istanbul, had explicitly warned us about paying for information. "If you pay in cash, expect to have to double check everything you are told." I still remembered the words he'd used. We were training for administrative positions, but we'd still received three months of basic security, self-defense and anti-kidnap training.

At the next traffic lights he turned to me. "Passport?" he said, looking at me with a frown.

"What?"

He replied by pointing up ahead. A stream of stopped cars filled the road. I squinted. Beyond them I could see the barrel of a tank, pointed towards us.

"Army," he said, as we slowed and joined the queue.

I counted the cars ahead of us. There was at least twenty. And they weren't moving.

16

Henry Mowlam was on duty that Saturday morning. He'd arrived early at six-thirty. Getting in before his team was important. He could allocate tasks and get a feel for what the day would bring.

That morning it was all about Egypt. The general, who had been President of the Egyptian Republic for less than a year, had been helicoptered to the Montaza Palace, a wedding cake style building in the eastern suburbs of Alexandria. President Mubarak had installed an underground control room there. It was an ideal location to oversee the crushing of any revolt against his rule.

Henry read the latest short report from the British Embassy in Cairo. It indicated that twenty civilians had died in the Tahrir Square massacre the night before and that six security personnel and nine armed rebels had died in attacks on three military installations the previous evening.

But these numbers were tiny in comparison to the population of the country, ninety-two million by the latest estimates. The most populous country in the Arab world had suffered a blow, but it was an injury that could quickly be recovered from.

If nothing else were to happen, that is.

Chatter on Arabic websites and social media, translated overnight by the security services translation team, supervised from the Swindon intelligence unit, showed that most Egyptians were not likely to join any revolt at this time. The decisive handling of the attack on government buildings in Tahrir Square had stopped the rebels. But two issues were still of concern to the embassy.

One was the possibility of a new demonstration that afternoon and the second was the shift in the alliances at the top of the Egyptian state. The rise of Ahmed Yacoub was noted. His possible elevation to a position in the Executive Council of the Egyptian Republic, where real power in Egyptian life lay, was now a distinct possibility.

Ensuring British interests were protected in Egypt would require that good relationships with Yacoub be firmly established.

Henry brought up his profile on another screen to see if anything had been added to it. The coffee he had brought with him to his desk was getting cold.

He read about the event in the Great Pyramid planned for that morning, and looked through the list of Egyptian security camera systems he still had access to. Relying on satellite images was not going to be enough today. He remembered Isabel Sharp had told him she was heading to Egypt to look for her husband.

Where the hell was she?

He took out his phone, laid it on the desk. He would call her, but first he had to allocate tasks to his staff. Two of them were already at their desks. They had to be directed towards monitoring the situation in Egypt, and in particular to finding out if there were any chance of a further destabilization there.

There was too much at stake right now. Nothing was certain anymore. Old alliances could not be counted on in the way they had in the past. The United Kingdom had to rely on its own intelligence, its own resources.

17

I looked at my watch. We were inching forward. The driver had turned on the air conditioning, as the heat was building up outside. The sun was over the horizon. Car horns were blaring.

The driver turned to me. "We will be twenty minutes more here, madam."

I took my phone out called the number the taxi driver had called me from. He answered quickly.

"I'm on my way. Please ask the nurse to wait. I'm stuck at some military checkpoint."

"This is bad, very bad." He paused. There was music in the background. Egyptian pop music. He was in his taxi, probably outside the hospital, waiting for me.

"How much cash will I need?" It was the question I should have asked on the last call.

"Ten thousand Egyptian pounds, but he prefers five hundred American dollars. It is the same for you, almost, yes?"

I groaned. I had a thousand Egyptian pounds in my purse, from the money I'd changed at the airport.

"Bring him to the hotel after his shift. I should be there in half an hour." I'd spotted a small sign at reception offering to provide Egyptian currency for credit card users. Most of my credit cards were below their credit limits.

And it would be safer to meet them at the hotel.

"We will wait outside." He sounded angry. Was this a warning sign? Was I about to be ripped off?

I ended the call. If they wanted the money they would come.

The driver looked at me in the rear view mirror.

"You want to go to the hotel?"

"Yes."

His eyes stared at me in the mirror. I looked away. What the hell did the men here stare this way? But I knew the answer. Western women were seen as easy here. Some of them would assume, because I had the freedom to choose my own partner, that I could be persuaded to go to bed with them, just by their smile.

I stared out the window. What the hell was I getting myself into?

The van lurched forward. A helicopter appeared to the right, coming over the low dust covered two and three level houses, appearing through a forest of satellite dishes, TV aerials and the clothes lines that filled almost every roof.

Within a few seconds the chatter of the helicopter was overhead. If they were targeting us, we were ducks all lined up, and tied by our feet to the ground. Whoever was at the controls of the helicopter, an Apache gunship, could send us all to the next life with the twitch of a finger.

The whup of the blades sent a shiver through my body. Fear had filled my heart every day since Sean had disappeared. Since coming to Cairo it had started filling my head too.

18

Ahmed Yacoub pointed at Professor Bayford. He took a step towards him to add extra power to his words. The conference room in the research center near the Great Pyramid was empty except for the two of them. Below, visible through the window, were four black armored Toyota Landcruiser J200's.

"You can bring anyone you like to the ceremony." He jabbed his finger into Mike's white shirt. "But when I see her I will tell her what I think of the British Security services sending a spy to watch over us. They should stay out of our business." Spittle flew from his mouth.

"Isabel Ryan is looking for her husband. She thinks he's in Cairo. Whatever her job is, that part is true."

Yacoub shook his head. "You are so naïve. That is the most obvious cover story I have ever heard." He pressed his finger into Mike's shirt again.

"She's a honey trap. And you've swallowed the honey."

Mike looked down at the Landcruisers. Two men were loading white plastic boxes into the last vehicle. There were three more boxes nearby waiting to be loaded.

"But you will meet her?"

Yacoub shrugged. "Yes. I'd like to meet this honey pot." He made a licking gesture on his fingers. "I have a liking for honey."

Mike glared at him.

"Will you help her look for her husband?"

"Let's get going. We'll be late." Yacoub pointed at the men carrying the last box. "Is everything the way we agreed?"

"Yes."

"And your team know nothing."

Mike nodded.

Yacoub's right hand became a fist. He placed it on the glass in front of him. "I don't trust anyone, professor." He lifted his fist away from the window, then banged it back onto the glass. The glass shook.

"Any mistakes, there will be consequences."

Mike stepped back. He looked a little pale under his tan. "There will be no mistakes. I don't do mistakes." He pushed his chin forward. "I don't even know how to spell the word."

19

The helicopter didn't fire. It loomed over the tank barring the road, then leaned to the side and roared away. Off to the next checkpoint around Cairo, no doubt.

I leaned forward. "How much longer will this take."

The driver shrugged. "Not long."

I tried the taxi driver's number again. I had to tell him to wait if I was delayed. There was no answer. What the hell was I going to do if he wasn't at the hotel? I willed the cars ahead to move, craning my neck to see if they were.

My phone buzzed. Thank God. The taxi driver was calling back. I put the phone to my ear.

"Mrs. Ryan. Henry Mowlam here. How are you getting on in Cairo?"

A light sweat broke out on my brow. This was the last thing I needed, Henry interfering.

"Still looking for Sean. But I'm alive. Was there anything else?"

Henry coughed. "You didn't get caught up in that incident in Tahrir Square last night?"

"No, but I saw flashes across the roof tops. I know what happened." I turned towards the window. "A lot of people died, didn't they?"

"Yes. It's not safe there, Isabel. The embassy is issuing a public notice that British citizens should not travel to Egypt, except for emergencies."

"This is an emergency, Henry."

"What are you up to out there?" Henry's tone had changed. "I'm pinging you off a mast on the road to the pyramids."

"I'm not sightseeing, if that's what you're concerned about." He was annoying me now.

"Go on, then. Tell me."

I thought for a second about giving him a story, but that wouldn't do me much good if I needed his help while I was here.

"I met Mike Bayford, who's doing research at the Great Pyramid. He has a press conference this morning. I was hoping to be at it." I didn't say why. The driver might report everything I said.

There was a pause, a clicking noise. Henry was looking up Mike on Google, probably.

"This is the guy who's sponsored by Ahmed Yacoub?" he said.

"Yes."

"Good." He left the rest unsaid.

"What does that mean?"

"Just keep your eyes and ears open. I'll call you tonight."

The line went dead. He didn't even give me a chance to respond. Typical. The need of the security services for information outweighed anything else. We lurched forward. We were near the top of the line.

"You have passport?" The driver was staring at me in the rear view mirror again.

"Sure." I pulled it from my bag, held it up. He held a plastic ID card with his picture up. Soldiers were standing to the side of the tank ushering cars through one at a time, leaning in, checking each driver, looking under each vehicle with a mirror on a telescopic stick, opening the boot of each and checking what they were carrying.

They were looking for guns, I supposed. They didn't want people fighting back today.

Now we were at the top of the line. They took my passport, gave it a quick look. The driver said something in Arabic. I heard Yacoub somewhere in the middle of it. My passport came back in the window. We were waved on. It looked like Mr. Yacoub had a lot of pull here. The road ahead was almost deserted. We reached the hotel ten minutes later.

It was twenty past eight. There was no sign of the taxi driver. I went to the reception.

"Are there any message for me?" I asked the smiling young man behind the counter. The reception area was almost empty. A few European tourists were standing near the door out to the street, with their bags. It looked as if they were heading to the airport.

He looked in a pigeon hole, then on the counter in front of him, then looked at me.

"No, I am sorry, Mrs. Ryan."

Can you give me some cash if I use a credit card?"

He smiled. "Yes, madam." He was slightly taken aback at the amount I asked for, but after calling someone on his phone he ran my card through a machine and took cash from somewhere deep beneath the counter. He smiled as he gave it to me. The exchange rate he'd given me was probably a total rip off. I didn't care. I had to be able to pay this guy.

I went to wash my face and use the bathroom. I didn't want to look a mess when they came. If they did come.

When I arrived back at reception the taxi driver was there. He looked out of place in his dirty white galabeya. He waved at me, his palm up and steady. I walked towards him.

"Where is this nurse?"

He shook his head. "He would not come here, but he told me what to tell you."

I pointed towards the wicker seats at the far end of the reception area. He shook his head.

"Come with me."

He led me to his taxi outside the hotel, opened the door for me, then sat inside. He started the engine.

"Where are we going?"

"My cousin has a restaurant near here. We will talk there."

We drove, took a turn to the left. This street was narrow, with balconies on the buildings and shuttered windows. At the next turn there was a restaurant on the corner with an ancient looking Coca Cola sign in Arabic on the wall high up. We stopped outside.

Inside the café a few old men sat at tables. A large flat screen TV dominated the back of the room. A glass case ran down the left side of the room. Behind it stood a woman. Her head was covered in a pale blue scarf. She was staring through the glass at us.

The taxi driver turned to me.

"We stay here. After, I drive you back." He paused, leaned towards me, his eyes widening. "You pay me now."

I swung my head from side to side. "No, you tell me what he had to say first. I'm not a fool." I felt for the door handle, glanced towards the woman in the restaurant. She was gone. There was no one behind the counter.

The driver pointed a nicotine stained finger at me. "No, you do what I say. You pay me now."

I pulled the door handle. "I'm going." Just then, a movement at the corner of my eye caught my attention. I turned my head. Two men were standing near the taxi. Both had dirty galabeyas on. Both were staring at us. She'd summoned his pals.

I pointed a finger at the driver. "The British Foreign office know exactly where I am. They are tracking my phone." I pointed at my bag. "If anything happens to me you will all pay."

"This is not a trick, madam." He pointed at the two men. "These are my friends. Talking is a thing that can get me into trouble here. Big trouble." He had a frightened look in his eyes now.

A noise came from the other side of the car. A man in a baggy, faded black suit slipped into the seat beside me. I held the door handle, ready to run.

The man turned to me. He was about twenty-five, with a close cropped black beard and pock marks on the left side of his face. His hair was black and cut tight to his head so that it stuck out in spikes.

"I can help you," he said, in hesitant English. Then he reached a hand towards my knee.

20

The room was almost all white, except for the hospital bed, which had steel legs and railings all around it. Monitoring equipment rested on steel stands. Black screens showed numbers and blinking lines ascending and descending in rhythmic patterns.

The light in the room was low, emanating from a series of adjustable downlights built into the ceiling. Along one wall stood a large basin with a water tap and beside it a green medical waste bag in a steel holder.

Two drip bags stood beside the hospital bed. Transparent liquid dripped from the bags into tubes, which connected to the patient lying on the bed. One fed into each arm.

The patient had no sheet covering him. He lay on soft green rubber. The room temperature was warm. A fan, humming intensely in the air conditioning duct, filtered impurities from the air.

The door to the room opened with a loud click, as locks tumbled. Into the room walked a young man dressed in a green hospital gown, with his hands held in front of him, high up.

His hands were covered in thick green gloves. He let the door close behind him, walked to the back of the room and pulled a steel, chest high table towards the bed.

On it there were needles and steel instruments in a row, as well as a see through plastic box with a warning sticker in Arabic on it. Behind the box was a white cooler box, with a clipped down lid.

He pulled the clips, opened the box, then went to examine the patient. He tapped the man's knee. There was no response. He lifted an eyelid. The man's pupils were almost fully dilated.

He held the instrument in his hand, paused. The last time he had done this it had taken longer than it should. This time he would get it right.

He bent the patient's head back, inserted a green roll of plastic beneath the patient's neck. Then he leaned over the patient and looked up his nose.

The nose cavity loomed bigger and bigger as he went closer to determine the exact route he should take as he went.

After a minute more he took the long steel scoop, with the small spoon shaped end and placed it in the patient's right nostril. Then he pushed it. There was a slight cracking noise as the membrane between the nose and the brain broke.

21

I slapped his hand away. He pulled it away as if he'd been scalded.

"He is only being friendly," said the taxi driver, his tone angry.

I made my hand into a fist. "If he touches me, I will scream." My mouth was dry, my hand trembling.

The taxi driver said something fast in Arabic, then glared at me.

"Do you want help or not?"

"How can he help me?"

"He saw your husband. Is that not enough?"

"How do I know he's telling the truth."

The driver sighed. "Why do you think we are talking here and not at your hotel?"

I looked out the window. The men had stepped back from the car. One was watching one way down the street. The other was watching the other way. Whether they were on lookout for someone who might interfere with me being ripped off, or some other danger, I had no idea. Warning klaxons in my brain were ringing so loud I wondered if everyone around me could hear them.

"Not convinced."

He reached towards the glove compartment, opened it, pulled out the now folded and bent picture of Sean. He passed it to the man in the back, who was eyeing me as if I was a snake that might bite.

"I see man," he said, taking Sean's picture, looking at it, then holding it towards me, his hand shaking. Then he looked out the rear window. There was a hunted look in his eyes.

I reached for my bag.

The man shook his head. "No money." He looked offended.

So that was why the taxi driver wanted to be paid in advance. I looked at the driver. He shrugged, smiled at me.

"You pay me for finding this one," he said.

I looked back at the man beside me. He was staring at Sean's picture.

"I see him. They put him in special ambulance. I never see again."

Something inside me broke open. A rush of emotion filled my chest. I pressed my lips tight as relief poured through, as if water had been handed to me after weeks in the desert.

But I had to be careful. I had to be sure.

"How did he look?"

"Bad." He looked at me, a sadness deep in his eyes.

"How bad?" A new fear rose inside me. What if I was too late? What if he'd been brought here to Cairo, but he'd died?

The man shook his head, slowly. "Bad," he said again.

Another wave of emotion passed up my body. This one made my eyes blink tears away.

"Where was he going?"

He looked at the driver. The driver was staring at him, his eyes wide, as if warning him.

The man reached for the door handle. As he got out he said one thing.

"I saw the bird." Then he slammed the door behind him.

The taxi driver put his hand out towards me. He grinned. I felt a shadow at the window. One of his friends was leaning against my door, his body stopping any chance of me getting out.

Then the other man was at the other door. Leaning at it. I was trapped. But I knew what they wanted.

22

Henry Mowlam stared at the report on the smallest of the two screens on his desk. The larger screen showed live images from Tahrir Square. The square had been closed for most of the day as workmen cleaned up blood and mended holes in the concrete from the night before. Cars were passing through it again and a semblance of normality was returning.

The only notable thing was the flowers passersby were dropping in front of the steel barricade, which the army was manning in front of the Egyptian government buildings.

Henry's gaze flicked occasionally to the larger screen, then back. The report had been written by a member of the British Embassy Cairo staff. It was about Ahmed Yacoub. He peered closer as he took in what he was reading.

Yacoub Holdings research and development division have been building capability over the past decade in the pharmaceutical sector. They have recruited scientists from Germany, Italy, Turkey and the United Kingdom. The focus of the research has been to prove the effectiveness

Laurence O'Bryan

of a variety of traditional Egyptian medical treatments.

Dealings with United Kingdom Universities have mainly been through the Yacoub Foundation, a registered grant bestowing charity. Grants have been allocated to almost all the main United Kingdom Universities with leading edge pharmaceutical laboratories.

The only other research grant the Yacoub Foundation has given out is to a Dr. Susan Hunter, Head of the Ancient Text Translation department at Cambridge University Archaeological Museum. That grant has been renewed each year. Dr. Hunter has visited Cairo on a number of occasions and has met with Embassy staff. Our understanding is that she has helped researchers at the Yacoub Foundation to translate various Egyptian, Greek and Byzantine texts discovered in Egypt and beyond.

Henry looked away. Dr. Susan Hunter. She was the researcher who had translated an ancient manuscript Sean and Isabel Ryan had found in Istanbul. It had proved to be a most interesting find. Parts of it were written on human skin, with invocations of devils and demons. Other parts were about making people well again, if they were close to death. Another section appeared to be a record of the trial of Jesus in Jerusalem.

The bound manuscript, with its sections sewn together with animal gut, had been assessed as being part of the Imperial Treasury of the Byzantine Empire. It contained some of the most valuable documents from a thousand-year Empire that began at the time of the Roman Emperor, Constantine the Great, in the early fourth century.

Henry looked at the large screen. Crowds were passing by in Tahrir Square. Most of them were dropping single white flowers he noticed now. A carpet of white flowers was growing across the square.

He looked at the list of live video feeds coming in from Egypt that glowed down the side of the screen. One showed the exterior of the Great Pyramid. It was tagged **Yacoub Holdings Press Conference**. He clicked on it. His main screen blinked, then showed a milling crowd in front of the Great Pyramid. An elevated speaking platform had been set up under the entrance to the pyramid. It had Egyptian flags in a row behind it. In front of it there was a scrum of what looked like private security officers.

They had a distinctive black uniform. He clicked on the zoom option. Two men were walking towards the speaking platform. One of them he recognized. It was Ahmed Yacoub.

23

I leaned forward, pointed at the taxi driver. "I'll give you half, that's all. Your friend was due half the money, and he doesn't want it."

The driver raised his hands. "We made a deal. I expect you to keep it."

"Even if the nurse doesn't want the money?"

The driver leaned towards me. "Maybe his family will want it."

"You know his family?" It sounded unlikely.

"No, but if something happens, I will."

"What do you mean, if something happens?" He was leaning so close, I could smell his breath, a mixture of tobacco and something spicy. I leaned back.

"If he dies, madam." He spoke softly, raised his eyebrows.

I thought about that for a few seconds. Was this all a trick? The main road was near enough to walk to. But it would definitely be better to get him to drop me back at the hotel, or take me back to see what was going on at the pyramid.

"You think he might die, because of what he told me?"

The driver shrugged. "It is possible. The bird he spoke about is the symbol of some people who are very powerful." He lowered his voice, as if some of these powerful people might hear him if he spoke too loud.

"What people?"

"The Brotherhood."

"You mean the Muslim Brotherhood?"

"They will kill us all if anything we say makes trouble for them." He drew a finger across his throat. "I do not want my family to end up on the street, because I help you."

I was torn. Maybe he was right. Maybe it was enough to have confirmation that someone had seen Sean. Maybe I should seek out the Muslim Brotherhood myself, see if they knew anything. And maybe there were other things this driver could do for me, if he thought he could make more money from me.

I reached towards my bag.

"Will you drive me the Great Pyramid if I pay you?"

He nodded. "Yes. You want to go now?" He smiled. His teeth were yellow and there was a gap on one side.

"I need the money before I take you." He pointed at the man on the right side of the taxi. "My cousin will keep it safe, just in case."

I was starting to believe he was afraid of something, or someone. I took the envelope with the cash the hotel had given me and passed it to him. It was an investment. I didn't have many contacts here who spoke English and Arabic.

"Where do I find the Brotherhood?" I asked, as I passed him the envelope.

"Do not contact them, please, madam. This will be trouble for you." He paused, shook his head. "You do not know them. They will not help you." He glanced down my body, as if implying that because I was a woman, dressed in un-Islamic clothes, my chance of getting help was close to zero.

He opened his door, passed the envelope with the money to a hand that reached inside. I still wasn't sure if I'd made the right decision, but the benefits of paying him seemed to outweigh the risks.

"We go now," he said. He started the engine.

"Yes. But there is one more thing you can do."

"What is that?" He turned, looked at me with narrowed eyes.

"Do you know the Brotherhood?"

"They are everywhere."

"Can you find out if they know anything about my husband?"

He pulled the car out into the traffic, heading back to the main road.

"This is a dangerous thing you ask. These people will do anything for their faith. Any stupid thing."

"I understand, but I will pay you. The same as you got today, if anyone knows where Sean is."

He shook his head. "I will want more. Double what you paid today. This is a big risk."

I thought for a minute, mainly to give him the sense that I was hesitating to pay his price. Actually, I would have paid ten or twenty times what he asked to find Sean. No, I would pay a hundred times what he asked and every last penny in every account I could lay my hands on.

When he stopped at the traffic lights he took the picture of Sean out of his pocket.

"Is this picture recent?"

I looked at it, then looked away. "Yes."

There was a group of men walking across the road. One of them turned to stare at me. He looked a bit like Sean. I couldn't look at him. I closed my eyes. Every time I saw a face like Sean's pain gripped me, as if my heart was being crushed from all sides. Images of him smiling at me swirled in my mind. Each one brought the same pain, a wound that wouldn't heal, that left me longing to see him.

The taxi lurched forward. I opened my eyes, mainly to stop Sean's face appearing all the time, haunting me. This goose chase had to be my last. I would follow these trails in Cairo to the very end, and then accept the truth, whatever happened. If I'd been ripped off, so be it. If there was nothing here for me, but for my desperation to be taken advantage off, so be it. And when it was all done, I would go home. Alek needed me.

"A checkpoint, madam. You have your passport?" He slowed as we approached the military traffic check, which I had been held up at earlier.

"Yes."

But they weren't stopping traffic going out of the city. They were stopping it going in and the line of cars waiting to be checked was double what it had been a few hours before. As I watched the cars waiting to be checked I wondered when the city would get back to normal.

Then I saw a car near the end of the line bump onto the thin grass strip that separated the lanes of traffic going each way. As we sped by, I saw three men in the car, all dressed in black. I looked out the back window. They had swung onto our side of the road. Behind them I could see the barrel of one of the tanks turning to face us.

24

Ahmed Yacoub bathed in the applause. In front of him sat a row of foam covered microphones with CNN, RT, BBC, AN, TN, 10 and a dozen other sets of initials and symbols.

The elevated speaking platform had Egyptian flags behind it and an emblem in front of it, the black bird on a white background symbol of Yacoub Holdings. In the invited audience, on ten rows of ten black metal chairs, sat a collection of well-dressed journalists, hand-picked Egyptian celebrities, and senior state employees, from the Ministry of Antiquities, the Tourism Ministry, and the Office of the President. Around the whole area was a red rope, beyond which security guards patrolled in pairs. A drone hovered at the back of the group. It was sending a live TV feed to Yacoub Holdings YouTube channel.

"What I have described for you is the biggest breakthrough in ancient Egyptian studies, of significance not only for all of us here in Egypt, but for the whole world too. And I am not just talking about tourism." He shook his head. Two senior executives of Yacoub Holdings hotel group were looking pleased at the back of the audience.

"The translation of an ancient manuscript found in Istanbul a few years ago, and translated at Cambridge University, shows that when the Byzantines ruled Egypt they investigated our Great Pyramid and made a number of discoveries, which they described in letters to the Emperor in Constantinople."

The audience looked up, as a helicopter with a bird symbol on it came over the top of the pyramid behind Ahmed Yacoub. It headed in their direction. Ahmed Yacoub didn't stop talking.

"The greatest of all their discoveries, is, without doubt the section in the manuscript which describes Egyptian medicines and treatments, all the secret things that were lost in the centuries between then and now." He raised his voice. "These exact medical treatments have been tested by our laboratories at Yacoub Holdings." He paused, raised his hands in triumph.

"And they have been found to be effective. But not only that, we have the exact compounds, which caused the effects and increase their efficiency!"

A female reporter, in a red dress, in the front row raised a hand, waved it.

Ahmed Yacoub smiled, pointed at her.

"What medical conditions do these treatments work for, Mr. Yacoub?" She smiled back at him.

"The most important treatment we have found works on one of the oldest ailments known to man or woman."

"What is that?" Another reporter shouted.

"Old age." Yacoub pointed at himself. "I have been taking this treatment for the past few weeks. Not only is my hair growing in a shade I have not seen in thirty years but I also have experienced an amazing flush of energy in other important departments." He looked down, as if embarrassed.

A buzz of conversation and laughter broke out in the audience.

An older man in the front row put his hand up. Yacoub pointed to him.

"Has this ancient manuscript been dated?"

Yacoub stared at him for a few seconds, then a grin spread across his face. "This is the very best part, ladies and gentlemen. Carbon dating of the papyri sewn into the manuscript shows a date of about five hundred and eighty in the common era, when the Byzantines still ruled in Egypt." He leaned forward. "And the opening section says that the report, about ancient Egyptian medical treatments, was copied from older documents from the time we call the New Kingdom, the period of Tutankhamun." He raised his hands wide.

"There are only a few papyri in existence anywhere from that period. This is the only one any of our experts are aware of that speaks about the fountain of youth."

The old man in the front row had his hand up again.

"The fountain of youth is a myth, is it not?"

Yacoub shook his head. "Yes, the Crusader stories, and the stories from Alexander the Great about a pool you could bath in and become young again, are myths. But they were based on facts. The defeat of aging was one of the secrets of ancient Egypt. Were we not the founders of all medicine? Were we not the people who produced tombs, and mummification processes, which kept bodies from turning to dust for thousands of years?"

A woman had her hand up. She was blonde, looked like an American.

Yacoub pointed to her.

"When will we see the evidence for all this?" she asked.

"I will let Professor Bayford answer this."

Yacoub sat. Mike Bayford stood up.

"Our scientific evidence is first of all in the manuscript and secondly in the double-blind tests that Yacoub Pharmaceuticals have carried out on the medical treatments described in it. In addition, we expect we will also discover other items to prove these treatments in the chamber we will open up in the Great Pyramid today."

A forest of hands rose.

"Who will be entering the chamber?" a voice shouted from the back.

"Both I and Mr. Yacoub will be the first to enter. We will be donning special suits to avoid contaminating anything inside."

"How do you know what is inside the chamber?" a woman's voice called out.

"We have sent two robots inside and from what we have seen, this is the eye of the pyramid, which archaeologists have long predicted would be found."

"What has been seen so far?" The old man was leaning forward in his seat.

"Our robots were unable to reach far into the chamber, but they have seen carvings of Imhotep, one of the Egyptian gods of healing and," he took a deep breath, "symbols for the dispelling of Ukhedu, poison, all carved on the passage walls."

An excited buzz rose up, as if a swarm of bees was passing through the crowd.

Yacoub stood. "That is all. You will find out more later today."

He shook hands with Mike Bayford as flashbulbs went off.

Someone shouted. "Has a hall been discovered or just a passage?"

Many of the crowd already had phones clamped to their ears.

25

My eyes were fixed on the tank, expecting at any moment to see a flash and a puff of smoke, then the car that had slipped away to our side of the road explode in a puff of smoke.

But nothing happened.

This wasn't Mosul. This wasn't a suicide attack. And soon the car and the tank had disappeared behind us. As we came closer to the Great Pyramid a helicopter flew over us. It had a bird emblem on its side. It flew towards the city, then circled back.

My driver slowed, pulled in. Up ahead was the entrance to the pyramids. A sign in Arabic above a high metal gate separated the walled area of the pyramids from the streets of shops and houses, the outskirts of Cairo, which lapped around the pyramids. A crowd of maybe fifty people was waiting at the gate. They were mostly Egyptian men in long galabeyas, but a few were dressed in suits and could have been from any country.

The taxi driver turned to me. "I will call you if I find out anything. And next time, when I ask for the money you owe me, will you give me a problem again?"

Laurence O'Bryan

"No. No problem. Find out where Sean is and you will get your money quickly." I got out of the car. The heat hit me. I'd been in the air conditioned taxi for almost an hour. Sweat broke out under my arms and down my back. The taxi driver gave me a thumbs up and pointed at the crowd at the gate. It looked as if none of them were getting into the pyramid compound.

I waited away from the crowd to see what was happening. Then the gate opened a little and two soldiers came out. They had long black batons in their hands. The crowd moved back and slowly the gate opened fully. Two black Mercedes came out. Both had darkened windows. The gate remained open. Beyond it stood a row of soldiers. The crowd pushed forward, heading to one side of where the soldiers stood. A man in a black uniform started checking what looked like ID cards, which the men were holding up.

I waited until the crowd were through, and walked up to the man in the uniform. He held his hands up to bar my way.

"No tourists today," he said.

My phone was buzzing in my jeans pocket. I looked at the screen.

"Henry. What's up?"

"Did you go to the press conference with your friend."

I sighed. "Looks like I missed it. A taxi driver said he had some information on Sean."

"Did he?"

"He thinks there's a connection with the Brotherhood. He's trying to find out more."

"Be very, very careful, Isabel. That's a hornet's nest you'll be sticking your nose into."

"I know." I paused. Maybe it was time to pull in some help. "Can you get me a pass into the pyramid compound, Henry? I'm stuck at the gate."

Henry let out an exasperated noise. "The best advice I can give you is to take the next flight back to London. When trouble starts in Egypt anything can happen."

"Thanks, Hen…" I tried to sound as sarcastic as I could, but a buzzing from my phone cut me off.

"Have to go." I pressed at the screen, hoping not to miss the call. The 20 code at the beginning of the number told me it was from someone in Egypt.

"Isabel here."

There were a few seconds of silence. Was it the taxi driver?

"Mike here. Where are you?"

Relief rose inside me. "I'm at the gate to the pyramid complex. I can't get in."

"Was your trip into town worth it?"

"Maybe. I'll tell you when I see you. Can you get me in?"

"The press conference is over, but if you want to meet Yacoub we are getting ready to enter the pyramid. I will send someone for you. You're at the main gate?"

"Yes."

He closed the line. I stored his phone number under contacts.

I stood back from the crowd. Many had gone through the gate, but there were others who hadn't. One had a t-shirt on with OFFICIAL GUIDE written on the back.

About ten minutes later I saw a guard in a black uniform waving at me. I headed towards the gate. This time I was waved through. Some of the men around were muttering. One shouted something in Arabic. It didn't sound complimentary. The guard put a hand on my arm and pointed towards a black Toyota jeep pulled up beyond the soldiers.

"I can walk on my own," I said, shrugging my arm from his grasp.

He didn't reply, just marched on ahead and opened one of the back doors of the car.

By the time we'd reached a large tent set up in front of the Great Pyramid I was in awe. Only close up do you get a real idea of how massive the Great Pyramid is. It's taller than most buildings in any city and as large as a city block. I could just about make out the kink in the middle of the side facing me to see that it was actually eight sided, not four, which was a common misconception. The sun was hitting directly onto the pyramid and I could see its shadow stretching out behind it, like an arrow pointing out into the desert.

A half dozen black uniformed guards stood at the entrance to the tent. Others waited beside three black Toyota Landcruisers with tinted windows. A black Mercedes SUV waited near them. Its driver was leaning against the front of the vehicle smoking a cigarette. His suit had a bulge around the waist on his left side. I assumed this was a weapon.

The guards at the gate stood to attention as we approached. One of them pulled open a canvas door in the tent. Beyond was a series of tables laid out in a square and a group of men with their backs to me. One of them was Mike. The other three I didn't know. As I came into the tent Mike saw me and waved me towards the table. The other men were too engrossed in what they were doing.

In the middle of the table was a wide screen laptop. On its screen was a wire frame image of the Great Pyramid. It was rotating slowly.

A man in a shiny navy suit turned to me. He had black, slicked-back hair, and was wearing a red tie. His skin was smooth, but he still looked to be in his sixties.

Mike pointed towards the man.

"May I introduce Ahmed Yacoub, president of Yacoub Holdings."

I put out my hand. Yacoub grabbed it, squeezed it tight.

"They didn't tell me you were beautiful too, Mrs. Ryan." He bowed slightly, smiled at me. It was almost a leer. He pulled me towards him, planted a kiss on both my cheeks. I could smell his aftershave. It was something expensive.

Mike touched my shoulder. "We are heading up to the King's Chamber in a few minutes. You haven't missed anything."

"You are fortunate Professor Bayford has invited you to come with us," said Yacoub. "But I can see why." His grin stretched like a cut across his lower face.

"I understand you are looking for your husband." He shrugged. "Were your contacts in the British security services not able to do anything for you?"

I started right back at him. "They won't search every hospital in every country of the world, just because an ex junior staff member in a British consulate asks them to."

"I am sure you were more than a junior staff member."

I decided to push my luck. "I expect you would be able to open the right doors for me, though."

His smile widened. "I will do anything I can for you." He bowed, turned back to the table. The other men were muttering in Arabic to each other as the 3D image kept rotating.

Mike pointed at the screen. "As you can see, we have used 3D reconstruction to create an image of what we discovered from our infrared thermography study. This will be the first time we've shown the full 3D image publicly." He reached towards the screen, pressed at it with his fingers, then flicked his fingers open.

The image on the screen zoomed in to the top chamber inside the pyramid.

"A group of researchers in 2011 sent a robot with a snake eye camera up one of the shafts from the other smaller chamber, the Queen's Chamber. They discovered a wall with hieroglyphs in red paint. We believe that shaft is a red herring." He reached for the screen, using his fingers to move the 3D model around. "Our research has focused on the King's Chamber."

He leaned forward, touched the screen. "This is what the 3D modeling came up with behind the floor of that chamber."

The screen showed a shaft leading down to a rectangular chamber. At the entrance to the chamber there were paler shapes on either side of where the shaft entered the chamber.

"What are they?" I pointed at the screen.

"We don't know," said Mike.

Yacoub was pressing into my left side. "Perhaps they are statues, professor," he said.

"They could be pillars," I said. "I saw pillars at the entrance to an underground room under Hagia Sophia." I stepped back. Yacoub was a bit close for my liking. I could smell his lemony body odor.

"You've seen the chamber they discovered there?" Mike's eyes opened a little.

"I was there when it was discovered."

"Then you can tell us if there are similarities when we get to it today," said Yacoub. He looked at Mike. "You should have told me she was involved in the discoveries under Istanbul."

Mike shrugged.

"What do you expect to find here?" I pointed at the chamber.

"There are three things we may find, Mrs. Ryan," said Yacoub. "A royal tomb, unseen in five thousand years, packed with more treasures than Carter found in Tutankhamun's, or maybe a room full of long lost papyrus scrolls and if not that, at the very least a chamber with hieroglyphics all over its walls, as we glimpsed with a robot sent down one of the shafts. What do you think, professor?" He tapped Mike's shoulder.

"We cannot be sure what we will find. The chamber could be empty or it could be the greatest archaeological find of the century," said Mike.

"Did you know that the purpose of the pyramids was as healing centers?" said Yacoub.

I shook my head. "I never heard that before."

"Well it is true. Ancient medicine was founded here in Egypt. Alexander the Great invaded us to be treated. Most of the great Roman Emperors had Egyptian doctors, the clever ones. Those doctors learned their trade in the temples, which were managed by the priests who were in control of our pyramids. These pyramids were the centerpiece of the temple complexes."

"This is not all proven yet," said Mike. "But it is not unreasonable, and if we discover anything on these lines." He pointed at the chamber on the screen. "This will cause a revolution in our understanding of medicine and ancient Egypt."

I heard a noise behind us. Two blue suited medical types had entered the tent. Each of the men carried a steel box. They moved to the end of the table the screen was on and started opening their boxes.

"Everyone who will go inside is required to give a blood sample," said Mike.

"You mean now?" I blinked.

"We need to be sure that any DNA found in the chamber can be traced to one of us, or that is it ancient in origin. Are you okay with this?" He leaned close to me. "It will only be a pin prick." Behind him, the two medical personnel had taken out syringes. They were holding them up in the air.

He leaned closer. "We can also use your sample to identify you, should the end times come upon us, and we need to put names to the bodies of the left behind."

"You're kidding, right?"

Yacoub grinned.

26

The white robed technician held the syringe up. He closed his eyes and spoke the cannibal prayer aloud, slowly, so that each word bounced off the four brick walls of the room.

"The sky clouds. The stars are cloaked.
We feed on their organs, with their body full of magic from the Isle of Fire.
The Lord Slayer cuts.
We eat people. We live on them.
We eat their magic for morning and dinner and night.
We travel the two heavens in their entirety.
We endure among them who are risen."

He paused, showed the syringe to each wall, bowing in each direction as he did so. He walked slowly to the body lying naked on the hospital trolley in the center of the room. The body was that of a man. His head was shaved and he had bruises on his arm and a purple mark on his forehead.

The technician picked up the man's arm. He slapped the skin at the elbow until purple lines appeared. Then he inserted the syringe. He extracted blood, walked to a steel table nearby, emptied the syringe into a glass vial and then threw the syringe into a blue waste bin.

As he left the room with the vial in his hand he turned off the lights and adjusted the room temperature control down a notch.

The room went quiet. All that could be heard was the distant thrum of the air conditioning.

27

I put my arm out. The man in the blue uniform shook his head, pointed to the back of the tent.

"It will only take a minute, Isabel," said Mike.

The man in the uniform walked ahead to a table at the back. It had a small fridge and empty glass vials on it. He motioned for me to put my arm out. I rolled up my sleeve. He put the needle in. I watched as he took a syringe of blood.

Yacoub called at me, "It is time to go."

They were heading out of the tent. I followed. Mike was standing near one of the Toyotas. Beside him was a bald man with a high forehead. He had a peaceful expression, as if he'd seen all this before.

"Isabel, let me introduce Mohammad Messun. He is the son of the Minister of Antiquities. Without Mohammad this whole program could not have happened."

Mohammad bowed. "You are too kind, Professor Bayford." He turned away, got in the car. Mike motioned for me to get in after him.

I was in the middle in the back between Mike and Mohammad. I tried to avoid pressing into them, but it wasn't easy.

Mike leaned forward to give me more room.

"Mohammad will supervise our work today. No internally destructive activity has been allowed in the Great Pyramid since 2002, when robots were permitted to drill through a blocking stone in a shaft leading to the Queen's Chamber."

Mohammad moved his legs, pushed his thigh into mine. I didn't move, pretended not to notice.

"Your husband is missing?" he said, smiling at me, as if he enjoyed the fact that Sean was gone.

"Yes." I turned to him. "How long have you worked at the Ministry?"

"I don't work there." His thigh pressed further into me. "What hotel are you staying at?"

"We will be going to lunch at Yacoub's house, after this," said Mike, interrupting. "Would you like to come?"

"Yes." I stretched my leg out, so it wasn't in full contact with Mohammad's.

Yacoub was in the front seat talking in Arabic with the driver. It was a short drive to the base of the pyramid. Red and white barriers were set up by the steps hewn into the pyramid. They led up to a small opening in the middle of one side of the pyramid. A crowd waited around the barrier. Black suited guards stood on the other side.

Our car pulled up at the side of the cordoned off area. As Mike and Yacoub got out the barrier was pushed to the side of the car so we could walk directly to the steps leading up the side of the pyramid. I got out behind Mike. As I did I felt Mohammad touch my back.

As we walked up the stairs I looked up. The pyramid seemed to extend forever. The stones looked far too massive to have been moved there just by brute force. The crowd behind the barrier were using smartphones to take pictures of us. Mike and Yacoub led the way into a roughly hewn opening in the side of the pyramid.

"This is known as the robber's entrance," said Mike. "It was battered into the pyramid in 820 A.D. by Caliph al-Ma'mun's palace guard. The Caliph was told by a fortune teller that he could regain his lost youth if he could find a way into the secret chamber in the pyramid."

"This was the story you told my father, too," said Mohammad. "I hope you have more luck than al-Ma'mun." He was behind me.

After a short climb up a steeply angled, narrow, low roofed tunnel the passage opened up into a small high roofed area. The walls here were smooth streaked limestone. The air was cool. I felt a sense of calm, similar to the feeling I get in cathedrals, as if something bigger than us was watching, listening.

A passage led upward, but a man barred our way with his body.

Mohammad strode towards him waving his arms, speaking fast in Arabic. The other man stood his ground, waited for Mohammad to finish, then launched his own tirade. Yacoub joined in the gesticulating, pointing at the man, as if threatening him.

"What's happening," I whispered to Mike.

"This guy claims to be the new guardian of the pyramid, appointed by the Minister of Antiquities only yesterday. He says we don't have the right papers to do any investigative work in the King's Chamber."

The argument was getting louder. Echoes of Arabic bounced off the walls, reverberated, filling me with a sense of menace. There was a noise behind me. I turned. Two women dressed in black from head to toe were standing right near me. They were staring at the man blocking our way. Yacoub looked back at them, motioned them forward. The two women pushed past me.

The argument took a new tone as they came up and joined in, standing beside Yacoub. The man blocking our way eyed them as if they were snakes. He started pointing at them. Then he stepped back. Everybody went silent, and the shouted echoes dissipated into the air.

Yacoub spoke softly now, reassuringly.

"What the hell is happening?" I asked Mike.

"Yacoub has pointed out that he has brought his daughters to see the King's Chamber for the first time. He's also said that this guy can supervise our work in the chamber."

There was a pause. The man blocking our way stroked his beard. Then he held his hand above his heart and bowed.

Yacoub hissed something. The man stepped aside. I followed up a steep walkway right behind Mike. The gallery we were in had a high roof, which tapered inwards to a narrow stone ceiling maybe thirty feet above our heads. I could sense the weight of thousands of tons of rocks all around us. Why the hell had anyone created this high roofed passage, sloping upwards, its stones angled precisely at the same angle as the walkway under our feet and narrowing evenly above our heads?

Mike spoke in Arabic to the man in front of him as we went. I was looking at the walls of the gallery. The cracks between each stone panel were straight, with no visible gap or mortar between them. How the hell had the builders made a gallery like this thousands of years ago, when most of the world was living in mud huts?

There were lights set at intervals along the walls of the gallery and wires running nearby.

At the end of the gallery was a platform and a small square passage, we had to bend and scuttle through. It led to a rectangular chamber, stone walled and roofed, maybe twenty feet wide and twice that long, with a flat stone ceiling about twenty feet above our heads.

The air was dry, still. A faint smell and taste of dust came to me. The room was lit by electric lamps on two walls. Three pieces of equipment on sturdy tripods stood in the room. One was in front of a niche in the end wall, near the entrance to the tunnel. It had a square metal weight suspended from it on a chain. The other two had an electronic instrument on top of them. A sliver of red light ran from one to the other, about chest height. I guessed they were measuring something with lasers.

Mike stood by the tripod with the weight suspended from it. We gathered around, expectantly.

"Thanks to Yacoub Holdings and the Ministry of Antiquities, we are delighted to finally conclude the testing phase of our project here in the King's Chamber. As you know our measurement instruments have uncovered anomalies in the floor of this chamber, with the thermal readings indicating a shaft below us." He smiled. Mohammad was filming him with an iPhone, as was one of the two black clad women who had joined us.

I put a hand up. "I thought you said the thermal anomalies were in the walls, Mike."

Mike's smile widened. "I did, but we do still have to be careful of tomb robbers."

Mohammad shrugged, as if he thought Mike was referring to him.

Yacoub walked near to where Mike was standing, but on the opposite side of the tripod.

"Thank you, Professor Bayford." He pointed at the weight suspended on the tripod. "This metal is osmium, the densest material currently available in usable quantities. This block has twice the density of lead and about twenty-five times the density of water. This block" — He tapped the metal with his knuckle. No sound emerged — "weighs three thousand five hundred pounds, about the weight of a small car."

Mike leaned forward. "And we are about to drop it on the floor." He brushed a hand against the side of the weight, went down on one knee. "The impact force has been calculated, and the falling distance, based on the type of granite of this particular block, which is different to the others around it."

It did look different, paler than the other blocks of gray stone which made up the floor.

Mike pointed at the other two tripods. "These instruments measure minute changes in the position of the floor slabs they are standing on."

Yacoub pointed a finger at a red button on the top of the tripod he was standing beside.

"It is my duty to start the test."

Mohammad took a step forward. "This is wrong, Mr. Yacoub, too destructive. As the lead partner in this enterprise, it is the ministry's duty to prevent any studies which might destroy any part of the pyramid."

The man who had tried to stop us entering the King's Chamber, said something in Arabic. Mohammad replied, nodded. He stepped towards Yacoub and pointed his finger at the tripod.

"You will not start this test."

Yacoub took a step towards him, his chest puffed out. For a moment I thought a fight was about to break out. Then Mike intervened.

"The procedure for this test had been agreed and set down in writing. I am the person who will initiate the test, not Mr. Yacoub. I will take responsibility for any damage to this floor stone. I assure you, our studies show that the stone will simply fall away with the weight placed on it. All this was made clear when we applied for permission. Your ministry specifically agreed that a weight bearing test was allowed."

I was wondering how much Yacoub had paid to get the test approved. I was also wondering how they got the osmium block into the King's Chamber, especially if there were any question marks about what it would be used for.

I leaned forward. There were lines along the face of the osmium. It wasn't a solid block. It was a stack of thin plates.

I waved at Mike. "Why will you drop it on this block, not that one or that one?" I pointed at the other floor blocks.

"This granite" — Mike pointed at the lighter block under the tripod — "has a high quartz content. I believe there's a reason it was placed here. This pressure test might give us some answers."

He stepped forward, pressed the red button. Nothing happened. A thin red beam of light had emerged from the top of the tripod and was pointing downwards. Strangely, it also came out at the bottom of the stack of osmium plates. There had to be a hole in the center of the plates. Presumably the laser would measure the impact the osmium would have on the granite.

"We're going to find something under here," said Mike. "That's my prediction."

"No more talk," said Yacoub. "Do it." He nodded at the two women he'd brought with him. One of them had a smartphone out and was pointing it at him, filming everything, most likely.

Mohammad also had a smartphone out and was filming. Yacoub waved at something behind us. I glanced around, saw another camera on a tripod. It had a red light on too and was filming everything.

Mike pressed the button again. The plates fell, crashed into the block beneath them sending a wave of dust around our feet and a faint shudder through the floor. Mike and Yacoub were nearest the tripod. They peered into the dust. All of us did.

I could see the top of the osmium. It seemed not to have made a dent in the block beneath it.

"Has it moved?" said Yacoub, expectantly.

"No," said Mike.

"I thought you said this weight would crack it." There was more than a hint of anger in Yacoub's tone.

"I never said that." Mike was staring at the tripods behind us. I turned. The red light between the two tripods was vibrating, just a little, but there was definitely something going on.

I lowered my voice. "How did you get them to agree to this test?"

He lowered his voice when he replied. "Drilling and boring are specifically outlawed anywhere inside the pyramids. Pressure tests aren't."

"The floor is moving," said Yacoub.

Mohammad leaned down, placed a palm against the smooth stone block under his feet. He pulled it away quickly.

"We must leave the chamber," he said. He began waving at us all.

Mike was staring at the back of the room.

I followed his gaze.

One of the floor blocks, in the far corner, was now lower than it had been. It was only an inch lower, but it had definitely moved.

28

Henry Mowlam reached for the plate of sandwiches sitting in the middle of the meeting room table. Major Finch, their liaison officer with the Ministry of Defense, was talking. She liked to talk.

He listened, ate the cheddar cheese and red onion dressing sandwich. He might even have time for a second, he thought.

Finch turned to him. "Don't you agree, Henry?" Six pairs of eyes bored into him.

Henry swallowed. "Actually, I don't." He reached for a bottle of water. It was one of the new refillable bottles the security services had recently switched to.

"Elaborate," said Finch. Her lips were pressed tight together. She pushed a hand through her blonde hair, moving it behind her ear.

"I reckon it's all a scam, this fountain of youth stuff. This whole event in the Great Pyramid is a PR stunt for Yacoub Holdings. Gotta be. All they want to do is sell face creams and highly priced potions to old women in department stores all over the world."

One of the younger women, Anna, who worked for him piped up. "They'll be selling mostly online, Henry."

He gave her an acknowledging smile, then went on, "They won't find anything useful in the Great Pyramid after all these centuries. And if they do find another room, it'll most probably be empty, like all the others in the area. We should treat this as what it is, a marketing campaign."

"Henry, there's more to this than Yacoub's plans for saving us all from looking old." Major Finch placed her hand, splayed out, on the table and leaned across it. "He's positioning himself as the next civilian president of Egypt. And if we don't have a good relationship with him, then I have no idea what will happen to our Middle East strategy. Do you?"

Henry leaned back. "Our Middle East strategy doesn't rely on getting into bed with this snake oil salesman." He pointed at the large screen dangling from a ceiling mount behind Finch. On it there was an image from the Al Awari, Egyptian language news site. In the center of the image was a still from the press conference Yacoub had held that morning.

"He's a bit more than a snake oil salesman, Henry," said Anna.

"That's true. He's involved in a lot worse than selling snake oil." Henry wiped his mouth with a paper napkin.

"What do you mean?" said Finch.

"Another one of his employees has gone missing. This one is a doctor who's helping him with his research for these new products he's launching." He waved at the screen. "Some say this doctor is the head of the project to gain approval for his snake oil products in the U.S."

"Another one," said Finch. "How many is that now?"

"Twelve employees of Yacoub Research have gone missing in the past year. No bodies have been found, and

Yacoub keeps paying their salaries to the families. It's beyond the realms of coincidence. I reckon he's bumping off employees who could reveal what he's really up to. That's my best guess."

Finch leaned further across the table. "I want to know what he's really up to, Henry. We can't exert influence with guess work." She banged the table with her fist.

29

Mohammad was at the tunnel leading back out of the chamber. He was waving at us.

"We must all go. You are not allowed to stay here."

They sounded like the words of someone who used to work as a guide and was used to waving tourists out of sites.

We were all crowded around the stone in the floor that had moved. It was square, maybe four foot by four foot. It had gone down about an inch, maybe a bit more. Mike was peering at the ribbon of stone that had been revealed around the edge of the block. I bent down, too.

"What's that all about?" I pointed at a series of small figures in red, in a row on one side. They all had headdresses on, but the most obvious thing about them was the giant phallus each of them had.

"There's drawings like that all over Egypt," said Mike. "What interests me is that this crown here," he pointed at a small figure, "is an Atef crown. See the ostrich feathers on each side."

There was something like a feather on both sides of it.

"That's the symbol of death." He moved around the opening slowly, examining the four edges of the revealed stones. I followed him. Yacoub did too, shooing the women who'd come in with him out of our way. Mike had a smartphone out now and was taking close up pictures.

He pressed his hand onto the stone that had moved, tapped at it.

"This is probably the first time these have been seen in four and a half thousand years."

"How do we get beneath this?" said Yacoub.

"I'll work it out," said Mike.

Mohammad stood over us. "You will all leave now, or you will never be given permission to visit this pyramid again." He sounded desperate.

"Stay calm. We're going," said Mike.

Yacoub spat out some words in Arabic. He led the way back out through the tunnel. When we reached the gallery, after the passageway crawl, an official in a brown uniform waited for us. Beside him was a hooded figure, whose face I could not make out. She looked like a priestess from another era, in the long figure hugging black sheath she was wearing. The official handed each of us a sheet of paper. On it was the following:

YOU ARE REQUIRED, BY THE TERMS OF THE LICENCE PROVIDED BY THE EGYPTIAN GOVERNMENT FOR THIS TEST, NOT TO REVEAL ANYTHING YOU HAVE DISCOVERED INSIDE THE PYRAMID, WITHOUT FIRST RECEIVING WRITTEN APPROVAL FROM THE MINISTRY OF ANTIQUITIES.

I leaned towards Mike. "They expected you to find something, didn't they?"

"Yes. and we did."

"But what does it mean?" I said.

"You must come to my villa," said Yacoub, standing close to us. "We will discuss our next steps there."

I took a step towards him. "Will you help me find my husband?"

Yacoub put his hand up and waved it in front of my cheek, as if he would caress me.

"Of course I will. How could I not help you?"

I thought about saying something smart back at him but decided to bite my lip instead. I was missing Sean too much. I'd been imagining what he'd say if he was here. What he'd make of all this.

The emptiness inside, the sense that some very important part of me was missing was almost overwhelming.

"Thank you for the invitation."

"You will find a new home here, Isabel Ryan, and perhaps a new husband, too." He snapped his fingers, as if he would magic a husband up for me in seconds.

"I still have a way to go before I accept Sean is dead."

"Oh, I am sorry, but I believe he is dead. You must give up hope of finding him. Now excuse me, I will join you later. I must talk with my friend." He turned to the hooded figure, said something quickly, then walked towards Mohammad and started speaking with him in a low voice, his hand on his shoulder.

The other official waved at us and led the way out through the gallery and the tunnel to the outside world. Yacoub's words were spinning around inside my head. Did he know something about what had happened to Sean? How could he say with such certainty that Sean was dead?

Surely he had to be just guessing, right? Or was I fooling myself? Was I a grieving widow who couldn't accept reality?

30

2756 B.C.

The three priestesses wore red headbands, tight red cotton bands under their breasts and tight black dresses with rosette symbols woven into them in gold thread down the front. They stood in the gallery waiting, their heads held high. Each wore a wide neck band. The priestess in the center had a small gold head of a lioness on her head band. The one on her left had a cobra on hers. The one on the right the head of a vulture.

A low chanting reverberated from below. Two shaven headed priests were singing at the far end of the high-roofed chamber. Their hymn to Sekhmet was intended to soothe the beast ever present within the goddess.

The three priestesses bent low as the child was led up to them. It was clear from the boy's eyes that he was awestruck, but unafraid. The two bare chested guards who had brought him up guided him forward. He pushed their hands away. He was clearly as defiant as everyone said. His mother's instructions had no effect on him, it was whispered. He'd been warned countless times that he'd find out soon enough what happened to those who defied the order, no matter what their lineage.

The boy spoke in the dialect of lower Egypt, inherited from his mother. "Greetings, guardians of Sekhmet." His tone was imperious. He was clearly used to having his royal attendants follow his every order.

The priestesses bowed together as one. Their pendulous breasts glistened with the gold dust sprinkled on them. The boy's eyes drank them in. The priestesses straightened. Each put their right hand out to beckon him forward. He followed on his knees down the long passage to the healing chamber.

The chamber, when they reached it, was lit by a glowing orb at the far end of the room. Whether the source of the light was an oil lamp or the power of the goddess, as was claimed, was not easy for the boy to discern.

But he could see the three golden bowls set on the stone floor in front of the orb. Three statues to Sekhmet, with their lioness faces and human bodies, stood behind the bowls. On top of them, gold blades balanced.

The three priestesses went down on their knees in front of the bowls. The chanting from down the tunnel could still be heard, and it was changing, the tone becoming more insistent. The air was filled with the sweet smell of myrrh. The boy stared, seemingly unsure what was expected of him.

His eyes were wide. He'd been told these priestesses initiated princes of the royal house into the sexual mysteries, as the priestesses of Isis did for the young men who came to their temples.

He knew that each of the priestesses had been chosen for the purity of their hearts, as well as their beauty, so he knew he had nothing to fear from them. But he hadn't been told exactly what the ceremony he was about to witness entailed.

The priestess in the middle turned to him. Her smile was radiant. Her teeth white. Her lips bright red. Her eyes highlighted with kohl. She put a hand out towards him. He went towards her, almost involuntarily. She pointed at the space between the bowls and the orb in front of her. She motioned him to sit. Not one word had passed between them. The chanting emanating into the room was getting louder. Was one of the priests singing in the tunnel?

The boy sat cross legged, as the priestesses were. He had his back to the orb and was facing them. The three of them smiled at him. He felt a warm glow from their obvious pleasure at him being there. The chanting stopped. The three priestesses picked up the blades with their right hands. They pointed them at their left breasts and while he watched they each made a small incision near their nipples. They had the gold bowls in their left hands and each caught the rivulet of blood that ran from their breasts. When the bowls were half full they pressed at their breasts with their hands and the blood flowed even faster. When their bowl was full, each held it towards him.

He understood. He had to make a choice. The lioness, the cobra or the vulture. He smiled. The priestess in the center was the one he should go for. She was the most beautiful by far.

He reached towards her bowl, took it, put it to his lips, drank slowly. The two other priestesses stood, walked to the tunnel and left the chamber. He was alone with the head priestess of Sekhmet. She stood, loosened her skirt and waited in front of him in her full radiant beauty, her skin golden, glistening.

He licked his lips, stood in front of her. He was not as tall as her and felt for the first time that he was entering something he was too young to fully appreciate. She leaned towards him, opened her lips to kiss his mouth. He leaned towards her, felt a tingling between his legs.

He didn't see the knife she was holding, didn't have any thought of what she would do, until she was running the knife up his backbone. He didn't move as he felt its caress. But he cried out when he felt it slice into his neck.

Within minutes the floor was red, covered in his blood. The only people to emerge that day from the healing chamber were the priestesses.

31

When we arrived at Yacoub's mansion overlooking the Nile the backs of my calves were aching from the long crawl into and out of the Great Pyramid.

The Toyota Landcruiser passed through a high ornamental gate. It pulled up at a stone paved parking area at the side of the three-story white mansion. The building looked like something from the late Victorian era, when the British Empire occupied Egypt. The windows were strong black wood and the roof was a sea of red tiles. No other cars were parked in front of the building and with its shades down on every window the building had an abandoned air.

The two women who came with us, who'd been with Yacoub at the pyramid, were Sawda and Aisha, named after two of the Prophet's thirteen wives, or so Aisha said. Her sister, Sawda, did not speak to us in English.

The front door of the mansion was opened by a man wearing a white turban and a pristine white galabeya. Mike had clearly been here before. He led the way up wide marble stairs to a long room with high windows overlooking the Nile.

He spoke fast in Arabic to the doorman who had trailed behind us.

"I just ordered dates and coffee," said Mike. I was looking out at the gray expanse of the Nile. Long pleasure cruisers, tugs, and a variety of other craft, both rusty and sleek modern looking, were making their way up and down the wide waterway.

"Come, sit with us, we must talk," said Aisha. She led us towards the far end of the room, where three low red sofas were gathered around a huge ornamental marble fire. It had the Sphinx's head carved in marble above it in white, and two head high red marble pillars on each side. The wide brass grate had a thick pile of embers glowing in it.

"Surely we don't need a fire?" I said.

Aisha crossed her hands in front of her chest, rubbed them up and down her upper arms. "But the summer has not come yet. We feel cold, Mrs. Ryan." She looked at her sister, who was sitting beside her on the sofa to the left of the fire. Her sister copied her hand movements. Mike and I sat on the sofa on the other side of the fire. A turbaned servant appeared, followed by a second. A red marble table was placed in front of us, coffee was poured into what looked suspiciously like gold cups with solid gold saucers. We were offered sugar from a gold sugar bowl.

Dates, olives, three types of cheese, small rounds of crusty bread and dips in red, green and yellow were set in front of us.

I took the coffee handed to me. "How did you come to be working with Mr. Yacoub?" I said, smiling at Aisha.

She returned the smile. "Our mother was one of Ahmed's sisters. He had four sisters. She was the youngest. Then she died. We lived by the sea in Alexandria. Our father also died in the car accident that killed my mother. Uncle

Ahmed offered us a home, training and most importantly medical treatment for Sawda."

Sawda smiled, politely, at the mention of her name. I thought about asking what was wrong with Sawda, but Aisha told me before I could open my mouth.

"Sawda has acute leukemia. She has been given," she shrugged, turned to her sister, patted her hand, "only another two years."

I was surprised at Aisha's openness. Sawda looked into the glowing embers of the fire as Aisha spoke. Her sister's eyes glistened, and her voice trembled as she continued.

"Our uncle's research laboratories are the only hope for Sawda. We pray every day that he will find a cure." She bit her lip. "I don't want to end up alone."

"I hope he does find a cure," I said. "I feel for you both."

Aisha turned to me. "If there is no direct family member to speak for me, uncle has promised to find me a husband." She looked down at her hands, placed them together, as if in prayer. "He will decide who I shall marry, and where I shall live after that." She rocked forward. "He has a business in Mecca, a hotel. The manager needs a wife. I have not met him." Her voice trailed off.

"Can you say no?"

Her eyes widened. She shook her head. "For now I am looking after my sister. He will not part us until this is all over."

I put down my coffee cup. It's always a shock when you find out that people, who appear strong and vital, have some hidden secret that's destroying them.

Mike had been silent for all of this. Now he spoke. "Mr. Yacoub's research into blood disease will help millions, I am sure." He leaned towards me. "This is why we must do whatever it takes to help him succeed." He took out his smartphone, turned it to me.

"Do you see these hieroglyphs?" I leaned forward. It was his picture of the glyphs that were painted on the walls of the section of floor that had dropped in the King's Chamber.

"You've translated them already?"

Mike smiled at me. "I have. While we were coming here."

"And?"

His gaze lingered a little too long on my breasts. For a second I wondered if I'd left a shirt front button open. I put up a hand to check. It was fine. His gaze snapped up to meet mine. There was an almost apologetic look on his face.

"It was easy. These are hieroglyphs for death and life. One after the other all along one side. Here we have the sons of Horus, one after the other, and the symbol of Ka, the life force that comes into us with our first breath. What's more interesting, is what's below that stone. I want to find out."

"Do you think the authorities will let you?"

"That's why we have Yacoub. I've never encountered anything that couldn't be done without his help in Egypt."

A trilling noise filled the room. Sawda pulled a phone from a side pocket. She put it to her ear, spoke quickly in Arabic, then listened for a while. We all watched her.

She put her phone away and spoke fast to Aisha. Mike listened intently. After a minute he turned to me. "We will wait here. Yacoub is negotiating for us to re-enter the pyramid tonight." He rubbed his hands together. "I told you this man can do anything here."

It all felt a little hurried to me, as if Mike and Yacoub were going to get one last look at what they'd opened, before the whole project was shut down and the Egyptian government took over.

"Can you call Yacoub and ask him about my husband," I said.

Aisha leaned toward me. "It must be wonderful to be able to marry for love," she said.

"It is, but…" I couldn't go on. I bit my lip. It was too painful to talk about love, while I was searching for Sean.

"If your uncle can help me find him, I will be grateful forever."

Aisha turned to Sawda and spoke. Sawda's expression was hard, unmoving. Aisha seemed to be trying to convince her of something. Then she turned to me.

"What is your husband's name?"

"Sean Ryan."

"He was American, yes? What height is he?"

What did she need to know that for? "He's six foot two, and so handsome I had to beat other women off for him." I had a strange feeling, as if I was groping towards something in the dark. "Have you met an American like this in Cairo recently?" I waited for an answer, anxiety tightening my throat.

Aisha looked as Sawda, spoke fast. I heard the word American somewhere in the middle of the stream of Arabic.

"No." Aisha looked me straight in the eye. Her expression was passive, her gaze fixed, as if she was trying hard not to say more.

I opened my mouth to ask her again, but refrained. I simply looked at Mike, asked him the same thing, but in the back of my mind I was thinking fast. So maybe they had seen him, but where? And why wouldn't they tell me?

Mike shook his head. "No, I ain't seen anyone like him and I meet a lot of the expatriates who pass through here. They all want to know the latest on our research in the Great Pyramid. I've never met an American who came here, who didn't want to know what we are up to."

I leaned towards Aisha. "You must help your uncle a lot." I gave my best impression of a stupid smile, as if I'd completely missed her weird expression when she'd answered my question.

She stared at me. My heart was thumping lightly, as if a distant train was on the horizon, coming towards me, and on it was someone I loved. My spirits felt lifted. I had two things to go on. The nurse's sighting, and this denial. It was thin grounds for believing Sean was still alive, but it was something, and it all needed an explanation.

All my instincts said he was here in Cairo. But was I right?

Or was I fooling myself? Was this irrational optimism?

"Would you like to see some of the work he does?" said Aisha.

I nodded, instinctively. What harm could it do? I expected to be shown a YouTube video or a virtual reality tour of his manufacturing plants. Aisha stood up, motioned me to follow with her fingers. Mike and I stood. Aisha turned to Mike, put a hand up.

"This is for us women only, professor."

Sawda was ahead of her, opening the tall double doors at the end of the room. I wondered where they were going to take me. Beyond the doors was a wide marble staircase with an empty feel, as if no one ever used it. But it was spotlessly clean, as was the glass chandelier that hung above it. Each section of the chandelier was an Ottoman style curved glass lamp, which you could put a candle inside.

32

The King's Chamber fell silent. The scream that had echoed, and then cut off, was long gone. The only noises that could be heard now were the chopping sounds of a meat cleaver.

Three blue plastic boxes with hermetic seals stood to one side. Two of them were closed. The woman wielding the cleaver took the arms and head of the man she had dismembered and threw them in the box. She took the blood splattered rubber mat she had worked on and poured the last of the blood into the container, then folded the rubber and put it into the box, sealing it with the clamps on each edge.

Not even the Ministry official's mother would be able to find him now. She stacked the three boxes near the exit passage. Yacoub would have them removed before dawn. Questions would be asked, but everyone had seen the man go home to his apartment in the suburb of El-Monib, five miles from the Pyramids, after the events of the day had concluded.

And he was known to visit a mosque near his home most nights. Such cases of men going missing in Cairo, where the local mosque said they rarely saw the man, were put down to the existence of a second wife or mistress, who the man had decided to leave his first wife for, and trouble with her relatives.

The fact that he was involved in some project at the Great Pyramid would be of little interest to the local and overworked El-Monib police.

When everything was ready and not even a trace of the man's presence in the room thirty minutes before could be found, she went over to the newly revealed step down in the floor at the far corner of the chamber. She bent down close to peer at the lines of hieroglyphs around the square drop in the floor.

She ran her finger along the hieroglyphs. She imagined the priestesses who had been present when this keystone had been put in place. Another priestess in the same direct line of descent had to be present when this keystone was removed and the path down to the secret chamber unlocked.

Yacoub had been right to argue with this official and to give her a message to finish him and watch his expression change from proud to terrified as she pulled her hood back and approached him with the small cleaver she had taken from where it had been strapped to the inside of her thigh.

She enjoyed such moments, as the men who thought themselves far above her met their end.

A scraping noise coming from the exit tunnel made her turn her head. Yacoub was emerging from the tunnel awkwardly. She rushed to help him.

"I am good," said Yacoub, brushing her away, after she had helped him. He surveyed the room quickly. "Good, our friend will not trouble us anymore with his calls for foreigners to be here when the secret chamber is opened."

She bowed, spoke softly. "When will we look to enter the chamber?"

"Tonight," he said. "It must be tonight. Another official will be appointed by Monday and our guards will all change tomorrow morning. They will be able to say they saw nothing."

"Will we be able to take away anything we find?"

He nodded. "There are four trusted workers available to us all night to take away whatever we want." He put his hand on her bare brown arm.

"This is what we have been working towards for years, Xena. Everything has led us to here. Be happy for this moment."

She shrugged. "If we find the secret room of the priestesses I will be happy. This will make everything worthwhile."

33

The shrill siren of an ambulance filled the upper landing. Sawda was leading the way. She turned left, into a wide corridor with a red, oriental patterned carpet and black framed views of old Cairo on the walls. I saw a picture of a pharmacy with YACOUB in large western script above the door and Arabic script beside it. A man standing in the doorway had on a Turkish fez.

This must have been where Yacoub's family money was founded, back in the Ottoman era in Egypt, which had lasted for almost four hundred years, until 1914.

Other pictures showed old cars in the streets of Cairo, men in military uniform and an ancient looking laboratory with glass vessels on tables. One of the men in that picture looked Nordic. The other was Egyptian, with a well cropped beard.

At the end of the corridor, Sawda stopped. She pointed at a door. Aisha came up beside me.

"This is where our uncle takes all foreign visitors. I am sure he would have taken you here himself, if he wasn't busy."

Sawda opened a set of white double doors with gold paint along its edge. Well, I assumed it was gold paint. It could have been gold leaf. The door handles looked like gold, too.

The room we walked into was the width of the building, with windows on three sides. It looked as if it had been a ballroom. In the center of the room was a replica of the Sphinx, but complete, with nose and beard intact and rounded, not weather beaten shoulders. It, too, looked to be made of gold.

"Wow," I said. I assumed I was supposed to be impressed, and I was.

Aisha touched my arm. She pointed at the side wall.

"Do you like this?"

My breath almost caught in my throat. A golden emblem stood out in the middle of the wall. It was a square, with an arrow inside it pointing up. I'd last seen this symbol on Sean's computer. He'd been looking for occurrences of this worldwide, before he'd gone missing. He'd found it in the logo of a Japanese bank, in the foyer of a German one, and in the emblem of a little known American oil industry association.

What the hell was it doing here?

"You know this?" said Aisha.

My hands became fists, as I sought to stop them shaking.

"I know this very well. My husband was researching this symbol before he went missing."

Aisha nodded. "Yes, our uncle told us you were involved in finding the book this symbol was taken from. You found the book in Istanbul, yes, with your husband?"

"Yes." I stared at her. She knew more about this puzzle than I had thought.

"Is that why this symbol is here, because it was in that book?" I let my breath out.

Aisha nodded. "My uncle says the book you found is the most important record of Egyptian medical treatments ever discovered." She bowed. "Its discovery will help save millions of lives." Sawda bowed as well.

I walked towards the gold symbol on the wall. Below it, to the right, was a small white plaque. That was when I figured out where Aisha might have seen Sean's face. There was a headshot of him and an inscription that read:

The Symbol of the Life Force was discovered in Istanbul by Sean Ryan, a director of the Institute of Applied Research at Oxford University

It crossed my mind to tell them that it should also state I was involved in finding the book the symbol was in, but I didn't care. They could put what the hell they liked on the plaque.

"So you knew about Sean before I came here?"

Aisha stared at me, as if trying to work out if I was trying to trick her. "Yes, we did."

I wasn't sure now whether to trust them or find a way to get out of this place as quickly as possible.

I turned to the other exhibits in the room. "I am sure this symbol is on many walls around the world."

"Yes, I am sure, but…" Aisha hesitated.

I stared at her. Was she about to reveal something?

Sawda said something fast in Arabic. She had pulled a part of her head covering which covered her face aside. Her skin was honey brown, her lips full, pink.

"Go on," I said.

"Our uncle said there are pages missing from the digital copy of the book he received. He said your husband would be able to confirm this." She smiled.

I didn't see it as a smiling matter. "Did he try to contact my husband?" Was this what was going on?

Aisha shook her head. "I do not know. But if he wanted to speak to your husband he would have contacted him through the Institute he worked for, I am sure. Uncle Ahmed always does things the right way."

I walked over to the nearby window. It had a view over the Nile. Boats were passing up and down, and the sun was casting shadows across the gray green water. What the hell was I to make of all this?

Aisha came up beside me, touched my shoulder. "Our uncle is a good man. He only wants to help people."

34

The screen on Henry's desk blinked. Freddie Jones reappeared. He was looking over his shoulder.

"What's up, Freddie? Are you used to the Egyptian beer yet?"

"It's not their beer I'm worried about. It's the whole bloody country going up in flames. You know if Egypt gets torn apart the wave of refugees from Syria, which pushed into Germany, will be like a warm-up lap. There's ninety plus million people here. And at the current rate of growth it will be one hundred and eighty million people in twenty-five years. That's a faster growth than the whole of Western Europe."

Henry shrugged. "I'll be long retired by then, Fred. What I'm concerned about is what's happening now. Is there anything else you can tell me about this Yacoub character, which isn't in his official file?"

"Yacoub. It's about time someone back home paid attention to this guy. Did you see his press conference this morning?"

"Yes."

"That's was one clever publicity stunt. I reckon he's been taking lessons from one of Trump's advisers."

"So you don't think he's likely to actually find anything in the Great Pyramid?"

"No idea. If you believed some of the crackpots who come in to us, you'd think there was an alien spaceship underneath the pyramid. The one that carried our DNA from some star in Orion's belt."

"You get a lot of crackpots?"

Fred raised his eyes. "More every year. What are you looking for on Yacoub?"

"Anything you know. Anything recent. Anything we might have missed."

"You do know most of his money is from pharmaceuticals?"

Henry nodded.

"You also know his father was helped out by a Swiss bank, which had Nazi money filling its coffers at the end of the war."

Henry nodded again.

"Well, then you know most of the scuttlebutt about him."

"What do people think about his claim to have found the fountain of youth?"

"Anyone educated here thinks it's a joke, but," he leaned forward, "twenty-five percent of the population here is functionally illiterate, Henry, and more than that for females. They're his biggest market. If he can show images on TV and in supermarkets of him with ancient Egyptian medicine pots and the pyramids behind him, he'll make billions in the next few years."

"So it doesn't matter what's in his face creams?"

"I'm sure it does. But he'll have science and ancient medicine on his side if half of what he claims is true." He smiled. "You do know what the ancient Egyptians used in half their medicines, Henry, don't you? Did they teach you anything at that university you went to?"

"What did they teach you at yours, how to be a dick?" Fred's reference to the university he'd attended in south London was typical of him. Kingston University didn't have the cachet of Oxford or Cambridge, and anyone who went to one of those elite universities always took pleasure in casting subtle, or not so subtle digs at those who didn't.

"I did classics, Henry, and one of the things we studied in the year we did ancient Egyptian civilization was the Cannibal Hymn."

"The what?"

"The Cannibal Hymn. It's one of the most famous ancient Egyptian texts from the 5th Dynasty, from about two thousand four hundred B.C."

"What the hell has this got to do with Yacoub?"

"Well, if you were familiar with the ancient Egyptians you might put two and two together, Henry."

"Go on. Don't make a meal of it, Freddie."

"The ancient Egyptians used body parts in their medicine. Powdered human skull, for instance, that was popular."

"Yuck."

"You may say that, but our own King Charles the second had a personal tincture, with chocolate and powdered human skull as its main ingredients. His physician claimed it was an ancient Egyptian royal remedy. And if you think that's odd, did you know that in Germany blood from executed prisoners was passed around after the execution for people to drink. I believe that little ceremony went on into the twentieth century."

"So there could be anything in this guy's creams."

"Anything. You know homeopathic remedies claim you should take a little of something related to what ails you. Well that's the same thinking which explains why if you have a pain in your head you take powdered skull, or if you eat testicles you won't need Viagra. It wouldn't surprise me if he included minerals extracted from virgin's blood to make older women young again."

"Like vampires?"

"Exactly. A young count Dracula probably visited Cairo when he was a hostage at the Ottoman court. That's where he got his taste for fresh blood. Nowadays we just give blood transfusions."

"So, Yacoub really thinks he's identified some ingredient that will make people young again."

"That's what I think. And he's recently made all his packaging red, Henry. I wonder why?"

"So that's all you have on him, some theory about his packaging, and what crap he's putting in his creams? That's all our Egyptian intelligence officer knows?"

"If you think we should all become cannibals, Henry, the crap in his creams is not a big deal, but there's more to Yacoub than that."

"Go on."

"One of his competitors reckons Yacoub wants to be a new Saladin, to unify the Arab world and retake Jerusalem."

"But he's not a military leader."

"You can buy a lot of things, if you have enough money, Henry."

35

"I think Sean is in Cairo," I said.

"Why?" said Aisha.

"I showed his picture to people who work at the *Dar al'amal* hospital. One of them recognized his face. Then he said he was too scared to tell me more because of the Brotherhood. He mentioned the symbol of a bird."

"The bird is a common symbol in Egypt, Isabel. It does not just belong to the Brotherhood."

"Who else uses it?"

Aisha took my hand and pulled me towards the far side of the room. There was a small statue of a man with a bird's head inside a glass case.

"This is an early statue of Horus, god of the sky and hunting. He has the head of a falcon, as you see. He was born after the body parts of Osiris were put back together and his penis used to impregnate Isis. He is still revered in Egypt as the sky. The sun is his right eye. The moon his left."

"But the Brotherhood was specifically mentioned in relation to Sean."

"My uncle has a good relationship with the Brotherhood. If you ask him nicely he will ask them if they know anything about your husband."

I didn't reply. Perhaps the missing parts of the book we had found in Istanbul could be bait.

But could I be sure to get hold of them. Maybe it was time to call Henry.

"Is there somewhere I can go to have a shower? I badly need one." I gripped Aisha's arm.

She smiled, bowed. "Follow me."

She led the way out of the room and down a flight of stairs to the floor below. This floor had a modern feel, all white paint and shiny pale wood flooring. It made me feel as if we were in London or even New York.

Aisha walked fast down a wide empty corridor and passed her hand over a security sensor.

"Put your hand here, Isabel. The sensor will take your palm print and allow you in and out whenever you need."

I raised my hand to the black six inch square panel on the wall. The sensor blinked with a blue light across my palm. Aisha pushed the white door open. The room beyond was a guest bedroom. It had a large bed with a plump white duvet and pillow in the center of the room, a window overlooking the Nile, with ornate bars, which presumably were there to keep thieves out, heavy white curtains and a gold coffee table with red chairs around it to the left. It was way bigger than my hotel room.

Aisha pointed at a door on the right. "The bathroom is through here." She bowed, left the room.

I had a look around. The temperature in the room was controlled with an electronic screen beside the door back out to the corridor. I pressed a button on the shiny black panel. A large screen TV began to lower itself from the roof. The TV was on a single stalk with a ball at the end, which meant you could rotate it and watch TV from the bed of the coffee table.

I let it come down, turned it to face me, hunted for the remote control. I found it in a drawer under the coffee table beside a gilt-edged guide to Cairo, a copy of a Victorian era guide, but updated to include the new museums and metro.

I headed for the bathroom, stripped off and stood inside the glass walled walk in shower area. It would be nice to be staying here, not in the hotel. The bathroom even had a scent to it. If only Sean was here to enjoy it with me.

I looked in the gilt-edged mirror above the sink, imagined what it would be like if Sean was waiting for me in the room outside. I closed my eyes. The ache in my heart was growing again. It was always there these days, waiting. No matter how many times I distracted myself. All it took was for me to be alone, to imagine him with me, to close my eyes and tears wanted to come again.

Why did this have to happen to us?

But I knew that was a stupid question. Many good people got taken early. No one knew why.

A buzz sounded from my bag. Someone had messaged me on Facebook. I knew its distinctive noise. It was my sister, maybe, or one of those nice people in the bereavement group I'd joined on Facebook. Every time I thought about the group I felt a pang of guilt. I'd barely participated, after looking through it that first time. There were so many sad stories. So many servicemen's wives. So many widowers with tales of cancer I couldn't bear to think about.

I'd put my lack of involvement down to not being ready to accept what was now my story, too. But I knew I still had a lot to learn about dealing with my own grief, especially when it grabbed me tight, like a shroud around my soul.

I picked my smartphone from my bag, checked the message on the home screen. It was from the Institute where Sean used to work. They wanted to know if I was okay, if I was ready to meet with someone.

I knew what they meant, and who they'd send: Dr. Beresford-Ellis. He'd be all sympathy and charm, offering buy outs for Sean's shares in the Institute, and asking for advice on when we should hold a service for him, even though his body had not even been recovered.

There was another message too. A voice-mail. Could it be the taxi driver? Had he found out something? I pressed the message icon.

It took about thirty seconds for the voicemail to play. But it wasn't the taxi driver's voice that came on the line, it was a soft American accent, and for a split second, as I heard the voice say my name, I thought it was Sean calling me. It felt as if everything inside me was falling, until the voice carried on for a few seconds more and I knew it was Mike calling me from upstairs.

"Just checking you're okay," he said. This was why I liked him, had been willing to go wherever he suggested. His accent and his attitude were so like Sean's, it was weird.

I put the phone down on a marble topped table at the other end of the bathroom and stepped into the shower.

The glass walls of the shower room steamed up fast. I put my head back, stood in the stream of warm water as it sluiced over me. Sean. Oh Sean. What the hell happened to you? Nobody could ever replace you. No man was half the person you are.

A knock sounded from the bathroom door. As my mouth widened in alarm, I watched the door open towards me.

36

The diamond tipped drill cut into the granite with a loud grinding noise. Xena had goggles on, and had the drill speed set to slow, to ensure pieces of granite didn't clog up the bit, but it meant slower progress than she'd hoped. And this was their first hole.

One of Yacoub's site workers was holding the drill. He'd been recruited from a gold mine Yacoub owned in the Nubian desert in the south east of the country, near the Red Sea. It was only the second gold mine in Egypt, but it was useful not only for the cash flow it generated, but also for the quality of loyal workers it produced.

The man held the Bosch drilling machine vertical, sending it directly down into the granite floor stone. The fact that the floor stone had moved meant there was every likelihood there was a space beneath it. The fact that they had no permission for drilling didn't concern her. They had hours to find out what was under this stone, before the Egyptian government took back full control of the chamber.

The first drill hole was in one corner. The plan was to drill a hole in each corner to weaken the likely support for the stone, which held it in place. If necessary, further holes would be drilled along each side. After that further pressure would be applied to the floor stone. They needed to work fast. And they needed distractions in Cairo to keep all eyes away from the Great Pyramid.

Xena touched the arm of the man who held the drill and spoke in the Bedawai dialect to him, the dialect used by Bedouins from the Red Sea coast area where he came from.

He pulled the drill bit out of the hole. She picked up a Bosch hand held suction device and turned it on. The noise was like a small airplane taking off. She put the head of the device over the drill hole. There was a clattering noise as all the granite bits went into the steel drum at the back of the device. She flicked the switch, turned it off. The noise in the King's Chamber abated.

She peered down into the drill hole. It was six inches deep.

It was time to drill a new hole. She pointed at the mark she had scratched in one of the other corners. She had also drawn an arrow in the center of the block. There was no way of being sure if the sign she'd been taught about would work on this block, but it might. She'd seen the symbol work, both bringing good luck and solving puzzles like the one she was faced with now, how to get behind this floor block. She signaled to continue drilling with a downward motion of her forefinger.

The drill bit cut into the granite with a high pitched growl. Pieces of granite popped into the air. She reached towards the man holding the drill, held his upper arm.

"Slowly, Mohammad. We are nearly finished."

He pulled back a little, smiled at her.

She returned the smile, leaned towards him.

His eyebrows went up and he blinked with happiness.

Xena pulled out a cigarette, took one out, lit it, blew the smoke in his direction. It was too easy to get sheep like this one to do what he'd been told. Soon enough the whole world would appreciate the work that she was doing, the sacrifices that had been made.

Yacoub would facilitate the Goddess returning, with his cures for women and his anti-aging products.

The noise of the drill changed. It shuddered in his hand. She put her hand on Mohammad's arm. "Stop," she said in Arabic. "We need new drill bits. If you get them I will reward you." She stuck her tongue out at him. His eyes widened in anticipation. His gaze flicked to her cleavage.

"When you have finished staring at me, go to the Yacoub building and get me the package waiting for me in the security hut."

His head shook as he stepped back. There had been gossip about a demon security manager Yacoub used, but this was the first time he'd met her.

37

The building in the poor Northern suburb of Cairo on Sharia Shubra had a red drop symbol above its door. It had been opened a few months before and was known by the name *bayt alddam*, the house of blood.

The only people who were allowed to sell blood to the clinic were virgin girls, aged between fourteen and twenty-one. The mothers who brought their daughters here had to provide a doctor's certificate of their daughter's virginity, signed in the past twenty-four hours by an approved doctor, and their daughter's identity card to prove their age.

The locals were happy with the clinic. It was bringing money into the area and the clinic's relationship with a famous private hospital in the south of the city reassured them as to where the blood was going. After the January 25th revolution, which overthrew ex-President Mubarak in 2011, private blood donation services were set up in other parts of the city, but not up here in the north. The fact that the donation center was open only one day a week and then only for a few hours suited the local shopkeepers, and the koshary, bread and tea vendors never objected to the extra business.

The locals assumed the restrictive rules for blood donation were simply one of the reasons the *Dar al'amal* hospital had such a high success rate for curing its patients and vowed to go there, if they could afford it.

That Saturday the clinic was closed. The door was firmly shut and there was no one waiting outside. Until a police jeep pulled up and four uniformed officers got out, went to the door and began banging on it, and a few seconds later broke the door down.

What happened next was caught on camera by two passers-by equipped with smartphones. The first photo showed the only person who was in the building being led away with his head held almost between his knees. The second showed the moment a filing cabinet, which had been dragged into the street, was set alight.

Most people in the neighborhood made no objection to the clinic closing. It had been said by some that the clinic brought bad luck to the area, because no Imam had endorsed it.

38

I turned my body away from the door, reached for the water, turned it off. That was when I heard the knocking again. This time a reedy voice called my name, incorrectly. "Miss Ryan. Miss Ryan."

"Who is it?" I shouted.

"You must come."

"Why?"

"You must come."

I was clearly not going to get a better explanation. I picked up my phone from the table. If anyone was tracking me, Henry, for instance, he'd need me with it to have any chance of helping me.

Someone was shuffling outside the door. I pulled one of the giant fluffy white towels around myself and jerked the door open.

An old man, probably long past being interested in seeing me naked, bowed. He had a red fez on and a spotless white uniform. He spoke as he held his head down.

"Sorry to disturb, Miss Ryan, but we must all go to the basement emergency room right away. Please come quickly."

He raised his head enough to look me in the eye. His eyeballs were veined with red, as if he had some disease. He didn't blink either.

"Why? What the hell is going on?" I walked to the black window shutters and peered out. A gloom was descending over the city as night approached. Strings of light went from building to building opposite us, but below cars were moving and there were no crowds gathering.

"Earthquake, Miss Ryan." He looked at his watch and almost jumped. "We are late. Please come."

There was such as plaintive tone to his voice I didn't want to refuse.

"Wait outside." I pointed at the door.

He bowed low, went quickly to the door. As he closed it behind him he pushed his head back in and said. "Not a drill. Please be quick."

I got dressed as fast as I could. It would have been good to spend a little more time in that room relaxing, but I didn't seem to have a choice.

The servant led me down the corridor and through an ornate, gold rimmed door into a stairwell. The stairs were wide enough for two people to pass. On the walls there were hieroglyphics, as if we were in a stairwell in an ancient Egyptian temple. At each landing there was a small black marble table with a white marble statue of a seated jackal headed man on it.

We went down three flights. The servant was ahead, walking fast for someone his age, turning now and then, calling me forward. I looked over the banisters. There were at least another three floors below us. Yacoub had an elaborate basement area. What the hell was he doing down here with all these extra levels?

On the floor below a woman in a long white uniform came out of the door. I hurried past as the white door closed behind her. I saw a thin sliver of what lay beyond. It was an intriguing sliver. The corridor she'd exited from looked like a hospital corridor, all white and bright lights.

I stopped, looked back at the woman who had passed me going upwards. Her uniform could have been something from the era of Florence Nightingale, when good British ladies were expected to cover up from head to toe. But she definitely looked like a nurse. Was Yacoub running a clinic down here? Was this where he was doing his research?

"You must come," said a voice beside me. I turned. The servant I'd been following had his hand out and was about to pull at my arm.

"Don't rush me." I held my hand up, as if to keep him away from me.

He stepped back, a look of surprise in his eyes. Maybe women he met didn't fight back, but I wasn't putting up with any bullshit. Maybe, before Sean had disappeared, I might have been softer, laughed at what he was doing, but ever since that day a darker part of me had emerged, fully formed.

I could bite at people who pushed into me in the street and I'd even caught myself shouting at the TV. The old "nice Isabel" was crumbling into dust with each day that drifted into the next. And I didn't care. I was sleeping less and my grief was coming out in weird ways, changing me.

"We must go. They are waiting."

"Who is waiting?"

He didn't reply. He just kept going down.

We'd reached what I worked out as the third underground level when he pressed his palm against a security panel and the door to the corridor beyond opened. He held the door wide for me.

This level was more like a residential level. There was a red carpet on the floor in a flowery Persian pattern, gold side tables with small statues at intervals. The wall lights were scarab shaped. At the far end of the corridor was an ebony statue of a pharaoh with a long beard.

The servant knocked on a door on the left half way along the corridor. He held it open for me. I was interested in the statue. I walked straight past the door, muttered something, quickened my pace.

I was right. The statue had Yacoub's face and he was dressed like a pharaoh. I shook my head. So that was what he really wanted.

"It's a good likeness," said a voice behind me.

I turned, did a double take, rocking back on my feet. Yacoub was standing behind me, but it wasn't Yacoub. This man was a little fatter and he had let the gray hair stay gray at the side of his head.

"My name is Mustafa." He bowed.

39

The gate to the compound around the pyramid site was closed. Not only closed, but a tank stood in front of it, blocking the way.

Mohammad, who had been allowed to exit the compound, was now standing in a line waiting for permission to get back in. The line was not moving. At the top of the line a wire mesh gate was closed and padlocked. Behind the gate three black uniformed guards held their machine pistols as if they were about to use them.

On the far side of the entrance, beyond the tank, a fierce row was going on. Officers of the Antiquities police, in black with small gold epaulets, were inside the gate. Army officers, from the 15th Division, Special Forces Regiment, were outside, guns raised, pointing them at the Antiquities police.

As Mohammad watched, a Major aimed his pistol in the air, let off a shot. The tank in front of the gate moved forward, its gears grinding and black smoke coming out of the back.

A shout went up from inside the gate. The Major barked something into a black microphone at his shoulder, which he twisted to face him.

The tank stopped, its barrel pressing into the gate, bending it. The side gate barring the Special Forces from entering the compound was opened and the Major stepped through. He shouted more orders and the black suited Antiquities police officers moved to one side. Filtering among them were members of the Special Forces. They pulled hands behind backs and applied plastic cuffs to each officer.

Shouts went up from the line of men watching all this. Almost all these men were cleaners, working for the Antiquities Department, whose duties were about to start.

Another shot rang out. The major, who had taken control of the gate, shouted at the men through the wire mesh.

"Come back tomorrow. The loyal forces of the Egyptian army have taken over this site."

A muttering went up from the crowd, then some of the men started to leave. Mohammad had his phone out and was whispering into it.

40

"I am Yacoub's brother."

"You look very alike. You could be twins," I said.

"But we are not," said Mustafa, as he led me into a large, low roofed room, which could only be described as a veneration of opulence.

The walls, and the square columns dotted around the room, were covered in gold wallpaper, with hieroglyphics in black. The floor was black marble and black marble statues lined the walls.

They looked like originals. Plato and Julius Caesar were on the left. Pythagoras and Constantine the Great were on the right. At the far end of the room was what looked like a picture window looking over the Nile. But it couldn't be, not this far down. It had to be a print or a screen.

"This is a view over the Nile onto the city of Heliopolis at the time of Moses." Mustafa pointed at the houses. "See, they have the same flat roofs as we have, but without the television aerials."

"When was Cairo founded?"

"This reconstruction is from one and a half thousand years before Christ. The city here was thousands of years old already." He pointed under his feet. "The slab of rock this building was built on might even have been the foundation of a house Moses lived in. Certainly, it was the house of a magician. The hieroglyphs you see are reproductions of the ones found in an underground room near here."

"You found his name?" I looked around the walls for any sign of anything original. People would claim anything had an ancient connection, in my experience, if they thought they could make some money out of it from gullible tourists.

"Not the name you Christians call him, but there is a record of the Nile turning red in the hieroglyphs concerning a famous magic spell. Moses was trained by the priests of the holy mountain, that is what they called the Great Pyramid. He trained as a phykikos, a high level sorcerer, and surpassed all his teachers in the end. But you know this. It is all in your Holy Bible."

"I thought a dust storm turned the Nile red."

"Not every dust storm turns the river red. It happens once in a generation, at most. But Moses knew that this type of storm was coming. Prediction and the reading of signs are the work of magicians, are they not?"

"What about this earthquake your man told me about to get me down here?"

Mustafa pointed at a table in the corner of the room. "Look at the readings. Tremors have been coming closer together."

"I haven't felt anything."

"Come." He waved at me to follow him. The instrument in the corner of the room had a paper read out and what looked like the inside of a clock exposed. He pointed at the paper. Wavy lines certainly seemed to show some recent disturbance.

"Is this common?"

"No. That is why I asked you all to come down here."

A noise from the far end of the room made me turn my head. Aisha and Sawda had come into the room. They were walking towards us.

Aisha spoke, almost shouted, as she came near. "Is this another of your false alarms, uncle?"

"This time something is happening. Mark my words. You will see they are true."

I took my phone out of my pocket. There was no signal. Had I been brought down here to cut me off from the phone network? I was about to put my phone away when I saw part of a message. I flicked at the screen. Yes, it was a text message from Henry. It must have come in before I got down here.

CONTACT ME, was all it said.

I put the phone back in my bag, put my bag on my shoulder.

"I should leave you all now. Thanks for everything." I stepped back from Mustafa and his nieces and glanced at the door.

"I am sorry. I must insist, to protect you, you see. You must stay here for at least the next ten minutes, until we see if the next shake brings down the building above." Mustafa pointed at the paper read out. "See the frequency. The effect is growing exponentially every ten minutes."

It didn't feel right giving in to his bullshit.

"I can't stay down here. Whatever happens up above, I'll take my chances."

I stepped back. None of the people in this room could stop me if had to get out of here. I hadn't used the self-defense skills I'd been trained in for a few years, but I was confident I could stop these two women and their uncle putting their hands on me.

Mustafa put his hands up, as if he was defeated.

"You can go any time you wish, Mrs. Ryan. You are not a prisoner." He smiled, shrugged. "But before you do, please, I wish to show you one thing. I believe you will find it interesting." He pointed at the screens behind me. "Please, it will take only a few minutes."

"What is it?"

"Another view of our city. It's from a different time. A few minutes, that is all it will take." He began walking towards the window like screens on the back wall. He pressed at the remote control in his hand. The picture on them changed.

"Tell me what time period you think this is?"

The screens went black for a second. Now we were looking over a city at night. Torches lit up a citadel's walls in the distance. The shape of the roof tops between us and the high walls could be glimpsed by the light from occasional roof top braziers and torches set into the walls of some of the buildings, high up.

Above the city, stars glistened like pearls in a velvet sack.

I was mesmerized. The stars were moving, as if the night was unfolding in triple time. In the east, a star was rising.

"No idea. Could be any time."

"Watch carefully."

Smoke, mixed with red firefly like embers, burst from a roof top in front of us. Guards, in leather breastplates, and with bows on their backs, were illuminated along the roof of a nearby building. Out of the smoke and fireflies, which were pouring from a hole in the center of the roof, emerged a figure.

He was robed in Arab costume, an ankle length white shirt, and had a tight white turban around his head. He strode towards the center of the roof, uncovered a stone box, took a scroll from inside it, sat and began reading. He was facing away from us.

"No. Idea," I said.

Mustafa put a finger to his lips.

I got the sudden notion that this was a computer game I was watching, because in the distance, around the high walls of the citadel arcs of flame came up from ground level. Arrows with flaming heads.

A shout rang out. Then another. It felt like we were there, watching an attack. The four guards on the roof were gathered on the edge looking towards the citadel. The man in white was still sitting, reading. He hadn't moved.

In the distance the citadel burned. Flames leaped up from one corner, then another. Screams could be heard. It sounded as if women and children were in fear of their lives.

The guards on the roof had their bows out, arrows nocked. They were pointing them down at the street below. The man in white said something to them in Arabic. The guards lowered their bows.

"What is this all about?" I said, turning to Mustafa.

He pointed at the screen. "This is the tale of what your Jesus Christ did when he was in Egypt, here in what we now call Cairo."

"Jesus was here?" It sounded a bit far-fetched.

"Yes, yes. It is in your bible. Do you not know the story of Herod? The baby Jesus being taken to Egypt by Joseph to escape a massacre of the newborns."

"But he went back to Israel soon after."

"Who knows for sure. And where else would he have learnt his healing skills, bringing Lazarus back from the dead

and healing the blind and so many others. This is how he
became famous. He learnt all these things in the most
important center of medicine between here and China, here at
the temples of Osiris and Isis. I am sure of this, even though
it's not in any record."

"Why are you so sure?"

"Roman Emperors used Egyptian physicians. They
were the best in the world. This means our schools of medicine
were the best in the world. The majority of Jesus' miracles
were healings and cures. One and one makes two, Mrs. Ryan."

The screen in front of us changed again. The sun was
coming up. The citadel was burning in the distance, a plume
of black smoke rising.

The guards had gone away, but the white robed figure
was back reading scrolls in the center of the roof.

"This is all very well done, but I reckon the world will
need some proof, before believing any of this."

"I agree. That is what we are looking for." His smile
was about as sincere as a crocodiles, before it ate you.

"Why not use our telephone here, if you have an urgent
call to make." He pointed at a small table in the corner beside
the screen.

"I need some fresh air." I wasn't going to let him listen
in to my conversation with Henry.

"One moment." He went back to the device with the
earthquake detector. He turned back to me, waved. "Yes, the
moment I feared has passed. Please do go back up now." He
looked at Aisha. "Please show our guest out."

Aisha and Sawda accompanied me back up the stairs.
This time no one came out of the floor I'd had a glimpse inside
on the way down.

"Would you like to see Professor Bayford before you
go?" said Aisha.

"I'll catch him later." I had to get out of this place. It felt as if a fog had descended on me. A fog of bullshit. All that earthquake stuff was clearly a ruse to get me down to that room and show me their video collection. And that stuff about Jesus being in Cairo? It was a stretch, and who the hell cared anyhow?

I had to focus on why I was here in Cairo, to find Sean. As we reached the ground level my phone started to bing. Three new messages came in.

Aisha opened the door to the corridor. I wanted to look at my phone, but I didn't.

"Do you wish our driver to take you somewhere?" she said, as she opened another door and ushered me into a reception area with a huge glass chandelier above our heads. Her sister was right behind her. She didn't look happy.

"No, I can find my own way." Something about this pair made my skin crawl, and it wasn't just because I was a foreigner here. I'd met a lot of strange people during my time working in Istanbul and London. I'd rarely felt this off feeling.

"There is a taxi rank at the end of the street," said Aisha, as I opened the double height main doors. There was a short flight of stairs and a side gate below. This was a different way into the building than the way I'd entered.

"Thanks for your hospitality." I waved as I went down the stairs. Already I had my phone out. As I went through the gate to the street it was in front of me.

There were two messages from Henry. The first one said CONTACT ME. The second one said CALL ME. There was something urgent going on back in London.

Another message read URGENT NEWS. It was from my taxi driver friend.

41

The air in the King's Chamber was hot, unmoving. Xena was sitting with her back to the wall opposite the entrance. She had almost given up waiting for Mohammad to return.

Little progress would be made without new drill bits. It had been a gamble bringing the drill in, without a selection of drill heads, but it had been their best hope of avoiding too many questions.

Something must have happened to him. It was likely that the disturbances in the pyramid had been notified to officials in the Antiquities Ministry. They weren't all under Yacoub's spell. It was possible they'd shut down the area around the pyramid.

That made it even more important that she made progress tonight. But what the hell could she do on her own? The light from the torch on the floor dimmed. She turned it off.

Before she could switch it off, the chamber plunged into darkness.

She sat up. The torch wasn't the problem. The darkness wasn't the problem. There was something else going on, which had only just come to her.

42

I pressed the phone to my ear. Henry could wait. If there was a chance I could find out what had happened to Sean, or if there was any possibility he was still alive, I had to follow up on that first.

"Is it you, madam?" The taxi driver sounded tired, as if he'd been up all night.

"Yes. What news do you have?" I knew I was being a little abrupt, but I didn't care.

"Please, where are you, madam. I must come for you." I looked up and down the street. In the distance, beyond a set of traffic lights, there was a McDonalds. "I see a McDonalds restaurant."

"Do you read our Arabic language?"

"No."

"There are many McDonalds here, madam. Each one says what district it is in on its sign. I have a better idea. Take a taxi to the *Dar al'amal* hospital. Wait for me in the car park."

It took me fifteen minutes to find a taxi driver who would stop for me and who understood me. It was like being in a nightmare, trying to get somewhere and the world conspiring to stop me.

Eventually, I was moving. And the driver was turning, grinning at me, as if he thought he had found a new girlfriend. I kept my bag close to my side, felt in it for my steel pen. He was going to regret it if he pulled down an alley and tried something.

I took my phone out and rammed it to my ear. It was dark outside now, just before seven and the city was bustling with Saturday evening shoppers.

"Where the hell were you?" It was Henry's voice, reassuring, but he was angry, which wasn't what I needed.

"Just tell me why you messaged me, Henry."

"The whole of Egypt is blowing up, Isabel. We have incidents in every city. And." He paused. "The Great Pyramid complex has been taken over by the Egyptian army. They are not allowing anyone in or out. There are stories going around that something has been discovered inside it."

I finished his point. "And there's expected to be an earthquake happening here too, and they've been expecting a sandstorm since the day I arrived. This is nothing new, Henry. This seems to be what Cairo has always been like; chaotic."

"What have you found out?" His words hung in the air as the taxi driver took a sharp turn. We were in a smaller side street, but it wasn't an alley, yet.

I told him about being at the pyramid and being taken to Yacoub's house and meeting his brother.

"Yacoub has a brother? That's not mentioned in any of our reports. Hold on." I heard him tapping at a keyboard. It wouldn't be the first time our wonderful security systems had missed something basic about someone.

"Isabel, you said he was talking about the book you and Sean found in Istanbul." He sighed, as if he didn't quite believe what he was about to ask me.

"Yeah."

"Well, have you seen it? Did he say where it is?"

"You've lost it?"

"Not me personally, but yes, it's gone missing."

"So if he has it, it's stolen."

"Maybe, you see it really belongs to the Turkish government and they could have done a deal with him. You do know what thirty pieces of silver can buy, don't you?"

The taxi driver braked. I fell forward.

"We here, lady."

"I'll call you back, Henry."

43

Xena took her cigarette lighter out of her pocket. She lit it. The flame was low, but enough. She was right. It bent a little. Not much, but enough to tell her there was a breeze coming from somewhere. She pulled the pack of Cleopatra, Egyptian cigarettes, from the pocket of her black jeans.

She lit a cigarette, began crawling around the King's Chamber. There wasn't much time. If someone had taken over the pyramid compound they could send people in overnight. The most likely thing was that people would start arriving at dawn. It was a Saturday night. To get anyone to head into the Great Pyramid in the middle of the night would not be easy. To get a team to assemble at dawn was what would happen.

She flicked the lighter on again. Dawn would be at five-thirty. She had about ten hours. Was it enough time?

She held the cigarette over the indentation in the floor caused by Professor Bayford putting pressure on the floor slabs. The flame leaned to the left. Fresh air.

She lit the lighter again, looked around at the tools that had been left in the chamber.

Could she set the weight up again to press down on a floor slab? She walked across to the stack of osmium plates at the far end of the chamber. She could use the tray to get the osmium over the indentation. And she could use the winch on the tripod to lift it.

She tested the weight of the top plate of osmium. It was thin, but it felt like lifting gold bars. But she smiled. She could do this. She didn't need Mustafa, or Yacoub.

She might even have found hidden passages inside the Great Pyramid.

44

I paid the driver. There was a line of taxis outside the hospital. There were so many of them they almost blocked the road. People were milling around. It was way busier than it had been the day before. Presumably because of the attack in Tahrir Square.

The taxi driver had turned to me as we'd been stuck at traffic lights and said out of nowhere, after listening to what sounded like the news in Arabic on the radio, "This government must go. Too many dead."

I didn't answer.

All I wanted was to find Sean. Everything else was just getting in the way. Frustration rose inside me as I took in the scene in front of the hospital. Some of the taxis were yellow, like the one I was looking for, others were black and white, more run down, while others had a blue stripe. Presumably it all meant something.

There was a group of yellow taxis on the right, stretching from the front of the hospital all the way back to a furniture shop, with chairs hanging above the shop window. I walked along the line, looking for my taxi. I sensed someone behind, turned, just in time to feel a slap into my thigh. I made a fist, shook my head in anger as I stared into the face of the man who'd slapped me. He grinned, displayed some nicotine slicked teeth and walked on. He was in his twenties, I guessed. I stepped between two of the taxis, a sudden feeling of vulnerability rising up inside me. I didn't like it.

But I had to be careful. Young men here didn't have the same respect for women on their own as young men in the world I came from. Here they saw Western women, in particular, as sexually easy, not the tightly controlled commodity women were in Muslim countries. Feminism definitely hadn't arrived here.

I walked fast towards the entrance to the hospital car park, went down the stairs, found the place where the taxi driver had waited for me the last time I was here. This had to be where he meant. Not wanting to just stand there, I started walking purposely on downwards, as if I was heading for a car. After I'd walked down onto another floor, I walked back up again, past where we'd parked and up further.

My breathing slowed as I walked. Did it mean anything, what Henry had said about the book we'd found going missing? And how the hell had Yacoub got hold of a translation? Was his interest in the book any clue into what had happened to Sean?

I kept walking. It made me feel better. The knot in my stomach, which had tightened hard after what had happened outside the hospital, was easing. The waves from two Egyptian women who were heading for their cars also helped. One even wished me a good night, in English.

I was heading back down for the fourth time when I spotted the yellow cab. It was pulled up, blocking the space we had parked in before.

My driver rolled down the window as I approached, leaned his head out. A cigarette was dangling from his lip. It looked as if he hadn't shaved since I'd last seen him, possibly hadn't gone home at all.

"Get in, madam." He looked me up and down.

"Don't tell me what to do."

He shook his head. "I have news for you. You want my help or not?"

I stood there, crossed my arms. He wasn't going to find me an easy person to lead around, as if I had a ring in my nose.

"Tell me, here, now. We're not going anywhere until you do."

He threw his hands into the air, exclaimed something in Arabic, which I took to be an insult, and got out of the taxi. I stood back. He pointed at me.

"Madam, you are much trouble. I bring you news and all you want to do is argue." He raised his hands, palms towards me. "But I understand, you must be careful." He looked around, as if expecting that we were being observed.

"But we all must be careful, madam. The people I have been asking about your husband are not soft people." He made a cutting motion across his throat.

"If you want to find your husband you will come with me. One of the men I spoke to has news. Important news. He is from another group, not the Brotherhood. They also use a bird symbol."

"What news and how much will it cost?"

"If I knew what he will tell you I would sell this to you myself."

"How much will I have to pay?"

"Ten thousand Egyptian pounds."

I shook my head. "How much of that is for you?"

He looked wounded. "I ask only for something to help pay for the time I am losing driving around trying to help you, madam. I ask a small part of this."

"What part?"

"Half. And this will not even cover what I have lost these last few days, never mind what I will lose if these people think I have betrayed them."

"I will give you your five thousand, but only after you bring me back here, safely."

He shrugged. "Agreed."

"How far are we going?" I asked, as I got into the back of the taxi.

"Into the desert, not far. It's a village, a little south of here."

"Stop at an ATM machine on the way."

The traffic was terrible outside the hospital, but as we headed out of the city it eased.

He stopped at a petrol station. It was a Total station and had employees in red uniforms filling up the cars. They had female employees too. They were serving women drivers. The taxi driver pointed at an ATM machine on the wall of the station.

I went to it, stood in line. As I waited I called Henry. When he answered I heard the sounds of a London pub behind him.

"You do know it's half ten on a Saturday night in London, don't you?" he said.

"I'm surprised you're not working, Henry."

"I am. This is just my break. What happened?" A buzz of voices continued behind him.

I missed being back in London, the sense of security, of knowing what was going on around you. And I missed our home. Our easy Saturday nights watching a movie on TV or

177

having friends over for dinner. I didn't want to be here on the outskirts of Cairo, looking for Sean. A wave of emotion threatened. I pushed it away, pressed my hand into my stomach.

"The taxi driver who's been feeding me information is taking me to meet someone."

"Where?"

"In a village outside Cairo."

"Don't go, Isabel. It's not worth the risk. Women disappear in Egypt. They won't have any problems raping you and cutting your throat. You're an unbeliever and a Western woman. You're not protected in their culture."

It was my turn at the ATM. I put my card in. There were a couple of men behind me. I heard two of them muttering. One laughed. I was sure it was about me.

I pressed the buttons on the machine. "Henry, I have to do this. Can you get someone to track my phone?"

Henry sighed. "We're doing that already. You're making a mistake, Isabel. You're on a wild goose chase. Stop now, for the sake of your son."

I cut him off, took the notes that spewed out of the machine. I put a second card in. The maximum withdrawal limit was five thousand Egyptian pounds on each card.

I pushed the bundle of notes into my trouser pockets, felt the eyes of the men on me as I went back to the taxi.

As soon as I got in the driver turned to me and said, "Please, give me your phone."

"I can't do that."

"I cannot take you if you don't. You will get out here." He pointed at the road.

I looked out the window. I wasn't sure what to do. The two men who were whispering behind me at the ATM were standing near it now, looking at us.

The knots in my stomach were heading up my throat. My jaw felt stiff and my hands trembled slightly at what I suddenly knew I had to do next. I reached into to my bag. My hand gripped the steel pen I kept there.

"I will give you my phone." I slipped my hand out of my bag and leaned forward. I put one hand around his throat and held the pen in the other at the side of his neck. His stubble rubbed like a wire brush against my fingers. He let out a squawking noise, like a chicken, then tried to pull my hand away from his throat. I pressed the tip of the pen harder into his throat.

"I am not one of your vulnerable little girls, who you can fuck with." Perspiration was thickening on my brow. My heart was thumping fast.

"I will cut your throat and leave you bleeding into the dirt if you're lying to me."

"Madam, please, believe me." He gasped for air. His voice cracked with emotion as he continued, "I must take your phone before I bring you to them. I am only trying to help."

I looked out the window. The two men were walking toward the taxi.

45

Xena flicked the torch on. Its light was steadier now. Turning it on for ten seconds at a time had allowed her to do what she wanted to do, and extend the life of the torch. And now she was ready. She released the tripod's main lever. It was the easiest way to get the stack of osmium to drop on the block.

The thud, when the osmium hit, sent a faint tremor through the floor. But the stone block Xena was hoping would move didn't shift. Was it sitting on another block?

Xena sat on the stone floor and listened. The King's Chamber of the Great Pyramid had acoustic qualities, she knew, from her reading before she came here, but did that mean the noise she was making was likely to reach any new guards stationed outside?

She waited, listened. Nothing. No one was coming.

She went back to the stack of osmium at the top of the room. She would put more on the tripod at the other end of the room and raise it again. She would keep doing so until she had exhausted the pile. If weight alone could pressure a way through, she would succeed.

As she used the trolley to move the remaining blocks of osmium Xena noticed that the trolley's wheels were bending outwards. The axles were unable to bear the weight.

It took another ten minutes of sweaty maneuvering, in darkness and in light to get the osmium onto the tripod and to raise it, using the handle, turning it slowly with the torch off, and with difficulty, until the larger stack of osmium plates was a few inches above the stone slab again.

With a mouthed prayer to the Queen of Darkness, she turned the torch on, pressed the button to release the osmium and took a step back. It dropped with a resounding thud.

She turned the torch off. Again nothing had happened.

But then a thud echoed from the other end of the chamber. She moved slowly towards the exit tunnel, where the sound had come from. But the exit passage wasn't there. There was no exit from the chamber. A slab had slid into place to block it.

Her heart pounded. No one knew she was here. And it could be weeks before the Egyptians organized a drilling machine to break through the slab that had fallen to block the entry passage. By then all they would find of her would be rotting flesh. She shivered.

Was this how she would die?

46

I released the driver. "Let's go then." I took my phone out of my pocket and dropped it on the passenger seat beside him. As long as the phone was with us I could be tracked.

We headed out of Cairo on a dual lane highway heading south. Slowly my heart stopped pounding and my hand stopped shaking.

Palm trees lined the road in places. We passed a long line of industrial buildings with Arabic signs and then a military camp. There was a tank at the front gate and a few soldiers milling around. Eventually the buildings gave way to flat desert on both sides and darkness.

I looked through the back window. Cairo glowed orange and yellow behind us.

"How long will it take to get there?" I asked.

"We will be there soon, madam," he replied.

Again and again he stared at me in the rear view mirror.

"You are a dangerous lady, yes." He grinned at me.

"If I have to be."

He laughed, as if he knew something I didn't.

What the hell was I letting myself in for?

"Can you turn the heater on?" It was getting cold.

He reached to the dashboard. Warm air, with an oily smell, spluttered through the taxi.

Ten minutes later the lights of a village appeared on the horizon. Low roofed houses with dim street lights and a few shops came into view. He slowed as we approached. There wasn't much traffic now, just the occasional car or truck. A group of camels were sitting by the side of the road. A boy, he must have been no more than ten, was sitting on a white plastic bucket near them.

"Is this the village?"

"No, not this one."

We passed through the village and turned off, heading along a side road deep into the desert. The road was obscured by sand in places and thorn bushes appeared on both sides.

The next village had no street lights. I made it out only as we came close and the small collection of buildings blocked out the horizon ahead. As we came into the village the driver slowed.

"This is it, madam."

"What's this village called?" I peered out into the darkness. Every one of the shops and houses was closed tight to the outside world. The village looked deserted.

He said something in Arabic. I didn't ask him to repeat it. Henry would be tracking me. He'd find me on Google maps in seconds.

The driver pulled the taxi up in the center of the village, opposite a house with a sign in Arabic above the door. He killed the engine and turned off the lights. We sat there. My eyes began to adjust. As they did an array of stars, like a dusting of diamonds, appeared in the sky.

"What now?"

The driver raised a finger. In his other hand he had his phone. He jabbed at the phone, then put it to his ear. I could hear it ringing. Someone answered. They had a two word conversation. The driver closed the call.

"Where are going?" I looked at the houses around us. I felt that odd feeling, a shiver across your back, when you know you're being observed. Was this whole village under these people's control?

The driver looked me in the eye. "You will find out soon."

It was even colder now, not freezing, but in comparison to the heat of the day, the drop in temperature was noticeable. I was glad I had my jacket on. I buttoned it up, stood near the taxi.

After a few minutes the driver walked away, further on up the road, as if he was expecting someone to come from that direction. No one had appeared from any of the houses. The village felt abandoned, but I was sure there were people in the houses and that some of them were watching us.

A sudden, and intense loneliness came over me. If ever there was an idiot searching too far and too wide for her husband, I was it. I'd come from London all this way, to the edge of the wilderness, hoping all the time that everything would work out, that Sean would be found. It struck me now that I had to be fooling myself. That I had to be among the most stupid people on the planet.

Everyone; my family, work colleagues, Henry, they had all told me I was following a wishful fantasy. And they were probably right.

Headlights approached from the direction the driver had walked. I felt exposed. Anyone could stop and rob us, or worse. I turned away, pulled the thin scarf from my bag, which

I'd imagined I'd never need, and wrapped it around my head, pulling it over my hair.

My sister had given it to me when she'd taken Alek. "Just in case," she'd said. I was glad she had.

I was expecting the headlights to sweep past us, but they didn't. A white, dust covered jeep pulled up beside the taxi and two men got out. They were young, dressed in long dirty galabeyas and with small white turbans on their heads.

The taxi driver approached them, began talking fast in Arabic. One of them pointed at me. The driver waved at me, dismissively, then launched into another long Arabic tirade.

"Madam, come. These men will take us." The driver waved me forward.

I didn't want to go with them. I might be able to defend myself against the driver, but I had no chance against three of them. I put my hand on the door of the taxi. I was thinking about getting my phone. I tried the door. It was locked.

One of the men walked towards me. He pulled the turban off his head and bowed. When he spoke, to my surprise, it was with a south London accent. I let out a stifled gasp.

"Yes," he said. "I was brought up in Peckham. My name is Asim. I am here to protect you." He smiled, broadly. His eyes were electric blue.

"How long have you been here?" I asked, tilting my head to appear friendly.

"I moved back to Egypt to be with my family last year." He pointed at the driver. "I must tell you that you're better off with me than with this rogue. Has he given you any crap?"

The driver let out a stream of Arabic.

"No, not really. He just wants money for everything." I bit my lip. Tiredness was making me say more than I intended.

"Don't concern yourself with money now. This man would ask death for a commission, before bringing him into your house." He waved his hand towards the jeep he'd arrived in. "You will come with me."

I glanced at the others.

"Just you and me, Mrs. Ryan. The others will follow with your friend."

He opened the passenger door of the jeep. I hesitated. The words, *never get in a car with a stranger*, echoed in my mind. When I was doing my Foreign Office training we were sent to Hanslope, north of London, for security training. Much of that was about learning what to do in a variety of threatening situations, as well as the psychology of getting on with people when under stress. Following your mother's advice about not getting in cars with strangers was one of the security lessons, which made us new recruits smile.

I wasn't smiling now, as I put my hand on the door and looked back at my driver. He did not look happy. The two other men were standing around him. One of them was leaning towards him, speaking softly. Asim bowed as I got in his car. But his eyes were still on me.

Between the Devil and Asim's deep blue eyes. I wasn't sure if the Devil might have been a better choice.

47

Henry Mowlam pressed his finger onto the touchpad. His screen beeped. The office was almost empty, only the skeleton weekend night shift crew, who occupied the far corner of the main control room were doing anything.

He had waved at them when he came back from the pub.

"Looking for another promotion, Henry?" one of them had said when he'd passed them.

"I just need to check on something," he'd replied.

"Keep us in the loop, Henry," shouted the night shift supervisor, from a few desks away. He nodded as he went to his desk.

After he sat down, he clicked on the tracking service link on his main screen, and then on Isabel Ryan's name in the list on the left. The satellite service was tracking her signal all right, but the map location it gave was deep in a village south west of Cairo, not in the city itself. Had her phone been stolen?

He brought up the location on the global security mapping system, zoomed down. The image on the screen, from the last satellite pass, showed the roof tops and dusty streets of a typical, abandoned looking, Arab village. The resolution was clear enough to show faces, but not many people looked up when a satellite passed overhead.

And there was no sign of any vehicle at the spot where the tracking system had the phone at.

He hunched over the screen. Where the hell was Isabel?

48

Asim gunned the engine as if we were in the middle of the desert. Then he spun the car around in a hail of dust and sand. He was showing off for me. I sat back, checked my shirt buttons were done up, then kept my eyes on the road ahead, looking for landmarks.

"Your husband is here in Cairo."

It didn't sound like a question.

"Have you seen him?" My throat felt tight. Was he playing some stupid game with me?

Asim looked in the rear view mirror, then turned and winked at me.

"Yes, but I am talking about your future husband." He reached across and tried to pat my thigh.

I moved my leg away from him. His fingers missed me. What a bastard. To play games with me when he knew what I was doing here.

"I'll scratch your eyes out if you touch me again." I kept my voice low, but steady. I could injure him, for sure, but we'd both end up in a hospital or a morgue, if I did it at the speed he was driving.

"But I like you, Mrs. Ryan." The car jumped forward in the darkness. The road ahead was empty. A tube of light from our headlights showed only faded tarmac and sand coming in from either side.

I opened my window. I could see a little more, as the road rushed by; drifts of sand, stars up above and a dark ridge ahead in the distance, which ran all the way to the horizon.

After a few minutes Asim turned the radio on. Fast Arabic music filled the car. A woman was crooning, as if her lover had been denied her, and all the time he tapped his fingers on the steering wheel, keeping time.

He turned to me. "You like music?" He stared at me so long I ended up pointing ahead, in case we ended up in a sand dune together.

In my hand I had the steel pen Henry had given me. It was strong enough to break bones, he'd assured me, but I'd never had to do more than threaten with it. But I could feel the moment it might actually be used coming on. This was not how I'd imagined this mission ending. Driving deep into the desert in the middle of the night with a young Arab man who might well be a rapist.

I knew that rape was rarely reported in Egypt, as women who did so might be accused of bringing dishonor on their family. I also knew many men here knew the chance of being punished for rape was slight.

I could feel my muscles tightening all over my body. The question I had to face was, how hard should I fight back? If I put the steel into the asshole's eye and killed him, I might never make it back to my hotel given that his friends were in the vehicle behind, whose headlights were the only thing visible to our rear. Would this be the end of my search, buried in some desert grave, which no one would ever find?

Asim tapped on as the song changed. This time the music was softer, and a man was singing. I didn't have to understand the words to know this song was also about lost love. The road became straighter, with fewer sand drifts in front of us. Asim sped faster on into the darkness.

I looked behind. The taxi was still there, keeping up with us. The only reassuring thought I had was that Asim might not want to rape me in front of so many others. And he had to be working for someone, taking me somewhere.

If all they'd met me for was to rape me, surely they didn't need to drive on and on into the desert for that?

In the distance a speck of light grew larger. At first I thought it was a star on the horizon, but finally I saw that it was a single lamp under a tent canopy. The tent walls were open and there was a group of men sitting on the ground in a circle under the light.

One man stood as we approached. He stared in our direction. There were cars pulled up near the tent. They became visible only as we got nearer and the light from our headlights glinted off them. We slowed and pulled up beside the other cars.

"We are here, Mrs. Ryan. Now you meet my brothers."

I didn't like the look of this. I stared out of the car window. Five men were sitting on a red patterned carpet. Each of them had a beard, one longer than the next. The man in the middle's was gray and his head was bald. The other men had black hair. All looked as if they'd just come in out of the desert.

Asim got out, went around, opened my door. He leaned in.

"Don't worry. They won't bite, not like me." He made a snarling noise, showing the teeth on one side of his mouth, then laughed and opened the door wider. The men were all staring at me, as if they'd never seen a woman before. I adjusted my scarf, pulled it down further towards my eyes, to ensure my hair was fully covered. This crowd might appreciate such a gesture.

I followed Asim to the tent. A cool breeze hit me, then the taste of sand was in my mouth. I licked my lips. There was sand there too.

In front of the men there was a battered teapot on a small iron stand. Red cups sat in front of each of the men and a shisha pipe sat to one side. A finger of smoke rose from it, as if it had recently been used. The man in the center pointed to one of the men near him, said something to him.

The man stood and pulled some carpet covered cushions from behind him and put them near to him, patting on them. The rest of the men stayed sitting as we approached.

Asim stopped, bowed deeply. He spoke fast in Arabic. I heard my name mentioned, twice. I stood to his side, waited, trying to look as unafraid as I could.

Eventually he stopped talking and stepped to the side.

The gray haired man raised his hand to me. "Welcome to our tent and our country," he said. His hesitant delivery made it clear he wasn't fluent in English. He put his hand in front of him, as if holding something, then nodded.

"Please, sit," said Asim.

I sat to the right, next to a lightly bearded man who was staring hard at the carpet in front of him. So far, so good. But what they wanted with me, and what they might do next was what I was concerned about.

The taxi driver approached. He bowed deeply. The gray haired man waved him to sit down. He sat near me.

The gray haired man slapped his hands together. The man beside me reached in front, took a spare cup, poured tea from the pot and handed it to me. The same was done for the taxi driver and Asim, who was sitting on my other side. All the men raised their cups. I raised mine. We all drank.

The tea was bitter. Tiny flakes of leaf caught in my throat. I coughed.

"You need sugar?" said Asim.

He passed me a red bowl with cubes of white sugar. I put one in my tea.

The gray haired man raised a hand. Silence descended. The wind came in from the desert with a faint whistle. He smiled at me. His teeth were yellow. He leaned forward, his hand still up in front of him.

"So you are the spy looking for her husband."

49

Xena breathed slowly. There was no way out. The two star shafts leading up to the outside of the pyramid were big enough for a rat, perhaps a desert lynx, but she had no chance that way.

She turned on her torch again.

But now it flickered again before she'd counted to ten. She turned it off to let the batteries recover for a longer period. The darkness rushed in, like an animal enveloping her. She was used to darkness, but now it felt like death itself smothering her.

An urge to scream, to hope that someone might come and rescue her, she suppressed. She had this one chance. She had to find the fabled other tunnels and halls, which connected to this room.

She was thirsty now, and her mouth was as dry as sand. She unscrewed the back of the torch, pulled down her loose trousers and peed into the cup like plastic receptacle, which the battery cover for the torch was like. Urine was drinkable. It would taste bitter, but it would stop any panicking at the dryness in her throat.

But how long would it be before all solutions were played out? Forty-eight hours? After that she would be curled on the floor, panting for water.

And how long would it be before they broke through into the chamber?

Even if they moved fast, the process of approving and pulling together such a project in Egypt was no easy task. Ahmed Yacoub might press to speed it up, but he wouldn't want to be connected too closely with what had happened, in case he was implicated in damaging the pyramid, one of Egypt's greatest tourist draws.

She'd known what type of man he was for a long time. What he wanted was the most important thing to him. It had been for all the years she'd worked for him. When she'd slit the throat of that Imam in Cairo, years before, at his direction, she had been paid well, and why it needed to be done had been explained to her, but it had suited Yacoub Holdings and he'd kept his distance afterwards then too.

She flicked the torch on briefly, then walked to the wall at the end of the chamber. She traced her fingers around the edges of the blocks in the darkness. The blocks here were big, but as tightly fitted together as all the other ones. How it had all been done was clearly the work of a secret skill humans had long forgotten.

She traced the outline of more blocks, looking for anything that would give her hope. She reached as high as she could along the wall, then flicked on the torch, looked up to the roof. It was twice her height and the roof blocks were stained black in places, perhaps from torches thousands of years ago.

Her lip was trembling now. She didn't want to admit to herself that hope was dying, but she knew she'd have to make a decision soon. She could rest, conserve her energy or work on the stone that had filled the exit shaft and hope it might give way after hours of scratching.

Which was it to be? She waited, let her breathing calm, then flicked on the torch, went to the floor block they had managed to move, if only for a few inches, and started jumping up and down, pushing as hard as she could on the block.

Nothing. She was wasting her time.

She sat in the dark, held her arms tight around her.

The darkness was like a presence around her.

And that was when she heard it. A soft whisper, as if something was in the chamber with her.

50

I heard myself inhale. I forced my voice to flatline as I replied, "I am not a spy. I worked for the British Consulate in Istanbul a few years ago. I am not working for any government agency."

"But you work for Infofreed, the people who say they want to tell the world every secret, but what they really want is to find out who are the people who will leak secrets, yes." He waved his hand at me, angrily.

I looked down at my tea. I wanted to stand up and leave.

"We want the people in power to hear the truth about the things that are broken. We want wrong doing exposed. We want to stop corruption. These are all good things." My voice rose as I spoke. I sometimes surprised myself with how much I believed in what we were doing at Infofreed.

"Yes, yes, but you still all work for the British security services."

I could feel my face redden. Fear told me not to reply. Anger pushed me to say something.

"That's a lie." I leaned forward, stared at him. His eyes hadn't left my face since he started the interrogation.

The gray haired man said something fast in Arabic. The men around me hissed, clucked. The mood in the room had changed. I looked at the taxi driver. Would he take me away from here? Could he?

The taxi driver stared back at me, an angry look on his face.

When I looked back at the gray haired man my heart did a double beat. He had a black pistol in his hand. It was a heavy looking Heckler and Koch, like what you see on a German police officer's belt. He cradled the pistol in both hands, as if praying to it.

It was the first time I'd seen a gun at a tea party. A ripple of fear passed right through me, into my gut. I couldn't take my eyes off it. We'd been trained in how to use guns, how to react when one is drawn, including wonderful tips such as, make no sudden movements, but every time I saw one the questions were the same.

When would it go off? And in whose direction?

And I had no idea what the man holding the gun would do. Radical Islamists have different cultural beliefs. Liberty, equality and women's liberation are far-fetched concepts, to be openly mocked.

I glanced around. No one else seemed to be paying any attention to gray hair, except Asim, who nudged me, and when I turned to him, made a motion for me to stay quiet, a single finger pressed to his lips.

I looked back at gray hair. He was holding the gun steady now with two hands, pointing it at the ground in front of him.

His eyes found mine. "I do not want to kill another spy," he said. He sounded wistful.

I kept staring at him, my heart double beating. He could kill me, I knew it. The seconds crawled as I watched his face. The men around us had gone quiet. The wind whistled against the tent poles. The canvas creaked.

"But someone must die tonight." He sighted along the barrel and pulled the trigger.

The noise was almost deafening. My mouth opened in shock. It wasn't me he'd shot. It was the taxi driver.

I gasped, feeling slow witted, and put a hand out beside me, grasping at a ruffle in the carpet. The taxi driver, the man who had helped me find these people, had fallen backwards. Blood was pouring from a huge wound in his forehead. It was flowing into the sand. He hadn't even had time to say anything. His hands must have gone up in front of him. They were still raised in the air. As I watched they fell to his side.

A whiff of cordite reached my nostrils. The men around me hesitated for a moment, then whooped and raised fists high, as if death was a good thing.

Asim leaned towards me. "Your friend made a mistake helping you. We do not blame you for working for your country. But we despise traitors who help our enemy."

I was beyond angry now. "This is not right. You cannot just kill someone, because they helped me."

He shook his head. "No, you are wrong. We are obliged to do this. It seems you do not understand who you are dealing with."

"So, what will happen to me?" I glanced towards the other men.

"You will be questioned. And our leader will decide what to do with you."

Two men were already dealing with the taxi driver. They took him under each arm, dragged his body, still bleeding, into the sand towards a dune. The whooping was finished now. The gray haired man put his gun away. He addressed me when I looked at him.

"Traitors must die, Mrs. Ryan. That is our law. Do you not have a similar law?"

I just stared at him. I'd been trained in what to do if kidnapped. Disagreeing and getting into arguments was definitely not recommended, no matter how you felt about any subject. Kidnappers might just be looking for an emotional reason to justify violence.

"You do know that followers of Islam will be the largest religion in the world by 2030, and more than half the world will submit to us by the end of this century."

"Is that right?" I tried to sound mildly puzzled, but not doubting him.

"Yes, it is right. Your culture, your Western civilization, will be the minority soon and then…" He put the gun down, made an explosive gesture with his hands. "Poof, it will be gone. Your stupid ideas about equality and women's liberation have undone you. We won't have to fight one war to take control of Europe, and then America will be next. Your birthrate is declining. Your women are not even marrying anymore. They have no need for a man. They stand on their own two feet."

He shook his head in bafflement. "You know that I am right. We breed better than you. Your men are soft, and weak. And we are hard and strong." He raised his fist. The men around us raised theirs too. They shouted something together in Arabic.

I didn't like where this was heading. My skin prickled and a sick feeling in my stomach made me clench it tight.

"You are all doomed, Mrs. Ryan. I feel sorry for you, never to have the joy of submission. It's the path all women need to take. The path to belief. To faith. Our women believe.

Our men believe. We all have faith." He thumped his chest. "And we will gladly die for our faith. And this is why we will win. And when we do win, we will eradicate all your temples to your false gods, your Vatican, your St. Paul's, and here, we will flatten the pyramids, take their stones one by one and use them for new mosques, until there is nothing there but sand."

"You know what you want."

"We do, Mrs. Ryan, and we want something from you, too. Something you will give us tonight."

I looked him in the eye, to show I wouldn't give in easy. I still had options. I could stab the first man who touched me, right through his neck until my steel pen came out the other side.

I'd be lucky to survive the night if I did that, but I wasn't going to lie back and let them all take me. If I showed them I was weak, the devil only knew what they would do to me.

He started laughing. The men beside him followed his cue. Soon all the men were laughing. I kept my face as still as I could. Fuck them all.

"Mrs. Ryan, we are not going to rape you. We are not going to take you tonight. I am sorry to disappoint you." He suppressed his laughter. "You will help us with a job we have to do." He leaned towards me.

"I am told you have been in Ahmed Yacoub's villa."

I stared into his eyes. They were dark pools. What the hell did he want?

51

Henry Mowlam looked at the email he was about to send. It was addressed to the duty officer at the Almaza Egyptian air force base, north east of Cairo. The 533 helicopter brigade of the Egyptian Air Force had at least two of their new Russian KA-52 with their new radar systems on permanent standby, as well as at least six older Apache helicopters.

A KA-52 would be ideal for a search and rescue mission, should the drone looking for Isabel Ryan find its target. The Egyptian unmanned military drone, a Scheibel Camcopter, released from a routine mission searching for Islamist infiltrators on the border with Libya, was already in the air above the last location of Isabel's phone. It was following the most likely roads she had traveled on leaving the village where the phone was located.

It would then circle each possible location at a height that was high enough not to be seen or heard.

Isabel's disappearance complicated things. The worldwide reaction to the deaths of civilians in Cairo was beyond what everyone had expected. The United Nations had called an emergency security council session, though the

United States had not given its position on the French resolution calling on the Egyptian government to offer free elections as soon as possible.

The French, as usual, were talking the talk about democracy, when they knew all that would lead to would be an Islamic state with Sharia Law for all. That would leave a country of eighty-five million in a precarious situation. And they were adding a million a year in a population growth rate double that of Germany.

Islamist faction fighting and then a decline in the Egyptian economy could see millions heading to Europe across the Mediterranean again. And Europe had given up accepting massive Muslim migrations. Ensuring Egypt had a stable government, which could offer hope, jobs and entertainment to its citizens was the goal now.

And not just for the short term.

And if that meant a few hundred people had to die, so be it. Even a few thousand. The end justified the means. Tens of thousands would die trying to get into Europe, and in factional fighting, if Egypt descended into chaos.

Always think of the greater good. Finch had drummed that into him.

But for now, he had to make sure every agent they had in Egypt was protected. They each had a mission to achieve. Without them the whole country could disintegrate.

52

I looked down. Many Arab men did not like women who weren't submissive. I was not going to annoy this asshole, even if that meant conforming to his idea of what was right, until I got the hell out of this place.

"You will return to Cairo this evening. You will be with one of our younger brothers. You will ask the security guard to let you in, because you left something behind when you visited, your car keys perhaps, and you need them before you fly back to Europe." He stopped. I stared at him.

"Do you understand?"

"I understand." This was good. They would take me back to Cairo.

"So, let us go." He stood, started barking in Arabic to the men around us. They sprang up, began rolling the carpet, packing things away into large straw bags. Asim took me by the arm.

"You will come back with me." His grip tightened. "If you do anything to alert the guards at Yacoub's about what is going on, I have permission to kill you." His grip tightened again. "You will be shot three times in the belly. That way you are sure to die, but it will not come quickly. Usually it takes an hour of great torment that way." He pushed me towards his vehicle.

I stumbled, then straightened myself. I wasn't going to react to the asshole, to any of these assholes. I had to get back to Cairo. I had to tell Henry what they were planning.

Three of us got into Asim's vehicle. I was in the front with Asim. A boy of perhaps twelve or thirteen, beggar thin and with an innocent face, was in the back.

As we drove away from the tent I looked behind. The tent poles were coming down and the only light now was from the stars and the headlights of two other vehicles, which crossed over the sand where the tent had been.

I wondered where they'd buried the taxi driver.

"The jackals will eat your taxi driver. Even if we buried him deep they would dig him up out here, and feast on him."

I looked out the side window. A shudder passed through me. What a horrible way to go. I pressed my jaw together, shook my head in disgust.

"You do not like that way to leave the world? Perhaps you will remember that you are lucky it is not you getting eaten. Malak al-maut, the angel of death, is not picky as to who he receives." He reached towards my thigh.

I moved it quickly, crossed my legs. His fingertips slipped off the cotton of my trousers.

"But perhaps he would have enjoyed pulling your soul from your body."

"I came to find out about my husband. Perhaps you can tell me what I was promised now."

The car bumped on the road. Asim slowed. There was a lot of sand on the road, almost obscuring it. Our wheels spun, headlights tracing an arc across the desert. Asim wrenched the car back in a straight line. There was a smell in the car now. The stink of dried sweat.

I glanced at the boy in the back. He had a six inch long knife in his hand. It had a white bone handle and a dangerous looking blade. The boy was rubbing a smooth white stone along its edge, slowly.

He was also muttering to himself.

His off white tunic was stained in irregular patterns. It looked as if it had never been washed.

I knew where the smell was coming from.

"I am the one who knows about your husband, Isabel. Cooperate and I will tell you what you want to know."

He reached again for my thigh. This time I swatted at his hand, connected, and brushed it away, hard. We swerved again. The boy in the back grunted.

"I am not your whore," I said.

"But surely all Western women are whores?" He swerved the car around a hump of sand in the road. I couldn't help myself leaning towards him.

"No, be careful, we can be devils, who are not afraid to push your eyes out to punish you for daring to touch us." I stared straight ahead. "Would you like to see if this is true?"

Asim kept his hands on the wheel. "I simply thought you would be willing to be a little friendly, to find out what happened to your husband."

I didn't reply. What a sleazebag, trying to blackmail me to get what he wanted.

"He doesn't mean that much to you, does he?"

"If you know where he is, why don't you just tell me. Is this what you have to do to get a woman?" I looked out the window.

We drove on. The boy in the back was still rubbing at his knife. Asim turned the music up. It was Arabic pop, lots of emotional crooning.

We passed through the village where my taxi driver had stopped, then turned onto the main road back to Cairo.

Asim spoke again a minute later. It seemed he had been thinking about what I'd said.

"I don't need anything from you, Mrs. Ryan." He scratched his neck, pulling at his wiry beard. "I thought you might need comforting, especially after what I will tell you about your husband."

I took in a deep breath. Did he really know something, or was he playing games with me?

"Just tell me what you know."

"You will need to be strong, Mrs. Ryan."

"I am." But I didn't feel that strong. Conflicting emotions were bubbling up inside me. I pictured Sean, his smiling face, and felt a longing deep inside me to see him, to hold him. And a stark, physical sense of foreboding tugged at me as well.

He didn't look at me when he replied. "Your husband's body has been used for experiments by Yacoub Pharmaceuticals."

53

Xena was moving around the King's Chamber on her hands and knees. The torch was out. After hearing the noises, she'd turned it on briefly to see if there was something in the room with her, but she'd seen nothing.

But she'd definitely heard something. She wasn't going mad. The angel of darkness had not taken her yet. Something in this chamber had made a noise and touch might help her find out if anything was different, if anything had moved. She thought back to the last time she'd walked around the room with the light on, half an hour before. Every stone had been smoothly fitted to the one beside it.

So why was it that they all seemed to have cracks between them now?

Had something been disturbed in the relieving stones, which took the weight of the pyramid above and sent it to the sides of the chamber? Or was there something else going on? Was the chamber about to collapse? If it was, she would end up a smear of blood and shattered bones under the thousands of tons of rock above.

She stopped at a corner, decided to find her way back to the place on the floor where the stone had descended a few inches. She turned the torch on.

And that was when she knew something had definitely happened to the chamber. It was a little longer than she'd remembered. She walked to the far end. The floor was marked in a line about two inches wide. She bent down. The stone floor slab sections that had been revealed were paler. She touched the new strip of stone, which had been revealed, put her fingers to her lips.

A dusty taste filled her mouth. She ran her fingers all the way to the far wall. It was the same all the way along. She looked at the ceiling. That had extended too. Was this something the makers had designed? Was there more movement to come?

She went fast to the other end of the room. Nothing had changed there. She turned the torch off, walked around the room, her hands on the walls. There were definitely small cracks between some of the wall slabs. But they didn't feel intentional, as the extended section of the room did. They were not consistent. But were there more now than before?

She stood in the darkness beside the section of floor that had moved down. Suddenly, her feet shifted a little under her, and she rocked sideways and back, fear tightening at her.

She went down on her haunches, then reached for the slab in the floor in front of her, pressed at it. It moved, angled down, as if hinged in the center.

54

I stared straight ahead. Was he telling me the truth, or did he just want to upset me, and provide more reasons for me not to cause trouble when we got to Yacoub's villa?

"Yacoub is a real danger to the world, not just to people in Egypt." Asim spoke as if he was revealing some secret.

"How do you know my husband was taken by Yacoub Pharmaceuticals?"

"We watch all the players in Egypt, anyone positioning himself for power in our beloved country. We watch Yacoub because he is a player. He might well end up as president of Egypt. If nobody stops him. So, we have spies inside his villa." He looked at me, then shrugged. "I don't care if you believe me or not. I want to help you understand the type of man you are dealing with." He made a spitting noise. "You are dealing with a devil."

"What sort of tests are you talking about?" Dread was pulling at me. Could all this be true? Had something terrible, something irreversible, happened to Sean? Memories of him smiling came to me. A rush of images passed through my mind. A heavy weight, like a hand, gripped my chest, my throat.

Acid filled my windpipe. My stomach had turned. I wanted to throw up.

"All I know is that someone matching your husband's description was seen in one of the testing rooms at Yacoub's villa."

"That's where he's testing people?"

"Yes, in the basement levels."

I remembered the basement levels I'd seen at Yacoub's. It was possible he was conducting experiments there. A man in his position was unlikely to be questioned about such tests. Anyone enquiring about human tests could be dismissed as someone trying to stop the progress of a key part of Egypt's pharmaceutical industry.

Had Sean been there when I was there? Had I passed within feet of him? I shook my head. I wasn't going to let that thought get to me. This Asim character could also be lying.

We sat in silence as we headed up the highway back to Cairo. The clock on the dashboard said it was a quarter before midnight. The traffic was sparse, mostly trucks, some of them lit up like Christmas trees, some were new Japanese imports and the cars were older, mostly dust covered Mercedes and Renaults.

It was another hour before we were parked down the road from Yacoub's.

Asim pointed at the entrance, then pushed his finger towards my face. I didn't flinch. "You will get the front gate open, and this boy will deal with the two security guards. As soon as they are on their way to their promised land, you will open the side gate and wait. We will find your husband, Mrs. Ryan. Trust me."

I stared him straight in the eye. I wouldn't trust him to tell me what day it was, but what choice did I have?

"And cheer up, Mrs. Ryan. You are about to rescue your husband."

Asim grinned, reached across me and pushed the door of the car open. Then he closed it again. A car had come racing around the corner beyond the villa. It was a police car.

I stared at it as it raced towards us.

55

Xena went down on her knees, turned the torch off, and began to feel all around the block, moving on her hands and knees.

She was going to take this slowly. If she had discovered a secret chamber in the Great Pyramid, it could contain anything. It could be the treasure room of a pharaoh, or a passage to the fabled Hall of Records, mentioned by Plato as where the records of ancient, pre-historic societies were kept. The Hall of Records would prove why the Great Pyramid was built with such precise dimensions too.

The time of change could be upon the world, at last. And she, Xena, priestess of the Queen of Darkness, would be part of the revelation. She breathed deep. The mothers in her monastery in Ethiopia would be proud.

She switched her torch on. What she had to do now was make sure she didn't die, entombed with the records, and that whatever she found would not be locked away again.

She pushed down at the edge of the block in front of her. It shifted again. It seemed to have an axis running through the center of the block. She pushed the block more, peered into the space below. It was a pit. A square sided stone pit.

And no matter how much she held the light down into it, she couldn't see the bottom. Xena sat back, turned the torch off again. What choice did she have now? She'd checked every wall, every floor slab for another way out. Maybe she should check again. She was facing a big decision.

For the next hour she pressed and tapped at every other floor slab and the surrounding ones on the wall. She pushed at where they met the extended far wall and banged hard at the wall slabs that had moved. But in the end it was clear, there was only one way she was going to get out of here. Down into the pit.

But what was down there? Did it extend down to a chamber, to water, or just rock? Was it just a place they used to throw dead bodies? And most importantly, was there a way out down there? And should she wait here, hoping to get rescued, or try to find a way down.

She kneeled, bent her head forward, seeking guidance.
"Abatachin Hoy Besemay Yemitnor
Simmeh Yekedes
Mengistih Timta
Fekadeh Besemay Indehonech."

She repeated the words five times, then tapped her forehead five times on the stone floor in front of her. She knew what she had to do, but she knew too that it was a throw of the dice. Anything could happen now. Her future would be decided by the architects of the pyramid, and decisions they had made five thousand years ago or more. A coldness moved inside her chest. It had started deep in her stomach.

She remembered this feeling from long ago too, from when she was young and learning the prayers and the secrets. She had been left in the desert, bound by her hands and feet. The woman who left her there had ridden off on a donkey. It had been hours before she got free of the ropes. It had been cold then, and dark. And all she had to guide her were the stars and hope. She had walked for three days before falling into a village with her tongue swollen.

But she had survived.

And she would survive this, too.

She took the torch, turned it on, held it over the center of the pit. She released it. As it fell it illuminated stone walls going down and down and down. It fell for a long time. Then, with a distant echo, the light extinguished.

But there had been a split second where she had seen something. She closed her eyes, brought the memory back. What did it mean?

56

Henry adjusted the resolution on his virtual reality headset. They were still in test mode with them, but watching drone footage from a Camcopter was an ideal application. By turning his head he could see where he wanted to see, rather than asking the drone to turn to face something.

The image of the street outside Ahmed Yacoub's villa in Cairo, on the west bank of the Nile, between the Nile and the pyramids was pretty good, despite it being the middle of the night in Cairo. Sure, the picture was in shades of gray, but he could see the vehicle they had tracked from Isabel's last known location,

As he watched, an Egyptian police car raced past the vehicle Isabel was likely to be sitting in. Some incident nearer the Nile was bringing police cars together. Another attempt to assassinate a government minister, most probably.

But it could also be a diversion.

Was some operation underway at Yacoub's? Two other vehicles from the location this one had come from, were now sitting around the corner from his villa. And the police vehicle that usually cruised this block was gone.

Henry picked up the phone, pressed the speed dial number for the Cairo embassy on his screen. The duty officer answered.

"Initiate a personnel retrieval, please, Tony."

"Henry, you were always a late bird. I hope this one isn't a wild goose chase, like our last one."

"Just following procedure, Tony. An agent is at risk. Let's do this right this time. No pissing about with getting the ambassador to approve it."

"Just following procedure, Henry. Make sure you put the right status on it to avoid any problems this time."

The line went dead.

Henry began typing, fast. He took the location tracking data from the satellite link. As he pressed send, he whispered.

"Stay safe until we get there, Isabel."

57

My heart was thumping fast as the police car passed us. I half expected them to stop, pull out their guns and order us out of the car.

"Time to go," said Asim. He pushed my door half open. The boy in the back got out. He fully opened my door. I stepped out. There was a cool wind blowing.

The boy led the way, but he walked beside me as we came up to the steel gate with the buzzer and keypad beside it. He stood next to me as I pressed the buzzer. Nothing happened. I pressed it again. Was everyone asleep?

Or had they a policy of not answering when people came to the gate at night?

The boy reached up, pressed the buzzer, held it down. We waited. Another car passed. I didn't look at it. I was looking at the security camera above the far corner of the door. I waved at it. Were they assessing whether to open up?

Other thoughts crowded in. Should I make a run for it, ask Henry to send a team into Yacoub's building to search for Sean? But that would take hours to get ready, at the very least.

And it was possible that Asim might get in anyway, whatever I did.

Maybe it would be better for me to stay with this.

I hugged my arms around myself. The boy put his hand on my arm. A shiver passed up through me. I wanted to move his hand. Every instinct told me to, but if I did anyone watching might assume the boy was not a friend. I kept rigidly still, stared up at the camera.

I felt both uncomfortable and stupid now, standing here, with nothing happening. Maybe I should run.

Then, with a scratching noise, the steel door slid open. Two uniformed guards were behind it, one near the door. The other further back. The boy tugged lightly at my jacket.

"I'm sorry. I left my phone behind when I was here earlier today. Did you find it? I'm really sorry to disturb you in the middle of the night, but I really need my phone. It has my ticket details for going home and all my photos. Please, can you ask about it?" I was talking too much. He was probably getting more suspicious by the second.

The security guard had droopy eyes, a half beard and a belly that was pushing out his shirt above his waistband. He probably had a wife and three or four children all waiting for Dada to come home. I didn't want any part in something horrible happening to him, no matter what Asim was threatening would happen to me. I put my hand on the boy's shoulder, gripped it hard. Perhaps there was a way to turn this around.

With a shrug the boy slipped from my fingers. He stepped forward, his head bent down, as if looking at the guard's feet. The guard went back, but he was too slow. The boy's hand went up in a smooth movement and a splutter of blood and a moan came from the guard's mouth.

The guard behind was raising his machine pistol, stepping back. The boy went around the first guard and ran, as if spring loaded, to the second. That guard let off three deafening bullets before the boy's knife was buried in his throat.

The bullets echoed in the road, like an earthquake. I imagined every house on the road waking up.

Then everything slowed as the reality of what had happened struck me. The gunfire echoed into silence. Dogs barked in reply. A circle of dogs seemed to be instantly calling to each other. A car started up down the road. Someone shouted in Arabic. Asim was walking towards us and from the end of the street a car was cruising in our direction. I looked back at the carnage in the passageway leading into the Yacoub building. The boy was pushing the bodies to the side. Blood was flowing. A pang of revulsion turned my stomach sour. I felt a slap on my back.

"I thought you might run. I am glad you didn't. We would have had to kill you. That would have been a terrible waste." He pushed past me.

I followed him, vowing to make sure these bastards got what they deserved.

A clatter of feet sounded behind us. Four men with black scarves around their heads and mouths pushed past us. I followed them towards the villa. The boy, still behind, closed the steel door to the outside world and stayed with the bodies. The last I saw was him rifling through their pockets.

Asim gripped my arm, led the way to a side door in the villa, down a set of marble steps. The door opened without a key and we streamed in. A corridor led into the building. Was it possible the two guards were the only security presence?

We moved fast past closed doors on either side. We passed a security camera high up on a wall. It pointed towards us. If there were any other guards here, they'd be well aware of our presence now. Asim opened a door at the end of the corridor.

The men were all around me. One was behind me. I got a sudden thought that I would be a bargaining tool if they were pinned down.

We went through the door. I knew where we were. This was the ornate staircase leading to the basement levels, which I had been in earlier that day. Asim went down, pushing me ahead of him. His men followed. The iron rich smell of blood was still in my nostrils. Revulsion was still tightening my throat.

I half expected a troop of guards to appear from below or above. I kept shooting glances over the banisters, but it appeared there was no one else in the building. The only sound was the clump of shoes on the marble stairs.

We passed the first basement floor and pushed on down. At the next level Asim pressed his ear to the door, then leaned away. One of the men was standing beside me. We formed a semi-circle around him. He'd clearly been tasked with watching me when Asim wasn't.

Asim motioned at one of the other men. He tried the door handle. Then, when it didn't open, he reached into a small backpack he'd placed on the floor. He opened a plastic lunch box and placed what looked like putty near the handle. It had a small electronic timer embedded it. The man waved us to go back, then tapped at the timer.

We were all back and up the stairway, out of sight of the door, when the explosion went off. My ear drums reverberated, as if my skull was a bell. I'd opened my mouth before the explosion went off, but my ears were still affected and every noise was muffled. The dull wail of an alarm started up. I looked at the others, spotted ear plugs in their ears.

They had protected themselves. My arm was grabbed again and I was pushed forward and down the stairs. Asim was ahead. He had opened the door. It had a hole blown out of it about a foot wide, where the lock had been. Jagged pieces of metal littered the ground. A black stain covered the wall, the floor and the ceiling. Smoke lingered in the air and a strong smell of burnt plastic.

The others followed Asim. I went through too.

The corridor beyond was empty. A flashing red warning light lit up the corridor with an eerie glow. The alarm wailed. My head was still reverberating, but I was focused. I too wanted to know what was in this corridor.

Asim was walking ahead, opening the doors on one side of the corridor. One of the other men was opening the doors on the other side. I followed, peering in the doors. My blood cooled. In the middle of the first room stood a steel operating table. Around the room stood hospital equipment. Steel tables lined one wall. On them were blue sample boxes, a small fridge, small pieces of steel and white medical equipment. This was a facility to experiment on humans.

Asim had been right.

A shout rang out from the corridor. I knew what it meant.

They had found someone.

58

Xena rocked back and forward on her heels. She knew what she had to do. She'd seen the bottom of the pit. It had looked like sand. But the light had gone out too quickly for her to be sure.

And even if it was sand, it was a long way down. And the sand could be a thin layer above bedrock. And it didn't mean there was a way out.

She closed her eyes, felt forward to the edge of the slab, pressed it down, moved her hand around the edge, looking for hand holds, any indication that people had gone down this way thousands of years ago. She took her time. She listened, too. It was a long way to the nearest buildings beyond the pyramid compound, but there was the possibility that there could be running water deep down, underground rivers flowing into the Nile.

It was one of the things she'd heard Yacoub talking about, that water courses fed out from the Giza plateau to the river.

Now she was finished working her way around the hole.

She said a prayer, turned, extended her feet into the hole. If she was going down this way she would have to do it quickly. Her hands trembled. She gripped them together. The muscles in her arms and legs were tightening, as if she was getting ready to run through the desert, as she had done when she was a child.

She remembered the village women ululating when a baby was born, or when a villager died. She remembered how they'd taken care of her.

She believed in the fate her mothers had taught her would be hers and hers alone. She was the chosen one, the one who would find what had been lost.

She held her hand over the edge of the hole. There was definitely a slight breeze. There had to be a way to the outside down there. She pushed herself over the edge, let go quickly before the stone swung back into place and crushed her hands.

And she was falling into the blackness.

59

I went into the room. My heart wanted to stop beating. There was a body under a white sheet on a hospital trolley in the middle of the room. The siren had just stopped, creating an eerie silence.

Asim was standing by the body. He was bent over, as if whispering to it. I walked slowly towards him. When I reached the body a hush descended on the room. Two of the other men who'd come with us stood behind me. They'd been talking in Arabic. They stopped as I lifted the sheet from the face.

My heart was heavy, and I wanted to slow time, for it to go backwards, to not be here at all.

But the face wasn't Sean's. My hand shook so much I dropped the sheet back down.

Asim said something to one of the other men. He took a smartphone from his pocket and took a picture of the face I'd looked at. The face looked caved in, as if something had eaten it from the inside. Was that what they had done to Sean? I turned, ran for the door. I had to check every other room.

"Mrs. Ryan," Asim called, but I ignored him. I looked at the other doors. The one nearest me was open. I ran to it. The hospital trolley inside the room had no one on it. I ran to the next door, opened it. There wasn't even a trolley in this room. It was a store room.

There was only one more door. Asim was near me, walking fast towards it. He had his hands up, as if warning me not to follow. I didn't hesitate for one second. He may have been conditioned to think women should obey what men say, but there was no way I was going to put up with this bullshit.

I went through the door. There was another body on a table covered in a white sheet, but this was definitely a woman. Asim turned and growled at me, waved at me, as if he wanted me out of the room. Then he strode to the table and pulled the sheet away, exposing the head and breasts of a young woman, perhaps twenty-five. Her face was disfigured. Where her nose had been there was a bloody hole.

I reached for the sheet, pulled it from Asim's hand and placed it back over the woman's body.

The men grunted.

Asim shouted something in Arabic. They all trooped out of the room. I said a quick prayer over the woman and followed. Asim was at the end of the corridor, back where we'd come in.

"Be quick, Mrs. Ryan," he shouted.

We went down the stairs again. On the next level the door was open. As we passed through it I saw that all the doors, on both sides, were also open. Asim walked fast past them. I waited at the door back out to the stairs. One of Asim's men waited with me. He had an AK-47 slung over his shoulder. His hand was cradling it. He looked ready to use it.

He was now staring at me. Did all Arab men think Western women are easy, that they'll sleep with anyone?

I turned away from him. God only knew what would happen if we were in a firefight. Men have a nasty habit of letting their most repulsive instincts out when death is staring them in the face.

But where were Yacoub's other guards, and where were his two nieces I'd seen earlier? They had to have heard the gunshots up above. Then it came to me. They'd have gone to a safe room as soon as they knew they were under attack. They were probably waiting for reinforcements to arrive.

If Asim wasn't careful he'd be trapped down here.

He may have come to the same conclusion, because he ran back to where I was standing.

He shouted something in Arabic and we headed down again. The door on the next floor opened easily. This floor was just a large concrete open area, as if the rooms on this level hadn't been installed yet.

The next floor down was the floor where I'd been shown that video of the ancient history of Cairo. The door to that floor was open too. I ran fast to the end of the corridor. If Sean had been upstairs, they may have taken him somewhere down here when they heard the attack on the building.

Perhaps they had a panic room at this level. Perhaps it was linked to the room where they'd shown me the videos. There had been two doors on one side of the room.

I reached the door at the end first. Only Asim was behind me. The other men were checking rooms along the corridor. I tried the steel door handle. The door was locked. Asim came up beside me. He leaned his ear up to the door. Then he smiled, waved me to join him, to listen at the door too.

60

Xena hit the sand with a bone jarring thud. It felt as if every joint and socket in her body had been opened and closed. She'd been in a crouching position as she fell, and he fingers had come near enough to the wall on each side, that she could sense it rushing past.

It took her a few minutes to recover from the shock. She checked every limb and her chest and head for the tell-tale wetness of blood or the pain of something broken. She'd been lucky. Her bones and muscles ached, but there was no serious damage.

Then she pressed a hand into the sand underneath her. It was deep as she pressed. She looked up. She couldn't see where she'd come from, but the fall hadn't been as long as she'd expected.

Was that deliberate?

Was the well a test of people's faith?

If the walls inched together over a few dozen feet, it would look as if the well was much deeper than it was. Her relief was tinged though with the thought that she still didn't know how to get out of this hole. She felt for the walls.

She was hoping one of them had a tunnel leading to a way out, but as her hands ran along the final wall her heart almost stopped beating. The wall was stone. Each wall was stone. There was no way out. She was trapped, and worse than how she'd been in the chamber up above. All she could take was one step in each direction here and she was met with stone slabs.

She looked up again. Could she climb out?

Where was the torch she'd let drop? And where was that breeze coming from?

If she could only see how far it was to the top and if there were any hand holds, she had a chance. She went down on her knees, felt all around. She couldn't find the torch. She ran her fingers through the sand. Had she fallen on top of it? Had she moved it in the last few minutes?

She stopped, took some deep breaths, and started pushing through the sand in a more methodical way, starting in one corner.

And then she felt it. Just the edge, deep in the sand. She must have pushed the sand on top of it when she was looking the first time. As she reached for the switch to turn it on she said a prayer.

61

Henry tapped at the screen on his left. It responded by zooming in on the satellite image he had brought up. It was an image of the streets around Ahmed Yacoub's Cairo villa.

Though villa was probably the wrong word for the complex Yacoub had built on the western shore of the Nile, directly between the pyramids and the river. It was a complex, and the records showed that a lot of work had been done underground.

Whether that was because Yacoub wanted to hide what he was up to from people in Egypt or from competitors around the world was hard to know. Henry's satellite image flickered, then cleared. It showed a replay of what had occurred forty-six minutes before.

Two people had gone to the front entrance. One was younger, smaller. The other could well have been Isabel Ryan. And a few minutes later a group of four men had followed into Yacoub's villa.

It was very late at night, after midnight now in Cairo, for Yacoub to be having visitors. Henry tapped at a red camera icon further down the street. That would give him ground level images on whoever had gone into the villa.

The screen changed. He was watching the front of the building now. He pressed at the rewind icon. It didn't work. He tapped it again, his frustrating rising. Finally it started speeding through the feed. Cars went backwards down the street. People walked backwards from where they were now to where they had come from. He pressed the icon again for it to speed faster.

It did.

And he almost missed them. But a jolt shot through him and he tapped the stop button, just in time to see Isabel Ryan crossing the road, heading towards Yacoub's with a boy by her side, probably Egyptian.

He turned to another screen. The red EEAR – Embassy Emergency Assistance Request – box was open on the screen. He put in his ID number, name and details of his request. It would be up to the military attaché at the British Embassy in Cairo to determine if Egyptian special forces would be requested, or if U.S. or British Embassy operatives would be called on.

It all depended on who would be quickest to get to Yacoub's. It was clear Isabel had been kidnapped, and her life was in danger.

Rescuing her had to be the priority. And all he could do now was wait until he was informed who would deal with this in Egypt, hopefully in the next few minutes.

He flicked through the links in a secure email he'd received ten minutes before from the Cairo Embassy. One showed a headline that would be appearing on the front page of the largest daily newspaper in Cairo the following morning. He didn't read Arabic, but he knew Yacoub's picture and the

Embassy had helpfully translated the headline and sub headline.

"I will make Egypt great again. Ahmed Yacoub Stakes His Claim to the Presidency."

62

I stepped back. Asim had his gun in his hand. We'd heard voices on the other side of the door.

Asim pointed his gun at the lock, motioned with his head for us to go back further. His stance, knees bent, arms tight to his side, made me think he'd been trained in the Egyptian army. Could he be a double agent, or someone sent to provoke the Brotherhood, so they could be arrested and imprisoned?

The gun went off. Splinters of the door around the handle flew in all directions. I'd covered my eyes with both hands, but I only felt something hitting my trousers.

Asim shouted, "Allahu Akbar!" then pushed the door with his shoulder and went through into the viewing room.

Two of his men followed. The last one gripped my elbow and pushed me after him. The screens in the room were turned on. They were showing a news channel with a demonstration in Tahrir Square and Egyptian commentators talking over it. They sounded excited.

There was no one else in the room. Asim started shouting and the men fanned out, checking the screens, the walls, the kitchen area. They were looking for something.

I walked up to Asim. "I advise you to give yourselves up. I expect Egyptian special forces are up above us already. If you play your cards right I will speak for you. You don't need to all die down here."

"We won't die down here. And we have you, Mrs. Ryan, our bargaining chip. That is why you are here."

I stuck my chin forward. "They won't care about me if it comes to a firefight. We will all die." I said the last words slowly.

He pointed his finger at me. "Then so be it." He said it softly.

Then he shouted in Arabic again and the men replied. I walked towards the screens. Was this a live feed from Tahrir Square? The square was full. Black flags predominated. Was the Brotherhood about to take over again? I peered closer at the screen. Yes, I could the damage caused by the helicopters on Friday. This was live.

A shout came from behind me. One of the men had found something. He pointed at the wall. We crowded around. I didn't see anything until I peered close. Then I saw it. There was a hole in the wall, about the shape of a keyhole. Asim was tracing an almost imperceptible crack running up the wall near it. He was muttering to himself in Arabic, too. I could imagine what he was saying.

One of the men shouted. He was pointing back at the door we'd come through. Asim shouted back at him. Asim shot twice at the crack in the wall, where it appeared there was a lock. The noise echoed in the room, like a banging from the gates of hell.

Dust filled the air. I coughed. A soft hissing noise could be heard.

I crouched. My heart was banging high up in my chest, almost in my neck. My legs felt shaky. I touched the ground to steady myself. Asim had opened the hidden door. He was pointing his gun at me, waving me forward. I ran, half crouching into the passageway beyond. It led straight on through a gloomy, darkened section to a distant light, which illuminated a long corridor with rough walls and a curved ceiling. It looked like one of those escape tunnels you see in World War Two movies, but this one was tall enough that you wouldn't have to bend down to get through it.

Asim was shouting at the men we'd left behind in the room. Gunfire erupted. A scream echoed. I peered back towards the room. One of Asim's men was down, clutching at his stomach, but he was still firing. Two of the other men were in the corridor with me. Asim was talking in the ear of one of them.

I walked fast down the corridor. They were unlikely to shoot me. If I could get away from them now, while they were distracted, I should. I didn't look back. I was almost running, adrenaline kicking in, my heart pumping as if I'd run a marathon and my sweat, which had broken out on my brow, cooling fast as I headed down the tunnel. The light up ahead was growing in front of me. I could make out a gray door.

The noise of running feet behind me reminded me not to look back.

Suddenly, a boom shook the air. It blew me forward and I tripped. A concussion wave passed through me, making my ears pop and my bones shake, as if I was made of jelly.

63

Xena looked around, turning her neck one way, then the other. Each wall was solid rock. The only exit was a rat sized hole in one corner, which must have been used to drain water. She rubbed her hand in the sand beneath her. She'd felt lumps beneath there. What were they?

She pushed the sand away from one lump and flicked the torch on. Her mouth opened wide as she saw what the lump was.

It was the top of a skull. She felt all around it. There were other skulls buried in the sand, some upright, some on their side. And there were larger bones too. She peered down at the sand. It wasn't like the sand outside the pyramid. She held a handful up to her face. It was bone white.

A gurgling noise emanated from the rat sized hole. It sounded as if a bath was being emptied somewhere far off.

And then the noise was getting louder.

She raised the torch, looked up, wondering if there was any way she could climb back out. That was when she saw the square opening in one of the stone walls. It was about ten feet up. Far enough that anyone down here was unlikely to reach it. But near enough that it gave hope.

She looked at the walls around her. They were within touching distance if she held her arms out. And there were small cracks between the stone blocks that made up the walls. They hadn't been constructed with the same precision as the walls in the chamber up above. She could pull herself slowly upwards using the cracks. A shiver ran through her. She looked at the cracks again. The thought that they had been deliberately placed there came to her.

But that was impossible. Wasn't it? She placed her fingers as high as she could, found a crack. Her arms were trembling. She flexed her muscles, found the crack again.

Now her legs were trembling. Her feet were sinking slowly into the bone white sand. If she didn't move fast she would drown in the bone dust.

She turned her torch off, pushed it into the pocket of her black cotton trousers. She put both feet up into a half crack in the wall and slowly began to move upwards. It was dark, but she would feel the cracks with her fingers and toes. And she would feel the opening above her head in a few minutes and push her way into it. Even if she fell back down again, she knew how to get up here.

A gushing noise sounded, far off. The smaller hole below had to be a pipe leading to a water source.

She kept going up. Her shoulders were aching now and her fingers were numb, from pushing, inching her way up the ice cold stone.

Then another noise joined in. A sniffing.

The sniffing of a water rat, that had pushed through a tunnel and found itself in a well of bones, with little chance of any food.

The sniffing was joined by another. There were more of them.

Xena moved up the wall faster. She had to get out of this hole.

She paused, looked down.

Red eyes moving this way and that looked back up at her. She could not fall.

64

Dust filled my mouth. I coughed, bent forward. Someone banged my back.

"Come, there is a way out," said Asim. He was shouting, but my ears were filled with buzzing from the echoes of the explosion behind us.

I turned, there was just him and one of the other men in the corridor behind me. They were both covered in dust. I looked at my arms. They were gray with dust. Where we'd come from there was a mass of rubble. A noise sounded from the roof above us. It was time to move.

Asim reached for my elbow. I shrugged him away, started walking. The corridor was lit by fluorescent tubes about fifty feet apart. The fact that they were still on meant, to me, that they were powered from the end of the corridor we were heading towards. That meant there had to be a way out.

I remembered a scream echoing in the corridor as the explosion Asim had set off hit me. How many lives had been taken by Asim's actions? My heart fell, as I thought of all the families waiting for a father or a son or a daughter to come home.

What the hell right did Asim have to cause such suffering? I walked fast, anger bubbling up inside me. If I had a chance, he would get the punishment he deserved. I know an eye for an eye will leave the world blind, but for some people, death is a just reward. Bastards like Asim deserved to suffer.

I felt something cold in my back, high up.

"Make no mistakes, lady."

The gun pressed harder. I stumbled. I used the stumble to reach for the wall and crouch, looking up at him. There had to be a way to get this bastard.

"Keep moving!" he shouted.

"Fuck you!" I raised a fist towards his face.

He laughed. I walked on.

There was a red door up ahead. It looked to be made of steel. I reached it first, tried the shiny steel handle. It was cold, and when I pressed at it the door didn't open.

Asim shouldered me aside. He pointed his gun at the lock. I turned sideways to him. A bullet could ricochet anywhere down here.

He fired. The thunk of the bullet filled the corridor. It was followed by another thunk as the bullet hit a wall. Asim and his henchman had just stood by, as if bullets couldn't harm them.

Asim laughed, as if the devil was inside him. He kicked at the door and waved the other man through ahead of him.

I went through next. We were in what looked like a garage for the villa. There were three cars, a white Mercedes limousine, a red jeep and a blue Renault. At the far end of the room there was s steel shutter. Beside it was a large red button.

Asim walked straight to it and pressed the button. He shouted something in Arabic. The doors ground open slowly. Beyond was the sodium light of the street. It looked empty.

Too empty.

65

Xena closed her eyes, inched her legs up some more. She couldn't fall back. There were who knew how many rats down there. The water table under the pyramids of Giza was renowned for its channels and its rats.

Some of the slum dwellers, living in the Giza area, even ate them, when times got tough.

She wasn't going to let these rats turn her into their lunch.

She inched up again. Then she felt it. Her hand touched the lip of the opening. She'd have to pull herself into the hole. But she'd done it.

She pushed over the stone lip. Her shoulder muscles felt as if a hot knife was burning into them.

That was when she felt it. Something nibbling at her neck.

66

I looked both ways along the street as I walked out. We were just outside the villa's perimeter, further down the street.

I stood still. Nobody was walking on the street. This could have been because it was nearly one in the morning, but my experience of Cairo had been that every street had people on it, no matter what the hour was.

Asim and the other man had both picked up on the uneasy silence. They were walking in a circle around me, their weapons high, sighting along their gun barrels. Asim was talking in Arabic. His colleague reached towards me, grabbed my arm. Then he was pointing his gun at my head. I saw the black pit of death in the barrel in front of my face.

"Do not run, Mrs. Ryan. Do not do anything unless I tell you. Do you understand?" He screamed the last word.

"I'm not going to…" My words were cut off by a spray of red and a splatter of bone fragments, wet brains and blood on my face. I closed my eyes, wiped my lips with my forearm. God only knew what sort infections this poor bastard had.

"I will kill her!" Asim shouted.

He had his gun pointed at me. The other man was lying face up a few feet away. A pool of blood was collecting around his head. There was a neat exit hole where his third eye might have been. Someone was a very good shot.

A stream of Arabic from an unseen loud hailer washed over us.

Asim spun around, trying to work out where the voice was coming from. He shouted something back in Arabic, then came up beside me, grabbed me close to him and pressed the gun to my temple.

I was standing as still as possible, exactly the way I'd been taught on the surviving a kidnap course I'd gone on, before I was posted to the British Consulate in Istanbul.

The idea was that you were supposed to comply, and take up as little attention as possible from your kidnappers, so their vigilance might flag, and an opportunity present itself to run and escape.

There didn't seem much opportunity right now. And whoever was shooting might easily kill me in the process if I moved. A cold shiver ran through me. Was this where it would all end?

67

Henry Mowlam looked at his screen. It was 3:20 A.M. in London. The night shift he had agreed to take was due to end at six. It was the classic Saturday night watch. Not only did he have to assess international incidents, and decide if any of them required senior security services staff to be wakened. He also had to decide on the allocation of tight resources, and be ready to justify his decisions the following week.

The situation in Cairo was tense. Isabel Ryan was on the point of being rescued, but the team involved was not British or American. He would have to watch carefully to make sure they carried out their task swiftly and release her to the British Embassy as soon as possible.

He had another concern now, too. The lead story in both the Washington Times and the London Sunday Times was a profile of the Muslim Brotherhood, founded in Egypt and still agitating there and across the Middle East against Israel.

He clicked to the story the journalist in the Sunday Times had leaked to him. It showed a picture of Ahmed

Yacoub. Behind him a crowd held up the green flag of the
Brotherhood, with its crossed scimitars.

Much of the article was old news, but the fact that Yacoub, who was tipped to be the next civilian president of Egypt, had such strong ties to the Brotherhood was worrying. Extremely worrying. The new U.S. administration would draw the line on sending further military and other aid to Egypt if the story was true, and that could lead to an implosion in the Egyptian economy, and a mass movement of millions of refugees towards Europe, which would make the crisis over the Syrian refugees look like a prelude.

The Syrian population had been twenty million before their war started. About two million had become international refugees. Egypt's was eighty-five million. If ten percent of that decided to leave, that would be about eight million people heading for Europe. Europe would not be able to cope. Its military and immigration services would buckle. Italy and Greece would face an existential crisis, which could start a chain reaction of heavily indebted states looking for bail outs.

He read the article:

The Muslim Brotherhood was founded in Egypt in 1928 by Hassan al-Banna. Al-Banna was twenty-two at the time. Soon after, he sent letters to Adolf Hitler seeking support for his new party and explaining how he agreed with Hitler's views on the Jews.

When Hitler and the Nazi party assumed power in Germany they agreed to support the Brotherhood. The Muslim Brotherhood became one the Nazi regime's most important supporting groups in the Middle East. In 1938 membership of the Muslim Brotherhood reached two hundred thousand.

Activists in the Muslim Brotherhood became spies for Nazi Germany. The Grand Mufti of Jerusalem, a senior

245

supporter of the Brotherhood, moved to Berlin. He was treated as a VIP and lived in Germany from '41 until the end of the war. Facing arrest by the Allies, he fled to Egypt in '46. Prior to that, the Grand Mufti had a controlling role in launching several Muslim divisions within Nazi Germany's armed forces. These were incorporated into the Waffen SS as the war continued.

Other prominent Arabs also came to be influenced by Nazi ideology and to admire the extreme violent racism emanating from Germany at that time. The founders of the Ba'ath movement, which later came to power in Iraq and Syria, where the founding Assad family still holds power, are among those who also came to adopt Nazi ideas.

The Muslim Brotherhood numbered 500,000 members by the late '40's. They were responsible for the assassination of the Egyptian Prime Minister al-Nuqrashi and took a prominent role in the Arab-Israeli war of 1948, which sought to destroy the emerging state of Israel.

The Muslim Brotherhood was later responsible for the creation of Hamas, the leading Palestinian terrorist group currently, as designated by the U.S., E.U., Canada and Japan, because of its record of attacks against Israel and a refusal to renounce violence.

Under Hamas' charter it is committed to the destruction of Israel. Its policies would likely lead it to be designated as a Neo-Nazi party, should it exist with the same charter in modern day Germany.

In addition, a Muslim Brotherhood educated Saudi, Osama bin Laden, was the chief conspirator in the destruction and mass murder at the Twin Towers on September 11th, 2001, which caused the death of 2,996 people and, up to this date, is still the most serious terrorist attack on the United States ever conducted. A direct line from Adolf Hitler to 9/11 can therefore be drawn. Should Mr. Ahmed Yacoub come to power, supported by the Muslim Brotherhood, a number of significant after effects would occur. These include a speedy realignment in Egypt's relationships with the USA, the EU and Israel. This possibility represents a clear and present danger to British citizens, business interests and those of our allies.

<u>Recommended further actions:</u> See Appendix 1AA.

68

Xena launched herself forward, pushing hard and fast to get as far into the hole as she could.

She landed on her side, her ribs smashing into the stone edge of the hole. The winding effect almost saw her pass out, but her scrabbling hands caught the edge and she was hanging over it, half her body in the tunnel beyond, the other half hanging down into the pit with the rats. She felt herself slipping and jerked forward, even though she could feel that the tunnel she was entering was slanted, like the passage up to the King's Chamber.

Only this didn't have wooden slats on the floor to stop you sliding. Or the reassurance of knowing where you would slide to, if you did go down it head first.

Xena put her arms in front of her and said a prayer to the Queen of Heaven. She was sliding now, her momentum building, any chance of working her way back up the slope diminishing with every second.

But what sent her mind reeling was that she might be the first person in five thousand years or more to come this way.

The slide seemed to go on forever. Her heart was pounding fast and her elbows and knees scuffed by the granite walls and floor of the tunnel, the skin brushing away until it felt as if her bones would be exposed soon.

Her head was pounding, as if she was going underwater. Occasionally she was pushed through cobwebs by her momentum. She didn't want to think about the thin desert rats and the deadly yellow-limbed stalker scorpions, which lived in the sand dunes around Cairo.

Then she was falling, without any walls or floor, swinging her arms wildly for something to hold onto, her mouth open, a scream echoing for a second, until she hit a stone floor with a thud that blew all the air out of her and left her sprawled on the coldest, wettest stone floor she had ever touched.

She turned over, looked around. Everything was black. She could have been in a tiny hole, or a massive chamber. She felt in her pocket for the torch. Then felt in her other pocket. It was gone.

69

I kept my gaze on Asim, my expression slightly wide eyed, using the genuine fear bubbling inside me to show him I was no threat.

His expression was hard, his lips pressed tight, his gaze jumping about as he moved around me, trying to keep the sniper he knew was trying to get a bead on him, at bay. It wouldn't be easy to get a clear shot, with him circling fast around me.

He turned his head, shouted something in Arabic.

That was when I took my chance.

I jerked my hand up, gripped his gun, turned the barrel upwards in one movement. He had his finger on the trigger and pulled it as the barrel moved, but he was too late. Bullets whistled high into the air and from the look of pain on his face he would be releasing his gun any second.

That was the least of Asim's worries.

Something rustled through my hair and a red dot appeared in the middle of his forehead. A second later a thud echoed through the air and an inch wide red hole, with a jagged white rim appeared where the red dot had been. His expression crumpled. He fell forward.

Someone was screaming. I closed my mouth. The screaming stopped. A woman in a green hospital uniform, with a silver emergency blanket in her hands was rushing towards me.

I went down on my knees. Asim's body was twitching in front of me, his leg muscles exhibiting involuntary death spasms. A pool of blood grew around his head. Another pool of piss grew around his trousers.

Someone was whispering in my ear, pulling me backwards. I went with her. She had her arms around me. There were black clad bodies behind her.

"You're all right now, madam," she was saying, over and over. As we walked towards a white ambulance with a green stripe along its side, which had appeared at the end of the road, men in black outfits, with black steel helmets and bird symbols, walked slowly past us. I glanced back. A group of them were standing in a circle around Asim.

An assistant was opening the back doors of the ambulance. I looked behind again. A man, he looked like an officer, was walking fast towards us. When we reached the ambulance door I put my hand up, to indicate I needed to stop.

The woman who was holding me up touched my forehead, at the side. Her fingers felt wet as she touched me. She pulled them away and put them up in front of me. They were covered in blood.

My blood?

I nodded. She led me up into the ambulance. Had I been grazed by a bullet from Asim's gun? My knees were weak. I put a hand out to stop myself falling.

"Mrs. Isabel Ryan," came a man's voice in my ear. He had an almost perfect English accent. I looked to the side. He had a round baby face, a black moustache and close cropped hair under a black baseball hat with that bird emblem on the front.

"Yes." My voice was shaky, even saying just one word.

"Did they harm you, in any way? Did they torture you, or inflict any of their depraved demands on you?"

I knew what he meant. Had they raped me.

"No."

He put a hand on my shoulder. "I'm glad. You will go to the hospital now. We will interview you later."

The woman who had led me to the ambulance put her arm around me. She motioned for me to lie down on the trolley in the ambulance. It had stainless steel bars and an orange rubber mattress. There was a white sheet, folded up, at the end.

Above the stretcher was a shelf with electronic equipment. Wires dangled waiting for me to be connected up. The woman motioned me again to lie down. For a hopeful moment I wondered if I was well enough just to walk away from this. Then the woman took a plastic dish from a rack and came towards me with a white bandage roll in one hand and the dish in the other.

She motioned me to put my head back. I did. The doors of the ambulance closed with a bang and a few moments later we jerked forward and the siren was turned on.

The woman ambulance assistant placed rolls of gauze on the mattress beside me, opened one roll with scissors and began dabbing at my forehead with cotton wool. When she pulled the cotton wool away I saw dark red blood. I closed my eyes. She kept dabbing at me.

A graze from a bullet can cause long term damage, especially if your skull had been fractured. I could be in a far worse condition than I thought. Shock often set in after injuries from bullet wounds, which could even lead victims to believe that they hadn't been shot at all.

And one part of me didn't even care about what had happened to me. I had gone along too easily with Asim, because I'd thought he knew something about where Sean was. But all that had proved to be a mirage. It was possible Asim had made up the whole thing about Sean being held in Yacoub's villa, simply because he wanted me to cooperate.

So what was he looking for in the villa, if it wasn't Sean? Had we missed Sean, possibly by minutes? It certainly looked as if we had discovered that Yacoub did experiments on people. Was that all legitimate? Was it allowed under Egyptian law?

With every wail from the siren coming from the ambulance I felt myself more dazed, as if I was moving further and further away from where I wanted to be. I wanted to go back to Yacoub's, and I needed someone to help me search his place properly. If only I had my phone. I could call Henry, or whoever was on duty back in London. They could arrange for some help from the Embassy.

That led me to wondering if Henry had already intervened. Had the Egyptian security forces turned up because of a tip off from him?

I opened my eyes. The woman had stopped dabbing at my forehead. She was opening a green bandage package. As I watched she held it in her plastic gloved hands and placed it on the side of my forehead, securing it with a roll of white gauze going around my head a few times, like a sweatband.

The ambulance stopped. The intensity of the siren went up another few degrees. The driver blew the horn a few times. Then we were moving again. We lurched to the right, then to the left, as if we were rounding some obstruction. The journey was taking longer than I thought. Had we been that far from a hospital, or was the traffic that bad in the middle of the night in Cairo?

I closed my eyes, leaned back. All this chasing around. All these people dead. My taxi driver among them. Was I responsible for all these deaths?

I shook my head. No, I didn't kill any of them. The driver didn't have to suggest I meet Asim's crew. He could have dropped the whole thing. And anyway, I didn't pull the trigger. The person who did that was the killer.

The ambulance stopped, waited about thirty seconds, then started again and moved forward slowly. I got the impression we had passed through a security gate, and that we would pull up soon. Great, I could get access to a phone. I could call London. I could end all this. Get them to book me on the next flight out.

The ambulance stopped. The back doors opened. Floodlights hurt my eyes. I blinked. The view was not what I expected. We weren't at a hospital.

We were at Yacoub's research facility on the Giza plateau, near the pyramids.

70

Xena felt all around her, slowly. She didn't want to miss anything. She knew there were tunnels in the Great Pyramid, which had been lost for thousands of years. There could, without doubt, be a way to the surface, or to some chamber near it, where she might be able hear the tourists and the guides the next morning and alert them to her presence.

She'd been told when she was young that there were secret chambers in the Great Pyramid, waiting to be re-discovered. The proof was in a book by a Greek historian, Herodotus, the father of history, who was in Egypt in the fifth century before Christ. He wrote about vaults under the Great Pyramid and an island underneath it, where the body of a pharaoh lies.

The only current entrance to the pyramid, created in the early ninth century by Caliph al-Ma'mun's workmen, was the only time a tunnel had been cut into the heart of the pyramid. A Victorian Egyptologist had, apparently, tried to bore his way into the Great Pyramid, then to clear a way in with gunpowder, but he was stopped by his workmen, who were unwilling to see the pyramid destroyed. He only got as far as damaging a few of the outer stones.

If more tunnels were cut in the other faces of the pyramid, they would find hidden passages and rooms, but such work had long been outlawed.

She slowed her breathing, listening for sounds. The place where she had landed could be a long-lost chamber with the treasure of a pharaoh all around her, or it could be the Hall of Records said to be under the Great Pyramids by ancient commentators, such as Plutarch. He claimed the Hall of Records under the Great Pyramid held papyrus scrolls describing the founders of Egypt, as well as golden scrolls with a history of the lost city of Atlantis. Could that be true?

She felt sand on the stone floor all around her. In some places it was in drifts, as if it had moved around. In other places there was hardly any. Her right knee and shoulder were throbbing, from where she'd hit the floor. Gradually she expanded her search, moving one step forward, then one back in each direction.

And then she touched it. It was her torch. It had to be. She felt all over it quickly. The battery door was open. Her heart sank. The batteries had come out. They were somewhere on the floor around her. She had to work methodically. Even if she did find the batteries, the top of the torch was deeply cracked. That might mean the bulb was cracked and useless.

She recited her prayer to the great mother over and over as her hands reached out around her. The mother had helped her many times in the past. She would help her again. Xena was confident of that.

It took maybe half an hour for her to find both batteries. One rolled away from her when she touched it. The other one was way further from her starting point than she expected. Persistence helped.

When she was about to put the last battery in, she hesitated. What would be revealed? Had she fallen into the Hall of Records, or just some empty foundation hole?

Would she be surrounded in gold or unclimbable walls of granite, or skeletons?

She pushed the final battery in.

Nothing happened.

She felt for the switch, pressed it.

71

I reached for a handle inside the ambulance and clung to it.

"Why are we here, not at a hospital?" My voice was shakier, and I sounded more paranoid than I expected.

"Please come, madam. We have the best doctors and the best medical facility here. Please, Mr. Yacoub explicitly said we must bring you here. No payment will be required."

I hesitated. My head was throbbing. I also knew it wasn't unusual in the Middle East for a large corporation to have its own ambulance and its own medical facility. But I'd wanted to find a phone, to get Henry or someone else from head office to meet me. That mightn't be possible here.

The nurse looking up at me had been joined by the ambulance driver. He was looking at me as if I was mad. A side door I hadn't noticed in the building had opened and two other men, in green medical gowns, were pushing a steel wheeled stretcher towards me.

I touched my forehead, looked at my fingers. They were red, wet. My blood was oozing through the bandage. I stepped down from the ambulance, looked around. The siren stopped. A second ambulance man, tall and with a bushy beard, was stepping out of the ambulance.

That was when it crossed my mind that there were no other patients visible, or cars. It was a very quiet medical facility. He had a lot of staff here for just the occasional company patient.

My knees felt weak at that point and they almost buckled. The two men in medical gowns raced the last few feet to me and took my arms. They helped me onto the stretcher.

"My name is Doctor Salliah, Mrs. Ryan. Please tell me where you feel pain."

The young doctor smiled at me and put his face close to mine, almost too close, as they wheeled me fast through the doors. Inside it was all bright lights and a long corridor.

"I…" I touched my head. Was I in pain?

"No need to talk. We will take you straight in for a CAT scan, Mrs. Ryan. I saw pictures from a security camera we have in each of our ambulances. I saw the blood, as I am sure you have, so it's important we get your head scanned, in case you have a fracture. That is why you are here. We have a CAT scanner."

We were in a low ceilinged room with white walls and a reception area. Doors at the far end were marked in Arabic and English. One of them said TESTS. Another said, ADMINISTRATION.

I tried to lean up. The doctor pushed my shoulder back down.

"Relax, Mrs. Ryan. It's important we get this done as quickly as possible." He raised a hand, clicked a finger, spoke fast in Arabic to a nurse who had appeared.

"We will give you a light sedative, Mrs. Ryan. It is important that you do not move inside the scanner."

I blinked. When was I going to be able to get to a phone?

He held a green plastic clipboard in front of me.

"We need your consent to treat you and to carry out the CAT scan. Please sign here." He pointed at a row of dots.

I took the form. It was in Arabic and English. They must be used to dealing with foreigners here.

"Where did you study?" I stared at the doctor.

"I spent six years at Imperial College in London." He smiled back at me. "And I did my clinical placement at St. Bart's."

I leaned back, touched my head again. It came back bloody again.

"We will be bandaging you up first, Mrs. Ryan, but we can't do anything without your signature."

I looked at him, then at the nurse smiling beside him. I picked the pen from where it was held at the top of the clipboard, read the form, signed it.

I was wheeled into a room with beeping medical equipment. My head wound was cleaned, then bandaged.

After that they wheeled me down another white corridor and into a room with a giant white CAT scan device, a giant donut on its side at the far end of the room. The walls were white tiles. Through a door on one side I could see a control panel.

A nurse with a white face mask came out of the control room. She was wheeling a metal trolley. She leaned down to me.

"You are safe here." She pulled my sleeve up, tapped at the crook of my elbow, then took a small steel needle from the tray, tested there was no air in it and put it near my elbow.

"Take a deep breath, please, and hold it."

"What are you injecting me with?"

"A very small dose of anti-anxiety medication."

She looked at me quizzically.

"Will it put me to sleep?"

"It is not that strong, Mrs. Ryan."

A minute later everything felt right. I was in the right place. There was no need for me to hurry. I had lots of time.

I saw the white donut moving towards me. Then I was inside it. The voices in the room were gone. There was a clicking. Then a whirring. Then it was over. A face loomed over me.

I felt someone pick up my wrist, hold it. Then I was being wheeled out of the room.

"We are taking you to a ward," said a voice. The nurse was smiling, leaning towards me, walking alongside.

The ward was empty. It had four beds, no windows, lots of equipment. I was hooked up to a drip, a monitor. I had to sleep.

In my dream I saw Sean. He was holding his hand out to me, pleading with me, soundlessly.

72

Xena's mouth opened wide. She was in a hall that looked like an underground temple. It had rows of tall pillars with bulging lotus leaf capitals. Each pillar had paintings on it. One row of pillars was all yellow. Another was a faded red. Some had only hieroglyphs on them.

She looked up. Above her head was a round opening in a roof made of rectangular stone slabs, similar to the King's Chamber, where she had come from. In this case the slabs rested on the tightly packed rows of pillars.

She looked around. She was in the middle of a bowl shaped depression in the floor.

Was this how people to be sacrificed were brought into this hall? Or was it a way out they had been told about?

She looked along the rows of columns. A feeling of awe came over her. The columns extended to the width of a football field. They were all perfectly uniform and about twenty feet tall. The hall was the biggest underground temple she had ever seen, even bigger than what they usually showed in movies.

And at each end of the row of pillars there was a giant statue. At one end it was clearly Isis, wearing a white horned headdress with a gold circle. Her costume was faded gold and red. At the other was a statue of Osiris, his face and hands pale green, a dust flecked gold crook and flail in his hands.

She looked through the gaps between the pillars. A row of gold covered boxes, higher than her, perhaps the size of an SUV, went one way, then the other.

This had to be the fabled Hall of Records. In each of these boxes there would be scrolls lying on shelves. She walked through the row of pillars and went up to one of the boxes. It had hieroglyphs embossed in its gold panels as well as symbols of Isis and Horus.

The front of the giant box had a split down the middle, with an iron rod as a bolt keeping the doors from opening. She touched the rod. It was cold, dusty. She pushed it to the left. The left door swung open with a loud creak, which made her jump and look around, as if she was expecting some guardian to appear from between the pillars.

Inside the box were shelves with papyrus rolls of various sizes stacked up. Many of them had crumbled to dust, but some were still intact. There was a passage down the middle, so you could walk into the box. She held the torch forward. Shadows sprung back, as if angry. Dust mites swam in the air. There was something dark at the back. A sweet smell assaulted her. Then she knew what it meant. It was a giant ant's nest at the back. A big one.

She closed the door over, gently, then moved to the next box, cracked the front open. The sweet smell that struck her was stronger than in the last golden box. She closed the front again without looking inside. Were the ants eating the papyrus?

She kept walking. Between every box there was a thin pillar with snakes intertwined all the way up. Each was as high as the box. Each had a different hieroglyph at the top.

She moved the torch around constantly, then stopped, swinging it behind her. She thought she'd heard a rustling, far off.

About half way towards the statue of Isis there was a break in the wall of pillars. She moved towards it. There was what looked like an empty pool beyond the pillars here.

She walked towards it. The pool was long and narrow, like one of those underground swimming pools they had in some hotels, where there wasn't much space. There were marble steps at either end. The bottom of the pool had sand in it. In front of the steps were marble seats at each end. On each corner of the pool there was a pillar with snakes intertwined.

It looked as if it had been an ancient healing pool.

She peered down into it. The wall of the pool was either made of gold or had a sheath of gold covering it, into which were carved hieroglyphs.

That was when she saw the sand moving.

73

I woke feeling half dead. I tried to turn on my side, but my arms and legs were strapped down. I arched my head up. I was in a semi darkened room. The red and white dots from electronic monitoring equipment cast an eerie glow over the bed. I looked at my feet. They hadn't even taken my shoes off. What kind of a hospital was this? My anxiety rose fast.

I'd been a fool to allow them to sedate me. God only knew how long I'd been out. I shouldn't have trusted that doctor. I had to get out of here. I pulled at the straps binding me. They weren't as tight as they could be. They weren't military grade. They weren't cable ties either. They were hospital straps, not intended to restrain prisoners.

I worked both arm straps from side to side. There was a half inch of give in them and with some persistent pressure I should be able to get my hands free. I had to act fast. If someone came in and found me in the process of trying to break out, my reward might be another stronger dose of sedative.

That had to be avoided at all costs.

My hands shook as I forced them again and again against the leather. I stopped for a moment, my heart beating fast in my throat, when I thought I heard something in the distance. Then I heard the noise again. It was something creaking in the air conditioning.

Every time I thought my hands might slip out I pushed them hard into the gap, but still they wouldn't come free. My skin was raw, blistered. But I kept pushing, kept going, ignoring the burning sensation in my wrists.

And suddenly one hand was free.

That was one of my worst moments.

If anyone saw me now, they would know I was awake and trying to break free. I used both hands to push and pull at the other strap. My heart was beating fast. I took long, deep breaths, willing it to slow down. But it wasn't working.

Then the second strap was free and a minute later my legs were free and I was stepping down onto the tiled floor. I could just about make out a door in the dim light. There was a crack of light under it.

I tried the handle.

It opened. I held it a finger's width open and peered out into a brightly lit corridor. This was a different part of the building than I'd seen before. It had observation windows along the far wall. The rooms beyond the windows were all in darkness.

The rattle of a trolley sent a shiver through me. I closed the door, slowly. Someone was coming. My mouth was dry. I looked around for a weapon. The rattle from the corridor grew louder. I stepped behind the door, hoping to surprise whoever came in. I prayed it wasn't some giant of a nurse I could barely scratch. I held my fists up. They were shaking.

74

Xena stepped back. Whatever was under the sand was progressing towards the far end of the pool. Was the sand filled with snakes? She turned, made her way back fast to the main part of the hall.

She reached the statue of Isis a few minutes later. It was bigger than it looked from far off, perhaps fifteen feet high, and made out of red sandstone, like many of the other giant statues in Egypt.

It had a wide base. She sat on it, turned her torch off. She wanted to see if there were any cracks of light, any indication that the hall had an exit to the surface.

But the darkness descended like a cloak. Nothing could be seen in any direction. She switched the torch on again. Shadows all around her jumped back, as if they were alive. The torch light was dimmer than before, but thankfully it still worked. She would have no hope of getting out of this hall in the dark.

She walked around the statue. There were hieroglyphs on its back. She stood on the base and looked at them. A memory came back to her.

The hieroglyphs were the Cannibal Hymn, the Old Kingdom hymn her mothers had taught her in secret, as proof that they were right to teach her to kill. She rubbed her fingers along a central part she remembered by heart, and recited the words out loud.

"Live on the fathers,
feed on the mother's every part,
so the bull of heaven
rages inside.
Live on the being of every one,
Eat their entrails,
When they come, bodies full of magic,
From the Isle of Flame."

She stopped. It was enough. She felt an old warmth inside her. To find the hymn here meant the mothers were right. Taking life to feed your desires was the way every ruler operated. Those who denied it were fools.

To become powerful, you only had to do what the hymn said. You had to devour those who stood in your way. It was the secret that gave her the power to do whatever was necessary without ever questioning herself.

She took a few steps to the right, then to the left, looking all around, but there was nothing else to be seen at this end of the hall, so she decided to make her way to the other end and the statue of Osiris.

As she was walking back she turned the torch off a few times, to save the battery. The final time she did this, as the center section of the hall came near and the pool, she thought she saw something moving across the stone floor, something dark and swift.

She stopped, held the torch up and turned on and waited, her legs tense, ready to defend herself or to run.

75

The noise from the corridor passed. I let my breath out, counted to thirty, pulled the door open, slowly. There was nobody in the corridor. I stepped out into it. I had to get out of this place.

My head was still woozy after the sedative, but I didn't care. I looked one way, then the other. I headed for the end of the corridor, which had a smaller exit door. With luck this would be an emergency exit. As I passed each observation window I looked inside. They had trolley beds at the center of each room. I stopped at the last window.

The trolley bed in this room had white sheets and green blankets on it. They were hanging off the bed, as if someone had been taken from it in a hurry. My throat tightened. Had Asim been right about the experiments Yacoub was doing, but wrong about where he was doing them?

I ran as quietly as possible to the end of the corridor. I had to find out who had been in that room. The door at the end had a plastic sign above it. It had Arabic script and the word Ausfahrt, the German word for "Exit" on it.

I tried the handle. It opened. Beyond was a concrete walled exit staircase. I closed the door slowly behind me. There were no windows to give any indication of what floor I was on, but by looking up through the stairwell I could see two floors above. From what I remembered the building had two floors above ground level. I looked down the stairwell. There were at least three floors below me. Yacoub liked basements. Easier to hide what he was up to.

I headed down. The door on the next floor was the same on the one above. I opened it slowly, just a half an inch, enough to see into the corridor beyond. The corridor had steel cages on each side. It looked like a storage area. Inside the cages there were rows and rows of shelving with barrels on the lower levels, and above them cardboard boxes of all sizes and blue, yellow and red plastic containers that could have held anything.

I closed the door gently. I'd heard what sounded like a radio, tuned to an Egyptian pop music station. There was someone in there, guarding the stores.

I went down another level, cracked the door open on this one too. There was nothing beyond but darkness. I opened the door further, half expecting a shout at any moment, then put my hand along the wall, looking for a light. My head felt light, as if I was in a dream. I breathed deep to stop the trembling in my hand. I'd found the light switch. My finger hovered over it for seconds as I summoned to courage to press it.

A blaze of light lit another storage floor the instant I clicked the switch. I sighed with relief. This floor had steel cages with larger wooden boxes in them. Some were big enough to take a stretcher bed. At the far end was a glass walled office and a double width door.

No shouts rang out, so I assumed the floor was unoccupied. I turned off the light, closed the door, headed down the stairs again.

As I reached the next floor I saw I something different. The door on this floor had a steel padlock on it. I bent down and looked at it. I wouldn't be getting through this door so easily. I hadn't anything to even insert in the padlock to try to open it.

Should I go down again?

I looked over the stairwell. There were two floors below me. That was when I heard the alarm. It was ringing from a few floors above.

I headed down the stairs, fast. My legs felt weak. I knew what the alarm meant. At the next landing I tripped. I'd tried to go down too fast. As I lay with my cheek an inch from the concrete I heard a shout. I looked up. A man's face had appeared two floors above, looking down at me, pointing.

76

Xena waited. Whatever it was that had scuttled across the floor was not making another appearance in the light from the torch.

Who knew how many different creatures lived and died down here in the dark? She walked on. The statue of Osiris loomed in front of her. He had a crook and a flail in his crossed arms and on his head there was a tall cap, which reminded her of something you'd see on a patriarch or a pope.

The statue was carved from red sandstone like the statue of Isis and towered above her. It too had a base you could sit on. She walked around it. On its back were the same hieroglyphs as on Isis. The cannibal hymn had clearly been important to whoever took part in ceremonies down here. She got a flashing vision in her mind of priests and priestesses lined up behind the statues, intoning the hymn slowly, with resonance, using the hieroglyphs on the back of the statue as a reminder of the words.

What a sound that would have created.

She walked beyond the statue. Just like at the other end, the wall here was made of three and four foot high slabs of limestone, all darkened with age. She looked at the gaps between them. It was the same as in the King's Chamber up above, the blocks fitted together neatly, not allowing even air to get through the gaps.

But why did the air here not feel musty, stale? There had to be tunnels to the outside world. Xena followed the wall around the hall, all the way to where the pool was. On the far wall she saw a darker area in the stone.

She hurried towards it. Could this be a way out?

As she reached it she was running, her skin prickling. This was also in the area where that shape had been moving across the floor.

She stopped, stared, as she reached the darker area in the stone wall. If it was an exit, it was unlike one she'd ever seen. It was a large square area of dark stone, with a crack down the center. There was no obvious way through. She went up to the crack in the stone, tried to peer through it, but there was nothing to be seen. She banged the stone hard with her fist in frustration. An echo sounded from the stone.

77

I raced down the stairs. Multiple shouts rang out from above. I didn't bother to look around. I tried the handle on the next door. It opened. There was a corridor ahead. It was in darkness. I ran into it.

In the distance I could see another Ausfahrt sign, with no Arabic this time. It sent a dim glow down the corridor, showing doors on either side and a set of elevator doors at the far end. My lungs were burning now. My legs felt weak. Could I make it to the elevator, before they caught up with me?

A shout behind me, then another, told me it was going to be a close thing. I raced on, without looking back. Anxiety was spurring me on with each step.

God only knew what these people would do to me if they caught me. I spied the steel elevator door button to the right of the doors. I pushed myself harder, my arms swinging, jacket bouncing on my chest. I had to get to the button.

Then it was fifty feet away. Then twenty. I held my hand out.

But before I reached it, as if summoned by my will, the elevator doors binged and started to open.

78

Xena sat down. She needed a rest, and she needed to work out what she to do next. She'd walked to the end of the hall again. She sat with her back against one of the pillars. It felt cold behind her.

She turned the torch off. How long would the batteries last? They could go at any time. She'd been in many difficult situations, some even underground. She'd had to escape through narrow tunnels in Manhattan, and from being buried alive when her nunnery was captured by Islamists, but every time she had managed to burrow a way out.

Was this the moment when her luck ran out?

A distant noise, like an intake of breath, made her switch the torch on. There was nothing to be seen. She turned it off again, made her hands into fists.

The fact that the Cannibal Hymn was written on the back of each of the statues made her feel strong, connected to this place. If she could, she would go and tell her old teachers in the nunnery that they were right, that the gift of Jesus, the sharing of his body and his blood, was more than just a metaphor. It was his central message.

To partake of the Kingdom of Heaven, you must eat the flesh and drink the blood of the gods.

That was when she heard it again. This time the breathing noise was nearer. She switched on the torch.

79

Henry rubbed his eyes. It was three-thirty in the morning, Sunday morning, London time. He should have handed over the situation in Cairo ninety minutes ago.

He'd handed over everything else. But he couldn't on this part of the operation. He felt responsible. Responsible for getting Isabel into all this. Responsible for Sean going missing too. If Henry hadn't arranged for Sean to speak at the conference in Nuremberg, then hadn't agreed to Isabel using security services search facilities to look for private planes leaving Nuremberg after Sean had disappeared, she wouldn't even have gone to Cairo.

The other duty officer was at a desk opposite him in the control room in Whitehall. He was typing at his keyboard, glancing occasionally at Henry. He was most likely writing a report about Henry, probably asking for him to be removed from any future work on the series of incidents involving Sean and Isabel Ryan.

He was probably right, too.

If Isabel had uncovered a network in Egypt, connected to the plot in Nuremberg, it was more than likely these were the people pulling the strings behind much of what the Ryans had uncovered.

That would all go down as a plus on his record, countering any negatives.

As long as Isabel Ryan returned safely, the mission ended without loss of life and this Yacoub character was stopped in whatever he was planning to do, especially in his attempt to gain power in Egypt.

Which was the reason why Henry had to stay all night and have multiple reports written up on him if necessary.

His earphones crackled.

"Permission to engage, sir." The Royal Marine Commando unit were in position. The unit, based on HMS Albion, which was coordinating patrols off the eastern coast of Libya, was better equipped and trained to undertake the task ahead, against possible stiff resistance.

Performing an armed search and recovery mission in the capital of a foreign state required surgical precision. Permission to carry out the mission had been granted only after Henry had promised they'd be no more than one hour on the ground, that Egyptian special forces would accompany them, and that their role would be described only as a supply and support mission, should the media find out.

One hour was not a long time. But it would be enough.

"Permission granted. Code green." Henry spoke softly, looking across at his colleague. He was fiddling at his earphones, clearly listening in.

His hands raised from the keyboard and he looked directly at Henry. Then he smiled. The signal was clear. If the unit succeeded Henry's career would be saved. If it didn't, he'd be filling and shredding at the Milton Keynes security services historical review unit within a week.

Another crackle sounded from his headphones.

"One man down. Unit two, engage." The sound of gunfire came clearly into Henry's ears. Rapid and repeated bursts of gunfire.

80

I jabbed at the buttons, my fingers pumping at them, as if by pressing many times the doors would close quicker. I didn't care which direction I went in either. Three guards in black uniforms with bird insignias were running towards me. Behind them, a woman in a green medical uniform was following.

The doors of the lift closed. We were heading down. I looked at numbers on the panel. There were ten floors. The building had only two floors above ground. That meant the stairwell I'd been on didn't go down to all the underground levels.

I'd pressed the number four. I stood back as the doors opened, not knowing what to expect. They opened on a small room with only bare rock walls. My hand hovered over the buttons. If I went up, and those people following me had pressed the button calling the elevator, in a few seconds the door would open on their floor and they'd have me.

I had to try the other levels. I pressed three.

The door pinged open again on another small room. I held the doors this time as I peered around. It looked as if it had been constructed as a test point in the rock underneath the research center. This room was bigger than the one above and the far wall was rough and had small round holes all over it, as if it had been used for testing something.

I pressed two. This opened into a longer room, reaching maybe fifty feet in front of me, into a far wall barely lit by the light coming out of the elevator.

I stepped back, pressed the one. This was it. My last chance. The door pinged open. A long passage, wide enough for three people to walk abreast, had been cut into the bedrock. The walls were rough gray. They looked as if they'd been cut in great slices, as if whoever had made them had been using some giant butter knife, capable of cutting through limestone.

In the distance the passage bent to the left. It was lit though, with bulbs at regular intervals. And they were on.

Anxiety had made my hands into fists, and I held them tight at my side. A part of me said, *go back*, but I had to see what was down here. I couldn't turn around now. I walked forward.

The door binged closed behind me and the elevator made a clunking sound as it started back up. I had to move fast. I half ran to where the passage turned. As I came towards the bend I saw the walls changing. It seemed as if they were cut into a softer rock now, paler limestone.

As I neared the bend, a shout echoed from behind. I didn't look back. I ran on.

81

Xena stood. A shadow, moving fast across the floor, was all she had seen, but she knew it meant trouble. She pointed the torch around the area by the door, focusing the dim light on each part of the door in turn.

There was no obvious handle or clear way through. But there were holes in the wall on either side. They could have been torch holes, or hand holds for people climbing the wall. She looked up. The roof, a series of stone beams, was twenty feet above her. She shone the torch upwards.

There was a ledge up above, cut into the stone wall above the door. She looked at the holes. She could climb up.

She put the torch in her deep trouser pocket. She left it on, so the light came out through the dark cotton, illuminating the wall. It wasn't ideal. But she couldn't do this in the dark.

She put her foot in the first hole, about knee height off the ground. She reached up to a hole above her head, put a hand into it. Her other foot went into another hole.

As she went up she heard a rustling on the floor below. She didn't dare look down. When she reached the level of the ledge she had to go above it, then use a hole above as a hand hold to clamber onto it.

The ledge was as wide as her body, and bare, except for what looked like a bowl above the center of the door. She crawled towards it.

It wasn't just a bowl. It was black inside. Perhaps it had been filled with oil and lit when the hall was in use. She looked up. The roof above was stained black. She lay out on the ledge, then turned the torch to the floor below. Her mouth opened.

Two areas of dark shadow were moving around the floor, as if they were ghosts. She peered down, trying to make out what the shadows meant. Then she knew. At the back of one of the shadows, giant ants were scurrying to join the shadow. As they joined, they disappeared into the mass of ants.

The shadows merged, stopped below where she had climbed up the wall.

A shiver ran through her.

A part of the shadow went up the wall, as if others below were supporting the ones above. The shadow seemed to be reaching for the first hole she had used to climb up.

She drew back along the ledge, looked around for a weapon, then looked back down. The ants hadn't reached the next hole. The smooth wall had defeated them. She lay back, closed her eyes. How was she going to get out of this place?

82

I stopped as soon as I got around the corner. In front of me there was a cave-like room with an opening on the far wall. The rock around us was various shades of gray.

The far opening was wide enough for ten men to get through side by side, but the roof of the cave was only a few feet above my head. Was this an underground entrance to the pyramid complex?

I walked fast towards the opening in the far wall. Beyond it was a ramp, angled downwards. Someone had put wooden rails on the left hand side. The angle was about forty-five degrees. You could run down it, but you would be lucky to be able to stop at the end. The roof of the ramp was a little shorter than my height.

I went to the left, started down using the wooden rails. Maybe there was another way out here. Or maybe I'd find out what the hell Yacoub was digging for.

A string of widely spaced lights lit the ramp with a phosphorescent glow. As I went down the air was heavy, hot. Sweat was prickling all over my body. A grinding noise echoed. At the bottom of the ramp, a glow of light pulled me forward.

I wondered for a moment if I was just walking deeper into trouble, but I knew I had no choice. The effects of the drug they'd given me hadn't fully worn off, but the knowledge that they could do anything to me, including kill me in my sleep, had sent a strong desire to get away from these people, whatever it took.

I tried to keep quiet, as I went down, but it was difficult, as the wooden bands nailed into the walkway squeaked as I stepped on them. As I neared the bottom of the ramp, which must have been a hundred feet long, a flat stone area came into view. Another cave.

I slowed as I approached. There were lights on down there and the grinding noise was louder now. I bent down as I came near the end, trying to see into the cave below.

That was when Yacoub's two nieces appeared at the bottom. Each of them was holding a black Heckler & Koch machine pistol.

"Come down, Isabel," said Aisha.

I stood still for a few seconds, wondering if I should try to run back up. It's not easy shooting someone above you who is moving. So they'd told me a long time ago. But did I want to risk my life on their shooting prowess?

Another figure appeared, beside Aisha and Sawda. It was Mustafa, Yacoub's brother. He waved at me.

"Come," he said. "Meet your husband."

83

Henry's earphones crackled. He had a visual on his screen, a green tinged live feed from the infrared headsets the unit were using in the pre-dawn darkness on the edge of Cairo.

"Ground floor secure, alpha one." A long crackle interfered with the next words from the special forces team leader.

"Repeat," said Henry. All he could see on the screen was a room with elevator doors.

"We need to go down, sir. From what our local contact has told us, they've had reports of multiple underground levels at this location. Loss of contact is likely. Permission to proceed requested."

Henry drummed his fingers on the desk. He looked up. His colleague was observing him from across the room.

"Granted, code green." He took a sip from the plastic cup of water on his desk.

If he got this wrong, the United Kingdom's reputation was on the line. The last thing the government needed right now was the accusation of another failed foreign adventure.

84

I ran forward. I couldn't stop myself. There was a body strapped to a steel hospital gurney in the center of the cave. A drip line was attached to one arm.

Aisha and Sawda blocked my path. They tried to take hold of my arms. I swung them wildly. Two security men appeared. As I tried to dodge Aisha and Sawda they reached for me.

"Let me go," I screamed.

But my arms were held tight. I kicked out, caught Sawda in the thigh. My other foot was kicked out from under me. I fell back, held up only by the two security men. The pushed me back to my feet.

"Your husband is not dead, Mrs. Ryan. Not yet, anyway. But if you keep causing trouble he will be," said Mustafa, who was standing in front of me. He gestured at the two security men.

They gripped me tighter.

He said something in Arabic. The men pushed me towards the gurney. Hope and fear mixed inside me in stomach clenching waves. I wanted to see who this was. And I dreaded seeing who it was.

I looked away as the thought of what I might see struck me, but I turned my head back an instant later. I had to see. I had to know.

Then I knew.

"What have you done to him?" I screamed, as I looked at Sean's face. It was pale, thin. He looked ill, like a survivor from a concentration camp. There were purple bruises on his cheeks.

"He's alive, Mrs. Ryan. And having him here has helped us. We found out some time back that your husband has the same blood type of the family of the ancient pharaohs, A2, with the very uncommon genotype MN."

"What the hell has that got to do with anything?" My arm wriggled from the guard's grip. I raised my fist in front of me in frustration. It was shaking. One of the guards grabbed it, pressed that arm behind my back, painfully.

"Stop," I yelled.

Mustafa nodded, then pointed across the cave. Rocks were strewn around beneath the far wall. A passage lay between them heading into the wall. It looked as if it had only recently been dug. There were electric drills lying on the floor, connected by cables to a bright yellow power unit. I remembered the grinding noise I'd heard when I was coming down the stairs.

"What sort of shit are you pulling down here? Sean's blood can't help you with anything. Let him go, for god's sake. You can't get away with this."

"Oh, but we can, and we will," said a voice behind me. I turned. It was Yacoub, but there was someone else with him. They were coming down into the room from the stairway.

85

Henry watched his screen intently. His face was only away inches from it. Communications had been cut off with the team leader, but as only five of the team had gone down, there were still another five above ground.

The sergeant in charge of the second section was mumbling into his microphone.

"Speak up, man," said Henry. "What the hell are you saying?"

"Sir, there's gunfire echoing up the elevator shaft. If the elevator doesn't come back up in the next few minutes we'll open these doors and abseil down."

The screen was filled with the black carbon helmets and padded body suits of the team as they clustered around the elevator doors.

"Gunfire outside the building again, sir. Exit route may be compromised."

Henry pulled back from the screen. This was not going as well as he'd hoped. If they were under fire below ground and above, there could be casualties soon. It was going to take some explaining, especially if they didn't come back with the Ryans alive.

The elevator doors binged. The angry grunt from the sergeant echoed in Henry's ears. As the headcam he was watching through angled down he understood why. The entire five man team were lying on the floor of the elevator. Behind them, the steel clad wall of the elevator was pockmarked with bullet holes and plastered with blood.

They hadn't stood a chance. Someone had fired into the elevator as soon as the doors had opened. Had they even got any shots off in retaliation?

"Permission to go down alone, sir," said the sergeant in his ear.

He hesitated for only a moment.

"Permission granted," said Henry.

86

Yacoub and Professor Bayford walked towards us. Bayford spoke first.

"I'm sorry it has come to this, Isabel, but the work down here requires total secrecy. We're about to open the fabled hall of records. If anyone got wind of what we really had discovered here, the Egyptian government would shut us down within the hour. Things have changed since Howard Carter's time."

I couldn't help shouting my disgust back at him. "And it's worth killing my husband, and God knows how many other people, to keep all this secret?" I stared at him.

"Do you know what's inside the room?" Bayford's voice lowered as he came near me. He pulled out his smartphone, tapped at it, turned it to face me.

On the screen was an image of a hall filled with pillars.

"We put a fiber optic camera through the doorway, Isabel. There is no doubting this is the greatest archaeological discovery in Egypt for hundreds of years, possibly the greatest discovery ever. Our history books will change after this." He raised both hands. "We have seen papyrus cases. They are the types of cases that hold scrolls, Isabel. The secrets of how they built the pyramids are probably in there, and how they aligned them with magnetic north and God knows, if Plutarch was right, the history of Atlantis written on golden plates."

His face was inches from mine.

I wriggled an arm free, struck him hard across his cheek with the palm of my hand. "None of this is worth killing for."

The guards grabbed me, tighter.

Bayford's hand flew up, as if to strike me. Yacoub grabbed his wrist.

"Do not strike our guest, professor. She is here to witness a great event."

"Let my husband go and I will say I never saw this." I wasn't going to beg, but I had to try something.

"I am afraid we can't do that, Isabel. Your husband is here for a reason."

"What the hell reason could you have for bringing him down here? Are you all stark raving mad?"

"No, Isabel. There is a very logical reason for having him down here."

He smiled at me.

"What is it?" I shouted.

"You tell her, professor."

Bayford was rubbing his cheek. He grunted, then replied.

"We discovered a version of the cannibal hymn on a doorway through that passage. It states, in hieroglyphs, that the door can only be opened when an amphora of a pharaoh's blood is poured into it."

"That's sick," I said. "How do you pour an amphora of blood into a door?" I glanced at Sean on the stretcher. "Are you going to drain his body?" My hands were fists again. My skin was tightening across my chest. This was too much.

"No, we won't kill him. We've been collecting his blood every few days for the last few weeks. Today we have just enough to carry out the instructions and he is here if we need more."

"What don't you just break the door down?"

"The ancient builders knew exactly what an amphora of blood weighed. They may have set the hall to collapse and crush everything in it, if the door isn't opened in the right way." Bayford shook his head. "We have done all this in the most humane way possible. Your husband will not die."

"Unless you cause us a problem," interjected Yacoub.

I shook my head. "You're all mad."

"If we do find the fountain of youth, and learn how it worked, millions of people will praise your husband's sacrifice. I am sure of that." Yacoub paused, shrugged. "Billions possibly, once we start selling them our prescriptions."

"When can I take Sean out of here?"

Yacoub walked towards the gap in the cave wall. "When our job here is done you will be free to leave."

I didn't believe him for a second. "How long until that happens?"

"It should all have been done yesterday, but events have held us back. I hope we will get this all completed in the next twenty-four hours."

I groaned. "Why don't you let us go now? You don't need us here. You have all the blood you need."

"No, we cannot release you until we are ready and…"

The sound of gunfire interrupted him. All eyes turned to the stairway out.

Yacoub spoke first. "Come, professor. We need to finish this."

87

Henry watched the large LCD screen on his desktop. It showed a video feed from an Egyptian Air Force, Apache LongBow helicopter. It had been assigned to air support duty by the Egyptian military, for the upcoming raid on the Yacoub Industries research facility at Giza, near the pyramids.

The feed was showing a pre-dawn fire fight at the entrance to the facility. The British force was already inside, having overwhelmed the Yacoub security detail thirty-two minutes before. An Egyptian special forces unit, the notorious Unit 777, had been dropped by helicopter at the time the British forces were abseiled onto the roof of the facility.

The Egyptian forces, except for the commanding officer, had been tasked with holding the perimeter of the facility, in case any of Yacoub's other security units showed up.

What they hadn't expected was a suicide car bomb attack on the main gate, and a trio of Muslim Brotherhood SUV vehicles arriving with a dozen black clad terrorists jumping out.

When they did, the Egyptian unit had called on the Apache to take out the SUV's. The request had been instantly made available to Henry on his incident feed.

What Henry was watching was the failure of that request to elicit a response. The Apache was observing, but not firing. What this probably meant was that the air force unit had a different agenda to the special forces command.

Whether they were holding off to help the Brotherhood achieve its aim, in return for something else previously agreed at a high level, or whether this was simply a stupid mistake was still unclear.

Henry personally subscribed to the stupid theory of history, which said that most of the major cock ups in the world, odd deaths and weird preventable disasters, were the result of human stupidity, not some arcane conspiracy. But that didn't mean conspiracies didn't ever happen.

The image from the Apache blinked, then swung away. The Apache was disengaging.

It was time to send the two Lynx Commando support helicopters, which had dropped the British commando unit, and been sent to refuel at the Almaza Egyptian Air Force base, just north of Cairo. Flying time from there to the Giza facility should be less than ten minutes.

If the helicopters had been refueled. Henry tapped at his keyboard.

88

Professor Bayford went to the table Sean was lying comatose on. He unhooked the bag of blood from it and walked fast towards the hole in the cave wall.

Yacoub followed. "Come with us," he shouted at me. Then he said something in Arabic. The two men holding me pushed me after him.

I stumbled as we went into the passageway. Bayford was in the lead with Yacoub behind him. Mustafa was behind me. The passage was a little higher than my head. Rough yellow stone jutted out in places. About ten paces in, the passage stopped at a stone doorway. It had a recess in its front, in the oval shape of a small amphora and on the floor, in the corner, a cable had been pushed into the bottom corner, between the door and the wall.

The door itself was covered in faded red paint. Hieroglyphs stood out in white against it. They included over-sized glyphs of men with erect phalluses and other glyphs that looked like piles of bones. Isis and Osiris were in opposite corners.

Bayford took a black amphora shaped jar from where it stood in a corner, poured the blood in from the bag and held it up.

"Now we will find out everything the ancients knew. Technology that has been lost for thousands of years. How the great prophets lived for hundreds of years. How sound was used as a weapon. And many more things." He looked excited.

"Professor, let's get this over with. We don't know who is coming down on top of us." Mustafa was crowding in behind me.

I felt something brush against my ass. I made a disgusted noise and took a step away from him. What I really wanted was any opportunity to kill every one of these bastards. What Sean needed was a fast evacuation to a hospital, blood transfusions and a proper assessment of whatever else he needed to get better.

Every second that was all delayed meant he was in more danger. God only knew the effect of repeated blood extractions on the human body.

Professor Bayford put the cork back on the amphora and placed it in the recess in the doorway. It fitted exactly.

Nothing happened.

Mustafa grunted. "How soon will this open, professor?"

Yacoub leaned forward. "Ssshhh, brother. I hear something."

I leaned towards the door. A rumbling grew louder as we all waited. Every head was angling forward, listening. Then the floor started moving. I looked down, my knees almost going out from under me. The rough stone floor was moving backward, slowly, as if it was on rollers.

We were all moving backwards. Only a few inches, but when I looked at the door I saw that it was grinding open in the center. The two leaves were jerking as they moved, as if it had been a long time since they'd opened.

Yacoub gasped. He held a small torch up. The light from it illuminated a large space beyond the door and rows of pillars. They reminded me of the underground hall in Istanbul.

Professor Bayford took a step forward, as soon as the opening between the door leaves was wide enough to walk through. As he did Yacoub put a hand on his arm.

"Professor, I shall be the first one to enter."

Bayford shrugged. Yacoub shouldered past him. The hall beyond came more clearly into view. A black shape filled the floor.

It was moving. Moving towards us.

89

Henry's video link was dead. The Apache had peeled away, heading back to base to refuel. So they said. The Lynx helicopters, which had been sent to refuel at the Almaza Egyptian Air Force base had encountered a problem.

Refueling permission was needed from a general, who was unavailable. That meant Henry had five men in the building, engaging a dozen Muslim Brotherhood terrorists intent on killing all in their path fast, before more security services arrived.

Henry's radio link was still working though. It crackled now, like something from the 20th century.

"Requesting permission to head down after Sergeant Smith. Two men wounded so far. One seriously. We can get in the elevator right now."

Henry's fingers tightened around the armrest of his chair. He didn't like it, not knowing what was happening underground, but if this was what the unit leader recommended, he was not going to go against it.

"Permission granted. Code green." He picked up the white telephone handset on his desk. He needed someone in the Foreign Office to call that bloody Egyptian general. Whatever happened, he had to be able to get their men out fast when the time came.

As he spoke into the phone he saw his colleague across the room typing fast on his keyboard. No doubt preparing an early post mortem report on this debacle. He looked down at his desk. Would this be his last night in his post?

90

Yacoub was transfixed, his mouth open and in a sneer, as if couldn't imagine anything so small threatening him.

"Ants," said Bayford. "A swarm. Step back."

Yacoub didn't. He went towards the black shadow. "Ants don't attack humans in Egypt, professor."

The black shadow reached him. Yacoub began stamping on it. For a second it swayed, as if the shadow was one entity. Then it swarmed up him. In a few seconds they covered him in a black shadow, as if ink had been thrown at him.

He screamed in Arabic.

His two nieces, who had been behind me, pushed past and ran to him. That was when I saw the second black shadow on the floor racing towards Yacoub. This was ten times bigger than the first and moving fast, as if it was angry or hungry.

Sawda and Aisha were beating at Yacoub's clothes, and I could see clouds of ants falling from him, but every time they cleared one area of ants more poured onto him.

Yacoub screamed. Sawda and Aisha were shouting too. It sounded as if they were cursing in Arabic.

"We need to get out of here," said Bayford. "We have no idea how these ants have mutated down here. If they have few sources of food ants can become highly dangerous."

Mustafa was behind us, blocking our way back.

"There must be a way to help them," he said, glowering at Bayford.

"I have no idea. Let us pass." Bayford raised a hand as if he would push past Mustafa.

"You are not going anywhere," said Mustafa. He reached inside his cream jacket. His hand emerged with a small black pistol in it. To make matters worse, he pointed it at me.

"Fire is the only thing they'll run from," said Bayford. "I have a cigarette lighter and some papers in my bag, just back there." He pointed beyond Mustafa.

A scream pierced the air, like glass breaking. I looked back. Sawda was on her knees, beating at herself as if she had gone mad.

Bayford led the way back out. All I wanted to do was get help for Sean. I didn't care about what happened to any of the others.

Sean hadn't moved since we left him. There was no gunfire echoing in the cave anymore. Two of the security guards were at the entrance to the stairs, pointing their guns upwards. One of them shouted at Mustafa. He shouted back, then turned to Bayford.

"Be quick. Take your bag. We do this now."

Bayford picked up his rucksack and headed back to the tunnel and the doorway.

Mustafa waved his pistol at me.

"You will come too."

I was beside Sean now. I held his hand. "I am not leaving him again. You can shoot me if you want. You have guards here. What can I do."

He looked at me, his eyes narrowing. Then he let out an exasperated noise and followed Bayford.

A scream echoed faintly from the tunnel. I looked at the guards. Both of them had turned to face me. I put a hand out to them, as if pleading for help. One of them shrugged, as if to say there was nothing he could do. I looked at the other one, held my hand out to him. He looked away too.

I bent over Sean's body, put my ear to his chest. I had to hold steady for ten seconds before I heard the faint beating of his heart. They'd robbed him of his blood, but, thank God, he was still alive. A warmth filled me from inside, which I hadn't felt in weeks. He was alive. We were going to get out of here.

But how?

I started walking towards the guards, as quietly as possible. Both had their backs to me. I had one chance. If I could take one of their weapons I could kill them both. They wouldn't expect a woman to try to kill them. Egyptian women were a tough bunch, but mostly they were respectful to authority.

I was half way towards them when one of them turned to me. His machine pistol was in his hand. He was pointing it at me. I put my hands up, held both out to him.

"Water," I said. "Please."

He smiled, raised his gun to sight along the barrel at me.

Then he waved at me to step back.

I kept walking forward.

91

Henry's fist pumped the air. His screen was showing the ground, a jumble of flat roofed buildings as the Lynx Commando support helicopters, which had recently refueled at the Almaza Egyptian Air Force base, made their way from the airfield, north of Cairo, to the Giza plateau, to its west.

They were traveling fast, their noses down, rotor blades making a distinct whining noise as they reached their two hundred and twenty miles per hour maximum speed. They would only be able to sustain this for thirty minutes, but it would be enough. They would reach the plateau in fifteen.

He looked at the set of clocks on the far wall. They showed the time in London, New Delhi, Beijing, Canberra, Los Angeles and Washington. He wasn't concerned at the hour. What he needed to know was the exact time they would arrive.

A support call had been put in to the U.S. aircraft carrier, Harry S. Truman. It was on a routine deployment in the Red Sea, and could have a ground support aircraft, the Harrier II, over Cairo within an hour. A single Harrier had been released to travel up the Red Sea on what could have been a standard reconnaissance mission, ready to redeploy, if permission were given by the general command in Egypt and the British Government requested it.

This little operation was heading to become a serious international incident. The commando unit had gone silent, after going underground. There were four casualties already and the reputation of the British military was now on the line. He stared at his screen, willing the Lynx to go faster. Then a noise behind him made him turn.

"Henry Mowlam, you are hereby relieved of your duties. You are under arrest for failing to follow a direct order by your superior officer." The man standing behind him was wearing a captain's uniform. A captain from the Royal military police. The red hat and badge made that clear. The question was, what were they doing here?

"Gentlemen," said Henry. "You have no authority to remove me from my duties. I am in the middle of overseeing an important operation."

The captain spoke to the two other officers beside him.

"Put him under arrest and remove him from the room."

The two officers moved swiftly, as if they were used to detaining suspects. One put Henry's right arm in a hold and twisted him out of his chair. The other took his other arm and they both lifted him bodily into the air.

A shout rang out from across the room.

"Well done!"

Henry's attention was on the crackle coming out of the speaker on his desk.

"Requesting permission to proceed," said the voice.

92

Xena looked down from her ledge. The swarm of ants had almost engulfed Yacoub and his two nieces. She'd been tempted to jump down and try to help them, but she didn't expect them to have any real trouble with the ants. Surely they could help each other?

It should have been an easy matter to scrape them off. And now, what she was seeing, the ants in thick layers over each of them, turning them into black clad shrouds, made her glad she hadn't.

Yacoub was wiping at his eyes, frantically. For a few seconds they were free of ants. He saw her in her hiding place. A pleading scream ripped through the hall, echoing off the far walls. When Xena didn't move, his scream turned to anger, and his hand came up and pointed at her.

He was demanding her help. But Xena was no one's slave. She wouldn't die for her master.

Bayford appeared below her. He was carrying a crude torch made of papers, rolled together, with looser ones at the top, lit. Flame and smoke spewed from them.

Mustafa followed with a similar homemade torch. She didn't like Mustafa. He'd tried too many times to get her back to his house. The place where he entertained his mistresses. And he'd become more crazy with her when he saw her with Yacoub.

And there was another thing to consider. If these people had opened a door into the hall, and they were all killed, she would be the only one with any knowledge of this secret place. This could be her opportunity.

Bayford and Mustafa threw their torches towards Yacoub. Neither of them seemed to care about helping the two women. The dark shadows flinched away from the flames, then drew back even further.

Gasps came from the two men below her. She leaned forward to see why. Then she knew.

93

I stumbled as I came nearer to the guard. I let my eyes close for a second, then blinked them. I was tired, but not this tired. I saw his gaze flicker to the right, as if he was checking if the other guard was looking. I stumbled again. I needed water, but not this badly. I was near him now, my head bowed, as if I was beaten. I went down on one knee in front of him. He reached down towards me, his steel water bottle in his hand. It was the biggest mistake he'd ever made. And his last.

His machine pistol was pointed down. He was well trained, probably ex-military. They didn't like to cause civilian deaths if they could avoid it. I bowed my head, reached my hand forward and up. Instinctively his hand came towards mine to help me.

I looked up, grabbed for his gun hand. I had one second to get this right, before he filled me full of holes. I jerked the barrel upwards, sending his hand and fingers bending. He pressed the trigger. A deafening hail of bullets sprung from the gun. It shattered the rock above into a rain of shards, which clattered around us and sent his hand jerking, like a fish avoiding being caught. But I held on.

The guard was screaming in Arabic, a mixture of shock and outrage that I'd dared to take him on. His fist came towards me. I saw it in a blur and fell backwards away from it, pulling the muzzle of the gun around so the stream of bullets headed in the direction of the other guard.

The stream of bullets stopped, but the scream from the other guard made it clear it was too late. His face was white. A red hole filled his chest. He fell backwards. The thump of his head hitting the stone floor echoed on the stairs. I was rolling over by then, holding the first guard's gun hand, twisting it one way then the other, trying to force it from him.

He screamed again. Arabic curse words. I struck out with my hard tipped boot towards his genitals. I felt a connection with something soft. His shout changed from anger to pain. He released the pistol. I had it.

I turned it towards him, hesitated, saw him reaching for a handgun on his belt and shot him in the face. The bullets entered through his cheek and his forehead.

I felt a swift surge of remorse, but I knew how to suppress it. It had been my life or his. No choice there. They'd been draining Sean's life too. And he would have shot me if I'd hesitated. The fact that bullets had smashed into the roof proved that.

I ran back down the steps.

Mustafa and Bayford were busy down at the end of the corridor. This was my chance to get away with Sean. I touched his face. It was still warm, but only barely. I slapped him lightly across the cheek to see if it would wake him. His head went to one side.

"Please, Sean, wake up," I shouted.

I slapped again. Harder. I wouldn't be able to carry him. Even half awake, he could stumble in my arms out of here.

Then, on impulse, I kissed him. Not on the cheek. On the lips. I kissed him hard. I couldn't stop myself. I was so happy to see him.

And he responded.

His lips moved. I was sure of it.

94

Xena watched as hordes of ants poured in from all corners of the hall. Perhaps it was the blood that signaled them. Perhaps it was their own messaging odors. She knew ants could summon their kind.

Screams filled the hall as Mustafa and Bayford experienced what had happened to Yacoub and his two nieces, who were now just piles of dark matter on the ground with white edges, their bones sticking out. The mass of black on each of them had a red tinge to it, as ants, gorged with blood and flesh, came up to the surface of the hordes.

Xena watched, her heart beating fast, a rushing in her ears. Only the overhang and the distance to the ground had kept her safe from a similar fate. The question was, how would she ever escape them?

Further screams were like knives cutting the air. Mustafa's mouth opened as he spun around. Blackness filled it. He fell to his knees beside Bayford. They would be gone soon, too.

And still more ants were coming. How many generations had lived down here without sight or smell of anything larger than a rat or a desert fox? Had they some genetic memory of feeding on human flesh? Was that why this hall had been abandoned, blocked up?

The mass of black below her was twenty feet wide at least now. Part of it was circling the five mounds, where the last remnants of human flesh were being consumed. The outer edges began to peel away, in smaller shadows. One came towards where she had climbed up. She held her breath as they tried to scale the wall after her, following her scent most likely. But the wall was too steep, too smooth.

Another shadow streamed towards the doorway under her ledge.

She closed her eyes. Would it be better if they were distracted by eating someone out there, so she could get away? And should she follow them out through the door?

A new, higher pitched scream echoed into the hall. This had come through the doorway. And she knew who was screaming.

95

Henry was being bundled, in a deep underground garage, into a green van with the words Queen's Suppliers in small red letters on its side.

It took four men to ensure he was settled in the wire cage in the back. Two of them got in the front and headed for the ramp leading up to the bomb proof metal doors and the street. Within minutes he would be in a safe house in Elephant and Castle and would be unlikely to see daylight again until the security services investigation was complete.

On Henry's screen, back at his desk, an image showed the exterior of Yacoub Holdings research facility in Cairo. A group of Egyptian commandos were pinned down by gunfire near the gate. Muslim Brotherhood fighters had been reinforced with two more truckloads of men in black.

Unless air cover came in swiftly the Brotherhood would overrun the commandos, and the facility would be entirely in their hands.

As a sign of how imminent that moment was, the screen showed two black clad men planting something near the front door of the main building unimpeded. It was a black backpack. The men were doing something with whatever was inside.

"Request permission to engage," came a voice, over the speakers attached to the side of Henry's desk.

But no one answered, and a few seconds later the sound of bullets striking the Lynx could clearly be heard, and the flashes from several machine pistols pointed in its direction could be seen.

A moment later the helicopter swung away and headed back over the jumble of flat roofs, piles of garbage and TV antennas heading back to the airbase.

"Mission aborted," came an exasperated voice over the loudspeakers.

96

I pressed my ear close to Sean's mouth. His breathing was shallow, but there was something else I wanted to check. I felt for his knee, then tapped it hard with my knuckles through the thin blue cotton hospital trousers they had put him in.

Sean had been sensitive about his knees for a long time. I had no idea if it was genetic, or a sign that he was getting older. He'd be forty soon, God willing. I tapped again.

No reaction. I'd hoped for an intake of breath, even a shallow one, to say that he was conscious in some way, if even sleepily. But there was nothing.

A moan came from behind me. I turned. The guard, who the other guard had shot, was crawling towards me across the stone floor. A trail of blood was like a stream behind him. He was up on his elbows dragging himself, his eyes wide in pain. The other security guard's gun was only a few feet from him, twenty from me.

The gun I'd taken from the guard was at the end of the hospital trolley Sean was lying on. I reached towards it. Another groan sounded from the guard. I touched the gun, pulled it to me. As I gripped it I saw something strange, glistening, almost magical, appear from the doorway in the cave.

A black shadow was pouring out of the opening. It covered the ground, as if the light was being blocked. And it was heading towards me.

It took a few more seconds for my brain to catch up. This wasn't a shadow or anything magical, it was the ants.

The guard let out a roar. I turned back to him. He had reached the gun. He was lifting it and screaming, "Allahu Akbar, Allahu Akbar."

I bent my head down, my heart banging suddenly against my chest. If he let off a stream of bullets both Sean and I could be dead in the next few seconds. Instinctively I lifted my legs, pushed forward until I was covering Sean's body with mine. Ricochets would hit me now, not him. It was all I could do to protect him.

My breathing almost stopped. I was shaking as if I was ill. A great clattering, pinging, thudding sounded through the hall. I put my hands to my face, sure they were wet. But it wasn't blood. Sweat was slicking them.

"Allahu Akbar, Allahu Akbar." The screams were higher pitched now, as if the guard was under attack. Then the sound of the bullets stopped. I forced myself to look towards him.

All I saw was a mass of black writhing on the floor. I looked below the trolley. The ants were parting at the steel trolley wheels and flowing on towards the guard. Some ants were trying to climb the wheels, the rubber was black from where they were mounting on top of each other, but the steel legs were too smooth for them to climb. They reached an inch or two above the wheels, then they were falling back in tiny waves.

The guard wasn't so lucky. His hands were still frantically beating at himself, but they were red with blood.

"Allahu Akbar, Allahu Akbar." More shouts echoed in the hall. I looked up to where the stairs came down. Four men, dressed in black, with AK-47's, had stopped near the bottom of the stairs. They were staring open mouthed at the carpet of black almost covering the hall.

One of them laughed. He took a step down and started firing at the ants, as if they were one creature. Perhaps they were, because the next thing I saw was a wave of ants streaming up the stairs, first rising up that man's legs, then pursuing the other black clad men as they retreated, stumbling backwards.

Then the waves of black ants were leaving, heading up the stairs after the men. All that was left of the guards in the room were mounds of bones and flesh, as if the room was an abattoir.

That was when the smell hit me. It was gross, like rotting meat. I groaned, held onto Sean, put my ear to his chest. His heart was beating, but as faintly as the sound of the wind passing through grass.

Something touched the small of my back.

"Now is the time to pray, Isabel Ryan," said a voice. I knew the voice, too. I turned my head slowly, expecting a gun muzzle to be pointed at me.

But it wasn't a gun muzzle. It was a face peering down at me, with lips pressed together, dust on her hair and a hand held towards us.

Was Xena going to pull us off the trolley and let the ants have us?

97

Henry stood between two of the officers who had arrested him. They were standing by the side door of the green van. The steel doors of the underground garage in Whitehall, which should have opened to let them through were still closed.

The two other officers had gone off to see what the problem was. It wasn't unheard of for the doors not to open, and especially this early on a Sunday morning, when there might be a gang from a nightclub passing.

But it was unusual for there to be no response to the request the arrest squad leader had shouted into his headset. It seemed as if there was a communication blackout in the underground garage. If it had been a Monday morning there would have been street teams passing through every few minutes, taking vehicles from the underground parking spaces. There would have been people milling around because of the delay by now.

"How long is this going to take?" said Henry. He flexed his shoulders. Wherever they were taking him, it was going to be a long time before he got some sleep.

"Shut up." The officer to his right was fidgeting with his headset, as if trying to get a signal. He added, "sir," thirty seconds later, as if he'd only just remembered Henry outranked him, and was innocent until proven guilty.

A warning klaxon sounded. The steel doors began to rise, as a red light up above, at each end, whirled into action, sending red tinged shadows around the concrete apron where vehicles could drop off or pick up passengers.

The two men with him looked to the doorway where their colleagues had gone. Then one of them motioned with his thumb back to the green truck. The only reason they'd all got out of it was to show anyone watching on the security cameras exactly who was in their vehicle.

Henry pointed at the steel doors. They weren't opening to let them out. They were opening to let someone in. And whoever it was, they were driving an unusual vehicle. All he could see of it so far was a black steel roll bar and a black chassis. It looked like an armored Toyota Land Cruiser. He hadn't seen one of those on the streets of London in a long time.

The last time he'd seen one, was on a live video feed from Egypt.

"Are you armed?" he said.

The two men beside him nodded.

98

I blinked at Xena. What the hell?

"How did you get down here?"

"Through the Great Pyramid. How's Sean?"

"He's alive, but he won't be for much longer if we don't get him out of here. Do you know any other way? Those bloody ants went up the stairs. Have you ever seen anything like them?"

"No, and they'll be back. When they get their fill they'll head back to their nests."

"How do we know when they've eaten their fill?"

She smiled at me. I knew the answer.

"Do you know how to pray?" she said.

"Of course? Are you Christian, or what?"

"My people were Christian before Jesus Christ. Where do you think the cross and the holy mother of God came from?"

I shook my head. I didn't care. "How do we get Sean out of here?"

"We need a lure, to get them to go rush back past us. Then we block the passage."

"What would you suggest?" I could smell sweat from her, as if she'd been down here a long time. I looked up the stairs. The ants were nowhere to be seen, but that didn't mean they wouldn't reappear at any moment, if they found nothing more to eat up to the elevator.

"One of us could be sacrificed." We were standing on either side of the hospital trolley, Sean lying comatose between us.

She looked down at Sean.

I shook my head. "What about a trail of blood? They ran straight past me when that guy's blood was on the floor." I pointed at the pile of bones, still red from the last of the blood that had kept the guard alive up to twenty minutes before.

She smiled. "It could work, but you will have to be quick."

Xena went to the pile of bones and bent down. "Guards here usually carry a knife." She started poking around the bones. Then, with her fingers she moved them, pulled something black from the pile.

She walked toward me. She wiped the knife blade on her black trousers. The blade glistened.

"Be quick."

I took the knife, held it, shaking, against my arm.

"Not at the wrist," she shouted. "Cut into the pad under your thumb. You'll bleed, but you won't die, and it can be stopped quickly."

"How deep?" I was flinching now. I didn't like the idea of cutting into my flesh. I knew the pain that was coming.

"Not deep. Do it slow. But do it now."

I took a deep breath, blinked, spat on the knife, rubbed my spit into the blade, held my breath, cut the tip of it into the pad under my left thumb. Blood came out, but not a lot.

"Deeper," she shouted.

I pushed the knife into the cut. A razor sharp pain ran up my arm. I winced as the blood started pouring.

"Like this," she said. She reached over, took the knife from me, slashed it across her hand. Her blood came quickly, poured faster than mine.

"Now we walk back to the doorway."

We walked backwards, our hands held near the stone floor, our blood lines coming together. When we got to the door, I said, "Is this enough?"

"No, we go all the way through."

The pain in my hand was getting stronger, beating like a burning pulse, but I didn't care. If it meant Sean could get out of this hell hole it would be worth it.

When we reached the doorway, I looked briefly into the hall beyond. Whoever the archaeologist was who going to explore this, they were going to have the find of the millennium associated with them. Bayford had got close, but his name wouldn't be attached to this.

"This has to be enough!"

She shrugged. "Yes."

We ran back through the passage. Both of us sat up on the trolley, on either side of Sean, back to back. We waited. Then we waited some more.

"Do you think they've found another way out?" I turned to her.

Just then I heard a rustling.

"They are here. Now is a good time to pray."

I heard a mumbling from her.

I lifted my feet up, instinctively. A black swarm, thick as a carpet, was flowing down the stairs. My heart tightened in my chest and my mouth went dry. They came straight towards us. Xena's mumbling continued. It had an ancient feel to it, as if the same words might have been spoken down here millennia ago.

The black swarm kept coming down the stairs. It was thicker, more compacted now. Would they be able to climb on each other and reach us?

The swarm went around the steel wheels of the trolley. It stopped. I couldn't breathe. Each wheel became covered in black. The swarm, like a wave, rose up the steel legs. Nearer and nearer. I could see individual ants, but thousands of them. They had red eyes, pincers at their mouths and long antenna, and some of them were looking up. They were definitely trying to reach us.

I couldn't see the head of the horde any more, as they were mounting up right below us. I didn't dare lean forward any more, in case I toppled the trolley. My back struck Xena's and we stayed there, our backbones touching.

"You must pray hard," she said. "The great mother will listen to you."

So I prayed. It couldn't do any harm. I used to recite the Hail Mary when I was a child, so wanting to believe it, that a higher power was watching over us with care.

I repeated it three times, fast. It calmed me a little. I looked down again. The swarm was circling the trolley, and then it pulsed inwards, as if it had one brain and was pushing its members up the trolley legs to get more food.

I held my breath. This was it. We could all be eaten by this carpet of ants in minutes. There was nowhere to run.

I could smell the ants now. It was a rank smell, like rotten food or dead flesh. The stink filled my nostrils. I looked upwards. My mouth opened and I recoiled. A line of ants was making its way along a crack in the roof, clinging to the rough edges, some of them falling off, but most of them making it.

And the lead ants were almost above us.

I looked back towards the passage and where we had laid the trail of blood. Why hadn't they followed it?

Then I saw. There were some ants heading that way, but the majority had either smelt us, or seen us. Smelt us probably. They'd have a taste for human flesh now. Was this the way these ants had always been?

A groan sounded behind me. "Did you see the roof?" said Xena, softly.

I looked up again. The trickle of ants was getting bigger. And then some ants started falling on us. I began rubbing them away.

"Say hi to Sean," said Xena. "You should know, I prayed for you both before. I think you've suffered enough."

"Thanks, but have you any ideas about how to get out of this hell hole?"

"I do," she said.

I felt the trolley move. I was still rubbing ants off my arms and legs and from Sean's body, but I turned and saw Xena walking through the ants, heading for the passage. They were mounting up her legs already. As she walked the swarm followed her.

The last I saw of her was the swarm covering her entirely, but she was still walking down the passage into the hall beyond. My mouth was open. She had sacrificed herself for us. I looked down, humbled.

There were no more ants below me. I looked up. There were some ants on the roof, but not many. I turned to Sean, slipped down from the trolley, stood beside him. I slapped him across the face. I wouldn't be able to carry him up the stairs. I needed him even partly awake.

But he wouldn't wake. And now I was worried that the ants would return. I looked back at the passage. Even if I could close it, I might leave a way for the ants to stream through. I want over to the pile of bones. Perhaps there was a water bottle amid them.

But there wasn't. I went up the steps to the bones spilling down, where another guard had been devoured. There was no water bottle, but I saw the glint of a lighter. I picked it up with just the tips of my fingers. It was resting against a thigh bone.

I took it back to Sean. I didn't want to do this, but I had to. I picked up his hand, flicked the lighter on, placed the flame under his palm, started counting. Five seconds, please. It would be enough to wake an elephant.

I was right. I heard a groan. Sean's eye's flickered. It was enough. I took the brakes of the trolley legs, pushed it towards the steps.

"Come on, Sean. Wake up, wake up," I was calling, over and over, anxiety still gripping at me. When I got to the steps I let the trolley tip over towards them. He slid forward. I stepped in, caught his head before it cracked against the stone.

But his eyes were open. An enormous wave of relief rose inside me. He was coming back. Warmth gushed through me. I hugged him tight.

"Thank God," I said. "Thank god you are back." Tears welled through my eyelids.

He made another groaning noise.

"We have to go, Sean. We have to get up these steps." I took him under the arm, half pulled, half pushed him forward. His legs buckled, but he made it up a step, then another. Then he fell. I was lucky to stop his head hitting the steps. I shouted in his ear, "Come on, Sean. Come on. Let's go."

His legs straightened. I pushed forward again. We went up another step. After a few more stumbles we were at the top. I looked back down. There were ants again on the floor below.

Not the same grotesque mass as had been there earlier, but there were more coming from the passage. We had to go faster. We stumbled, fell a few times before we got to the elevator. It was the longest few minutes I ever remember. It seemed as if it would never end. But then we'd made it. When I pressed the button I turned around. Ants were all over the place. I hadn't seen them. I looked down. They were all over me. They were all over Sean, too. I pressed the button to call the elevator again. I started swiping the ants away from Sean.

Finally the elevator binged. I cringed. Three men, soldiers, were lying, dead on the floor. They were half covered in blood. I recognized the insignia on their arms. They were British. So this was what had happened to the rescue party.

I pulled Sean in, leant him against the wall. Then I felt for pulses among the men. None of them had any. Anger spiked inside me. Some evil bastards had killed my countrymen. All these men had been trying to do was to help me and Sean and do their duty. Tears filled my eyes. I wiped them away. I had to be ready for whatever was up above.

I reached down, took a black pistol from the holster of one of the men. It was a Glock 17, standard issue. It was shiny, black. Someone had taken good care of their side arm. I bit my lip, aimed it at the crack in the doors. The elevator binged. The doors opened.

I was facing out into the foyer of the Yacoub Industries research facility. It was empty, but what was weirder was that outside the windows there was a whirlwind of sand, rushing up against the glass.

It was the sandstorm that had been threatening the city for days. I half dragged Sean towards a chair nearby, then went off searching for water. The sandstorm had, hopefully, sent whoever had killed our rescuers away.

I found bottles of water in a small kitchen behind the reception desk. I drank greedily, then brought a bottle back to Sean. I propped his head on my arm, put the bottle to his lips. His mouth was half open. He blinked. I poured some water in his mouth. He spluttered. "Stop." His voice was stronger.

His eyelids flickered. I was staring into the most beautiful blue eyes in the world again. Another giant wave of relief ran through me. I beamed from ear to ear.

"Are you trying to kill me?" he said.

Epilogue

Henry Mowlam closed the taxi door. The early May sunshine in West London had warmed the inside of the cab all the way from Whitehall. He looked up at the terraced house off the King's Road. There was a security camera pod on a stalk at the roof line, another around where the side passage led to the back garden.

He pressed the doorbell. It was only a few seconds before Isabel answered.

"You're quick, Mrs. Ryan." He held out his hand.

Isabel shook it, smiled. "Come in, Henry. With the new camera we see everyone from the moment they enter our street."

Henry walked down the passageway to the kitchen. Upstairs, a TV was blaring. Some Saturday morning children's show.

When he entered the kitchen he paused. Sean was sitting at the kitchen table.

"Come in, Henry. Sorry I can't get up." Sean gestured at the wheelchair under him. "But it is good to see you."

"How is the physio going?" Henry came forward, held out his hand. Sean shook it.

"Good, I think. There's hope. That's the main thing."

"You do feel better, though?" Sean nodded. Henry had read the medical reports, they were part of the deep operation investigation his work with the Ryans was being subjected to. There was also the matter of a possible award to cover medical expenses, which the Ryan family were entitled to.

The medical report had said there was brain damage, following the lengthy period Sean Ryan had been sedated for, and the blood that had been extracted from him, leaving his red blood count dangerously low. But the damage was likely to be recoverable. The brain is an amazing mechanism, the report had said. New pathways can be generated with dedicated care.

Isabel was at the kitchen counter, a steel kettle in her hand.

"Coffee?" she said. "I got a new Italian yesterday. You can buy it by the brick." She grinned.

"Sounds good."

He sat opposite Sean at the kitchen table.

"Any news on when the Egyptian government will open that hall under the pyramid?" said Sean.

Henry shook his head. "Yacoub's son is making a pitch to be elected to the Egyptian parliament. He wants the announcement to be timed to just before the parliamentary elections."

"When are they?" said Isabel.

"Next year."

"I thought Yacoub's name would be mud after all the stuff he pulled," said Sean. "Hiding that dig inside the pyramid, the people who died in his research facility. He'd have been arrested, if he'd lived."

"But he didn't. And a big find like the hall of records has a way of smoothing out a lot of things. Anyway, when they finally eradicated those ant colonies, everyone knew he'd met a grisly end."

"Those ants were scary. Were they mutants?"

"Someone told us there were people in Egypt who wanted the colony maintained, so they could be studied," said Henry.

"They didn't do that?"

"No, but they got samples. A local entomologist thinks they're a sub species which only exists under the Giza plateau. He says they would have been bred for their blood sucking abilities and ended up eating flesh too. Apparently, they'd wondered for a long time why there were so few rats under the pyramids. Now they know."

Isabel placed a large white coffee cup, with a red band around its edge, on the table in front of Henry.

"Milk and sugar?"

Henry shook his head. "I'm trying to get healthy, now that my early retirement is approved."

"I hope it wasn't due to us," said Sean.

"I was lucky," said Henry. "A supporter from the Prime Minister's office turned up on the day you were rescued. She helped sort a few things out. Otherwise, I don't know what would have happened to me." He was not going to tell her about the moment the Toyota Land Cruiser had disgorged its occupant, the Prime Minister's private secretary, who had almost gone into shock when she'd seen all the guns drawn.

"I am sorry," said Isabel. "I know you loved your work." She sat down on the chair next to Sean, put her hand over his on the padded arm of the wheelchair.

"So that hall we found was somewhere people were rejuvenated?" said Sean. He leaned forward.

"That's what it looks like. You saw the brief report, the translation of the hieroglyphs?"

"Yes, we threatened to go to the press last week, if the authorities in Egypt didn't tell us what was going on. You do know the report they sent us was all of two pages?" He shook his head.

"But two very interesting pages."

"And they want to call that pool the fountain of youth." Henry nodded.

"It's a bit of a stretch, isn't it?"

"We think, from the hieroglyphs, that they may have been drinking blood down there," said Henry.

"Yeuuch," said Sean. "Why?"

"Well, you do know," said Isabel. "That if you transfuse the blood of teenagers to elderly people, they experience real physical rejuvenation, in many ways." She smiled.

Sen shivered. "The whole idea is creepy. It's vampirism." He picked up his coffee cup.

"Drinking blood was probably just one way they got young blood into their systems," said Henry. "They also found hollow needles in the hall. They might have been doing early transfusions."

"The section of the report about the ankh, the cross they found overlooking the pool, was interesting," said Isabel.

"That is a bit bizarre." Henry took a sip of his coffee. Then he continued, "Any claim that the Catholic symbolism of eating the body and drinking the blood of Christ at Mass, was an idea they got from all this cannibal Egyptian stuff, is not going to go down well in Rome or many other places."

"They also mentioned a square and arrow symbol was found down there."

"That symbol is a lot older than anyone thought."

"They say it is the hieroglyph symbol for the hall."

Sean paused. The sound of a plane passing overhead, on the way to Heathrow, reached them. "So, what will you do in retirement?"

"I'll be looking after Commander Smith's roses." Henry grinned.

"You two are getting together?"

Henry nodded. "You will be at the service tomorrow?"

"Wouldn't miss it for the world."

"I know the servicemen's families will appreciate it." Henry stood. "Better go."

"I see Xena is also mentioned on the list of people being commemorated. Does that mean what I think it means?" Isabel stood to show him out.

Henry shook his head, sadly. "If she'd played just one side, she might have survived, but she was worse than Mati Hari for switching allegiances."

"But she was working for us at the end? You wouldn't commemorate her life like this, if she wasn't." Sean's tone was matter of fact.

Henry stopped at the door. "I think her final act proves that, once and for all."

He stopped in the corridor, turned to Isabel. "His mind is one hundred percent," he said.

Isabel gripped his arm. "It could take years before he's walking again, Henry. But I know one thing about Sean. He won't give up. Ever. That's just who he is."

Henry kissed her cheek.

"Goodbye, Isabel. You are one amazing lady."

One last thing

I hope you have enjoyed this book. If you can be persuaded to write a reader review on Amazon I'd really appreciate it.

Reviews on Amazon are critical to the success of an author these days.

Made in the USA
Monee, IL
06 January 2021

56683042R00198